<u>Boomshot.</u>
Hunt for a Killer.
Paul G Jackson

CH00842534

A Carew novel.

Thanks to my family and friends for the inspiration to write. Thanks to Mandy Brennan for encouraging me to stick at this novel and helping with ideas. Thanks to the British weather for creating many scenes and different moods. Where would we be without a bit of rain? I have mentioned 2 special dogs in my story too. They are truly princesses.

All characters are fictional and any likeness to anyone living, dead or otherwise is a miracle.

Cover by Jasmin

© Paul G Jackson 2015
1st Edition 2015

1

'Lick shot. Boomshot. Boom boom shot!
Police brutality, in dis ya society,
Boomshot boomshot!
A wah me seh?
Mash Babylon to rasclaat.'

August 1999. Saturday.

Dave Martyn hated his fifty something, 'wanna be teen', mother. She made his life hell when he was a child. Nothing he ever did was good enough for her. So he dealt with her *his* way. It was one summer and the family had holidayed at their summer bungalow by the sea. Saturday evening his father had gone with his golfing friends to the club for drinks. His mother decided to remain at the bungalow to watch her favourite game show.

As she sat on the plush sofa a dumpy teenage Martyn in a track suit, had crept up behind her. He quickly wrapped a tea towel around her neck and pulled it tight. She choked as she struggled to get free. Hands clawing at the tea towel as her feet flailed wildly slinging her slippers off. He left it just long enough for her to fade into unconsciousness before releasing her. He didn't want her dead just yet. He carried her awkwardly through the adjoining door that led into her bedroom. Then he laid her onto the double bed and taped her mouth shut with strong duct tape. She began to regain consciousness as he ripped apart her night gown revealing her naked body and shaved bikini line between her legs. As she looked in horror he pulled down his jogging bottoms to reveal an erect penis.

Grabbing her wrists in a grip of steel he mounted her and fucked her hard until he came to orgasm. All the time he was repeating: "Matris, ego operor non have connubialis intercourse per men!" As he withdrew his ejaculating penis his sperm splattered over her body and face. She shut her eyes tightly as some sperm landed in them. There was a small trace of blood on his cock. She was going through her changes.

He punched her squarely on the jaw and knocked her out cold. Her limp body flopped back arms spread wide. Semen dripping from her belly and soaking into her silken night gown.

Martyn felt a thrill at the prospect of killing his own mother. His heart raced with the excitement and he was laughing. He had already planned her execution. Fire. Smoking in bed. It was perfect. His parents *did* frequently smoke in bed and any evidence would go up in smoke too.

From behind the closed curtains he opened the top window of the bedroom. A tumbler on the bedside table was half filled with whiskey and dropped near his mother's face. The tumbler rolled toward her neck where semen and whiskey mingled. Then he had a better idea. Martyn poured whiskey over his mother and the bed throwing the bottle on the floor. Hurriedly

2

he lit a cigarette, hands trembling. He placed it into his mother's mouth after ripping off the duct tape. The cigarette wouldn't remain in place between the limp lips. He managed to lodge it in the corner of her mouth precariously. He opened a newspaper to a random page and placed it near his mother's head. She was still out cold when he ignited the newspaper and whiskey. There was a burst of flame and it wasn't long until the bed caught fire followed by the room. Martyn watched as long as he could, satisfied that his mother hadn't survived. Body fat spat in the heat as her body crackled in the flames. Within minutes the bungalow was ablaze. All that was found were the charred remains of her body. Even recognition of the corpse was impossible apart from the two melted engagement and wedding rings on what remained of the blackened bones of her hand.

From outside, near the garage Martyn rang for the fire brigade. He then rang his father and acted distraught over the incident. Actually, it had been the best day of his life. A fuck and a 'snuff'. Magic!

It was eventually deemed that his Mother had killed herself accidentally by smoking in bed. The insurance paid for the bungalow rebuild much to every one's surprise.

At the funeral Martyn pretended to be grieving but behind his sunshades his eyes shone with delight.

July 2001. Tuesday.

Maggie Fairchild, prostitute, waited until she saw the car pull up. A saloon with blacked out windows. She strode arrogantly over to the car as she clutched her Prada handbag. Her leather jacket complete with motorcycling badges matched her torn jeans and biker boots in a biker chick sort of way. It was the handbag that looked out of place yet it went well with her streaky blonde hair and high pony tail. Her friends told her it made her look aggressive and called the style a 'Croydon face lift'.

Nothing was said but she was thrown into the back of the car. It disappeared down the labyrinthine streets of the Brockwell estate.

Her body was discovered a week later by a gay couple walking their German Shepherd dog. The dog dragged them over to a ditch. They both vomited upon seeing the corpse.

September 2001. Tuesday.

The Brockwell estate flats. A pale faced, nose ringed Faye Jaracz waited in the rain. She sheltered between the flats as best she could. Pulling on the the hood of her silver puffer jacket she looked furtively up the street. It was dark and the orange streetlight flickered before blinking out. A familiar saloon car with blackened windows pulled up. It was impossible to see the occupants. She ran over to it. There was a scuffle and she was pulled into the rear door by a shadowy figure. The car drove away.

She was found dead the following Friday by a lorry driver who had parked to urinate in the bushes. He noticed what he thought was a bundle of rags under one of the arches of the viaduct. He would have ignored it but saw a hand sticking out from underneath the rags.

Chapter 1
May 2015. Sunday

"Carew is a fucking nobody!"

The words echoed from the past. Who was it that had spoken those words? The answer was lost in the obscurity of passing time. The reason for the insult was long forgotten. However, there was a face to the voice. Podgy and freckled. Greasy hair and bad breath. Yellowy teeth. The name to the face had been forgotten for the moment and to be honest it didn't matter anymore to Carew because Carew had thumped the little shit, given him a bloody lip and not before time. End of the matter.

It was just a childish insult from those hazy pre teenage years and yet the poignancy remained. Carew, Julian Maxwell Carew, had always believed he was 'a fucking nobody' and not just because some random voice from the past had confirmed this. It had been the repetition of the insult, the constant bullying that made him fear going to school. It lasted years until one day he snapped.

It was the discarded crisp packet in the hedgerow that reminded him. Crisps reminded him of school and school reminded him of dark days and being bullied. Since school he had been known as Carew. Not Julian or Jules and certainly not Max, but Carew. That was okay because the name Carew was an old British name. As far as he knew it meant 'Dweller of the city'. How ironic. He was on foot at the moment, he didn't drive anymore, not since the accident. It wasn't that he couldn't, he simply didn't want to. Even being a passenger was uncomfortable for him. To any onlooker he looked like he had no real dwellings in any city although he didn't look like a tramp, he just had that dispossessed look in his eyes. He did have a home back in the nearby city, a two bed roomed house that he rented from a private landlord. However, that was another story that he didn't need to think of right now until he found the bastard he was looking for. All he had was a photograph on flimsy paper but this would be enough to get a positive recognition of the person he was seeking.

Up until now Carew had struggled with life. The guilt of displeasing his peers because of his life choices had marred his enjoyment of living. His parents eventually joined a religious cult. The cult emphasised that no matter what you did, it was never enough. There had been heartache too. Bitter sadness and even now, a chill wind screamed through his soul.

4

Carew was no saint. He'd killed people and sometimes brutally. It hadn't been enjoyable but more a sense of justice being served. In some cases the crueler the better.

Carew stopped walking and gazed at the countryside in the twilight. A nearby streetlight provided some added illumination to the scene along with the not so distant floodlights on the church. It was unusually warm for May and the nettles grew high in the hedgerow. He looked and wondered; Was that what they called 'kek' or common hogweed growing? It looked too large for common hogweed. Could it be giant hogweed? Heracleum mantegazzianum? The sap causes blisters, scars and blindness if it gets in the eyes. There he stood lost in thought.

Carew, 5'9" tall. If asked about how he viewed himself he'd reply 'Generic and mid range.' His good friends called him a 'pointy nosed bastard' in fun. Although he didn't appreciate it himself, when he smiled he could light up the world. It was his smile that girls had usually found most physically attractive about him. He was a 'one woman man' as he said and had never been unfaithful to a partner in a relationship. He couldn't! Monogamy had been hardwired into him by his religious parents. Carew hadn't had very many relationships and Amy Bell was the only one he referred to as 'soul mate'. To anyone looking he was an ordinary man and quite slim, deceptively agile and stronger than he appeared. He had a tendency to have his naturally black hair short cropped and swept back. Then he'd let it grow and it would become quite bushy. To avoid the prickly annoyance of stubble he would shave every morning leaving his thin, long sideburns and goatee. Carew sounded uneducated but gave evidence of a very wide vocabulary.

These days Carew had a far away look in his eyes and yet he carried greater pain than was evident. When he walked he had a very slight limp. There was a persistent ache in his left hip as a constant reminder of the reason for his inner turmoil.

The available light glinted and glistened like jewels across the still waters of Barnow lake. The lake was on the very edge of the town signposted as 'Barnowby'. The sign was at a slight angle because one of the two posts holding it up had been glanced by a motor vehicle at some stage. Someone had drawn a simple unhappy circular face on it in felt tipped pen followed by the words: 'Abandon hope'. Carew already had. A long time ago. However, he had reached Barnowby as intended. Would he stay long or would it be overnight? That all depended on what he found for his secret objective.

Geese flew overhead in their 'v sign to the world' formation. They were honking very loudly.

He saw a sign on a dry stone wall near a cottage that read 'Church Lane'. It was a short lane that led to the now illuminated St Matthew's church. Carew saw the steeple behind a couple of tall trees.

He slapped his neck as he felt the tickle of an insect on it.

"Fucking gnats!" he cursed.

A silver fairingless BMW R 1200 motorcycle zoomed down the lane. There were two riders on it. It was impossible to know what sex they were clad in their leathers and helmets. It was the local clergyman John Cruickshank and his wife Mona. Mona was the one driving.

Barnowby was once a small dark, smoke stained and grim village. The architecture was a mishmash of old and new. Nothing really matched. It was an eyesore. Once a small farming community inhabited by Saxons. More recently in history it became a town that had formed to house railway workers. That was in the days before Doctor Beeching had cut the amount of lines the railway used. Richard Beeching had been chairman of British Railways. Also known as Baron Beeching, he had died back in 1985. The famous 'Beeching axe' made Barnowby a victim of those line cuts in 1965.

'Abandon hope,' mused Carew. Hope was now an alien word to him. He remembered sitting in church praising the Lord. He recalled how one day he was looking up at the rafters when the pastor said prayers of intercession. He vividly recalls how he whispered to himself: 'God isn't there. No one is listening.' He had tried to retain his faith in the Lord but failed. It seemed that this so called loving God was simply as imaginary as a child's invisible friend. 'We are alone.' He thought, 'No one is watching or helping. Totally alone.'

It was then that Carew concluded this dog eat dog world carried no divine reward or consequences. Yet if God did exist then God is a psychotic creature. Surely God must be a 'Love and worship me or I'll kill you and torture you forever' monstrosity in the sky. A celestial Hitler. The thought was horrifying. The idea that we are alone to fend off the machinations of those that exploit others with no fear of retribution was a terrible thing to ponder.

Carew was thinking back. A car's tyres screeched in the distance and brought him back to reality. The crunching of wet gravel and grit beneath his feet as he walked continued but by now he didn't notice it. He looked at his footwear casually. Second hand British Army shoes. Mud splattered but still shiny and sturdy.

There were the sounds of the town at night that ebbed and flowed in intensity providing a veritable soundtrack to the scene. From a nearby Inn came the music of an Irish folk band playing a live concert. He thought he recognized the strains of 'Whiskey in the Jar'. Carew wasn't sure where the Inn was but he would investigate. It may provide a temporary place to stay for the night.

He took a small mobile phone from his pocket and looked at the screen. Nothing. It didn't matter how much he swiped at the screen or pressed the 'on/off' button, it remained dead. No light. The phone battery had now died adding to his feeling of loneliness and hopelessness. He cursed himself because he knew he should have charged it before he left the city to walk to Barnowby.

"Bollocks," he cursed.

He put his phone back into his camo combat jacket side pocket. He felt the small piece of carved wood in his pocket. He had been told this carving was a scale replica of an African ceremonial Voodoo mask. It was fashioned after the style of the BaKongo people's masks. Moira McNamara had presented it to him as a birthday gift three years ago. She knew he had a love of woodcarvings.

His fingers fondled the carving feeling over the smoothness and the bumps. It gave Carew a strange feeling of well being for a brief moment in time. He was not superstitious and did not attribute this fleeting feeling to anything spiritual emanating from the small replica. A small piece of grit in his pocket found its way underneath his fingernail. It was an annoyance that he at once removed by digging with his index finger's nail from his other hand. He flicked the nail pickings away with rapidity.

Carew walked into the small town down 'Venables Street'. If the Inn didn't provide lodgings then perhaps somewhere close would. If not, a hedgerow would suffice. It had been a long time since he'd been here and it had changed. Maybe he could recharge his phone though if he found lodgings. He had his reasons for arriving at the town in the dark but perhaps on reflection it wasn't the greatest idea.

As he began to walk, his mind wandered back to days long before. He recalled the girl called Moira McNamara. The girl of the woodcarving fame. He smiled. An Irish girl with jet black hair and deep brown eyes. She had the most beautiful smile he'd ever seen. She often worried that because her teeth were slightly crooked that her smile wasn't perfect. In Carew's eyes it only added to the uniqueness of that smile.

Carew had no romantic feelings for Moira. They were just friends and she was more like a sister to him. Carew was in love with another but that was a different story and one which haunted him.

He recalled sitting on the hay in the barn with Moira as he waited for her brother Frank to come and give him a lift home. Flies were buzzing. Ants were crawling. Birds were wheeling in the summer sky. Frank was a little older than Carew but quite youthful in appearance. Square jawed and swept back dark hair. In the platoon he was nicknamed 'Obvs'. Frank thought it was because he often carried out observations in the field of a combat zone. The reality was because of his incessant use of the word 'obviously' when he spoke. It was an 'in' joke with the other mercenary soldiers. Moira and her brother lived on the Brockwell estate in the city and shared the house they grew up in. Their parents had died in a car crash. Carew actually met Frank when they fought as mercenary soldiers together for those brief violent years. They trusted each other totally.

Bullied at school Carew felt he had something to prove and a balance to redress. He joined the British Army and later became one of the 'Dogs of war', as mercenaries were termed.

Yet the balance still remained the same; one sided and unfair. Perhaps the lack of self worth was too hardwired into him to ever be removed.

This summer encounter would be the last time Carew had seen Moira happy. On the matter of Carew going to Barnowby, they had sent texts to each other on the phone some days ago. Moira had sunk right down into a deep depression.

Carew walked down the incline and into the town. He passed a kebab shop that was brightly lit with neon lights and signs. It used to be a quaint cake shop he recalled. He walked past a cash point that boasted 'free cash'. This amused him because he knew it wasn't really 'free' as in the concept of a gift. The money would still be removed from his bank account. He gave a wry smile at the thought.

He followed to where the sound of the music emanated from. It was down the first side street over to his left. A blue car drove past him with blaring music coming from it. Was it music or just the thump, thump, thump of the bass drum he could hear?

'Bugger me,' he thought, 'Is that music or the bloody wheel bearing cracking up?'

Carew walked past a man leaning on wall outside an electrical retail shop. As he walked past, the man started to be sick into the gutter. Drunk. It wasn't even night time yet. He'll have a headache in the morning Carew mused. Carew shook his head in a mixture of disapproval and amusement.

A police car drove slowly by. As if in slow motion, Carew and the sweaty skin headed PC. made eye contact. The copper looked away with disinterest and continued driving. He turned into Mayfield Street. Carew recalled that face but not the specifics of how or why. It bothered him but it was best not to be obsessing over it as the answer would come if he put it out of his mind.

As Carew walked over to the Inn, a scuffle broke out in the doorway. There were shouts. Profanities verbalised loudly. Slapping sounds. Perhaps it was a fight. Three of the revellers looked at Carew and walked arrogantly over to him in a threatening manner. One of the suited men was hobbling slightly. The long haired shorter one came over.

"Oh, look. A stranger! We don't like strangers here!" The man was thick set with a face that resembled a Toby jug covered in grease. He wore a powder blue suit, had flaky skin and long dark center parted hair. There was a scar on his cheek. Carew had seen many such scars as a soldier. It was a bullet graze. He had two associates with him who remained a distance behind.

'Toby jug' raised his fists at Carew. Dropping his travel bag on the floor Carew lifted his hands with his palms faced down as if to say 'please stay away'. Carew relaxed his stance, knees bent, feet shoulder width apart.

Toby jug moved in to invade Carew's personal space. Toby snarled and threw an expertly aimed left handed punch.

Carew side stepped. In a flash slapped the punching arm at the elbow and diverted it, pinning it to Toby's body. At the same time he threw a springing back hand at Toby jug's neck. As Toby reeled in shock Carew grabbed his assailant's elbow with his left hand, spun him around, stepped quickly behind him and gave a hard palm strike into the floating rib. Now directly behind Toby, Carew grabbed his shoulders and kicked behind Toby's left knee. Toby was flung backward to the floor and his hands slapped the gritty road surface. Carew gave Toby a painful kick with his army shoes to the jaw, just below Toby's right ear. Carew held back from administering a head lock and further blows to Toby.

"Want more, you cunt?" Carew asked.
"Bastard," muttered Toby as he slowly rolled over and began standing up. He massaged his jaw and open and closed his mouth slowly in wide circular movements.
"Thought not! Now fuck off and leave me alone. If you or any of your fucking cronies come within one mile of me I swear to God I'll finish you the fuck off. Okay?"

Toby remained dazed as Carew looked around at the small crowd that had gathered.

Toby jug was the same face that was on the photo Carew had with him and he knew it.

'Bingo,' thought Carew. But now was not the time to start what he came for, there was a crowd of witnesses here. Best to wait.

"Well?" Carew asked the crowd, "Can I help you?"

The crowd dispersed. Toby ambled away with two other men who kept looking back at Carew. Carew made a mental note of their faces. One was grizzled and thin faced, short brown hair and a small moustache. The other was a squat fellow who carried an air of arrogance in the way he held his head up. He had prominent teeth that seemed to give him a permanent sarcastic smile. He was of similar stature to Toby but fatter. Both wearing tasteless yet expensive powder blue suits with double vent jackets. Toby had a silk handkerchief in his top pocket.

A white haired middle aged man approached Carew and held out his hand for a hand shake. Cautiously Carew accepted the greeting. He resembled Dick Van Dyke in Carew's view.

The man with the handshake spoke: "Hello. I'm Pete. Pete Silver. You just met the town's bully boy Dave Martyn and his cousins Mike and 'Other Mike'. Mike Kitter is the one that looks like a demonic mole. Mike Rolph is the 'Nosferatu potato' look alike. Martyn's a real criminal but no one has ever stood up to him before. Rolph had a stroke they say. That's why he walks a bit lop sided. No one questions them not even the coppers. Fear you see. It's because his family runs things around here. Hey, what were those moves? Karate?"

"Pleased to meet you, Pete. Dave Martyn and two Mikes. To think I had in my mind that Dave bloke was called 'Toby Jug'. I'll remember those names though. I don't give a shit about his family or who he thinks he is. If he tries anything I'll break the bastards face. I still might! Moves? Oh, no. I call it my dogs of war style Kung Fu and I was holding back! Sorry about my language, I just don't need any bloody hassle the moment I walk into a strange town." Picking up his travel bag Carew continued, "Bloody tired to be honest. Looking for a place to rest the night. Then I'm on my way tomorrow."

"Well, I don't know you or anything about you but if you need a place to stay you can kip in my shed the night. There's a camp bed and a light. Oh, and a plug socket too. I can't offer you more than that. Oh, and you can use the shower."

"Sounds good, Pete. Call me Carew. Tell me, why would you help me?" Carew fixed his squinted gaze into Pete's eyes as he spoke.

"Wow, that is a straight question. Yeah, I imagine it does sound suspicious now I think about it." Pete rubbed the back of his neck and said, "My son joined the army, he's about your age. Oh, and I live alone. The Martyn family have been nothing but a pain in the arse. It's part of the reason my son left. I'll never forgive them for that. Many times I have really wanted to stab the buggers but that isn't realistic. So anyone that stands up to the bastards is good in my book. I'll help that person. Personal reasons you see."

"I got you. You don't have to tell me anything about it. I'll give you some cash for hospitality and be on my way late morning."

***

"I'm going to get that stranger and get him good," Martyn said to the two Mikes. The two Mikes grunted in agreement. He looked back at Carew talking to Silver. They were two silhouettes in the neon shop lights. Swathed in the hue of blue and red flashing signs. Martyn watched the pair walk away toward Venables Street.

The three cousins all clambered into the cab of Martyn's white Ford Transit van. He had a car as well, a brand new Porsche 911 but he preferred to use the van on nights out. No reason to risk a scratch from a careless revellers drunken meanderings on his car or a door ding from a car parked next to him.

The two Mikes were talking but Martyn's mind was elsewhere. Instead Martyn was thinking back to how Pete Silver had been found out for the two timing bastard he was.

Dave Martyn recalled the night he returned home from his 'dealings' on the Brockwell estate in the next city. He'd planned to stay city side for the night but changed his mind and decided to return to their reasonably large country house. Silver had been employed as a handyman and gardener. His wife had been in hospital for some time as she succumbed to the cancer that ravaged her body. His son was just a weak fool.

He drove up to the house in his white van. Martyn had applied lipstick, crimson lipstick to his mouth very clumsily.The gravel crunched as he approached his home. There he saw a small red car. It was Silver's. The question as to why it was there puzzled Martyn as he parked outside the Greek style entrance. Perhaps there was a good reason. He scratched his stubble. Skin flakes floated away in the night air. Martyn farted and grunted.

He entered the house and all seemed quiet. That was until he went up the large staircase to his room. It was believed father was still away in Greece on business. Martyn didn't care where his father was.

As he walked past his step mother's bedroom he heard her giggling. There was a voice. It was Silver. Martyn narrowed his eyes and gritted his teeth.

Martyn in his pig headed rage burst into his step mother's room. There in the large bed with his step mother was Silver. They were having an affair he deduced.

"Dave!" his step mother screamed, "What are you doing?"

Her long curly dyed black hair was a mess. Her face was now drained of colour. Her wizened lips were pursed. She looked positively dessicated.

She was frightened and angered all in one go. Silver jumped out of the bed. Stark naked he quickly picked up his clothes as Martyn shouted at him to get out. Martyn threw a left handed punch at Silver. It only connected faintly to Silver's jaw. Without hesitation Silver ran to his car. He heard the shouting of the step mother and son as he left. There were slapping noises.

Martyn heard the faint sound of tyres spitting gravel and Silver was gone.

Dave Martyn decided there and then that the Silvers would suffer. He would see to it that they were run out of the area or better still, killed. However, other matters had had stymied his wish. For now.

In the distance a dog howled as simultaneously a bottle was smashed outside the Inn.

***

Pete drove his small red saloon car the few miles to his home which was situated in a short terrace of dark bricked houses. Carew felt ill at ease being a passenger in a car. He kept his calm and fought off the feeling of panic. He'd offered to walk but Pete had told him he'd have trouble finding the house.

They saw a fox run across the road and disappear into the bushes

Now, they were just outside the town, but there were still terraced houses here. Carew recalled that these houses had been built for railway workers in the 1800's. It had been trivial research on his part some years ago.

Pete led him to what was more of a summer house than a shed. There was ample room inside it for Carew to get comfortable.

"If you need the toilet in the night there's one outside." Pete pointed to a small outbuilding attached to the rear of the house.

He continued: "Just beware of the flushing mechanism; it takes a few tugs before it works. Old style chain job."

"Okay, Pete. I appreciate this, I really do. I'll not disturb you."

"Join me in brekky in the morning if you want. I get a bit lonely. The neighbours are a bit insular around here. In fact I have no idea who lives in the end house now. Never see them."

There were no lights on in any of the neighbouring houses.

Carew mused this small road, in itself, seemed like a ghost town. It wasn't all that late at night either.

The idea of some sustenance in the morning was appealing as he was hungry now. Luckily he had some beef jerky, biscuits along with some breakfast bars and bottled water in his travel bag.

"Join me for a cuppa?" asked Pete, "We have some Rich tea biscuits if you like."

After leaving his travel bag and jacket in the 'shed', Carew agreed to have supper with Pete. Both men went into the house.

"Milk and one sugar in tea," Carew said as the door closed behind them.

Not far away, a train rumbled by and into the tunnel on its journey west.

Then, a peaceful silence fell.

Chapter 2
Monday.

"Carew is a fucking nobody!"

Those words echoed into obscurity as Carew woke up from his turbulent dreams. It was those same bloody words again. Why were they haunting him? Perhaps he'd never know. At this time he was not going to obsess over them. He had other things to do.

It was the alarm on his phone that woke him up with the sound of a cock crowing.

Bleary eyed he swiped it off. The warning at the top of the phone display declared "Fully charged". He removed the charger wire. He wondered if it did the phone any harm to be left on charge longer than necessary. He had slept soundly not hearing it beep when charged.

The words, 'Carew is a fucking nobody,' seemed to be amalgamated with the alarm going off.

Why were those same bloody words haunting him to this day? At this time he was not going to obsess over them. He had other things to do. He'd promised Pete he would be on his way today. Carew started to ensure he had all his belongings with him.

Then it hit Carew. The copper in the car. That looked like Bellamy. Yes. Phil Bellamy was the one that taunted him with that insult, 'Carew is a fucking nobody!'

His eyes lit up. A smile came to his face as he wondered if the copper was indeed the adult Bellamy. He knew he had to find out without drawing attention to himself. The easiest way would surely be to ask Pete. All in good time. At least his technique of not trying too hard to remember things might have worked.

The sounds of the morning came to Carew.

Carew thought back to when he first met Amy Bell. Her curly brown hair and hazel eyes had appealed to him straight away. They met at Moira's Christmas party. Frank introduced them. Amy had been a childhood friend of Frank and Moira. Carew wondered why he hadn't met her before. At first their chat was polite. He made her laugh with his wit. It became clear they had much in common. Their mutual love of art and music gave them much to discuss. Discuss they did, for hours sometimes. They had arranged to meet for coffee or drinks in the days that followed. Nostalgia gripped Carew. He sighed deeply.

As he gazed out of the shed window he could see Pete moving in the kitchen. Pete looked as if he was preparing food.

Pete gazed up and noticed that Carew was looking back at him. Pete waved at Carew to join him. With frantic movements, he indicated that his door was unlocked and Carew was free to enter. 'He really does look like Dick Van Dyke now,' thought Carew.

"Listen," Pete began, "You, er, don't have to leave today if you don't want to. You're welcome to stay longer. As long as you're not an axe murderer of course."

They both smiled.

"Well, a couple more days might be useful. We'll see. Thanks for the offer. I will remunerate you of course."

"That's good of you. If you want to get milk for tomorrow's breakfast then that's fine, otherwise there's no need to worry. I have all I need to live comfortably."

"You know you said about the local coppers being in league with or frightened of Martyn," Carew tried to look nonchalant and asked, "Who are your local coppers? Anyone in particular in Martyn's pocket?"

"Well, I don't think you'd know them to be honest."

"No, it's okay, I have some local knowledge. I know some folk from around here."

"Well. Let me see. The one that drives about a lot is Phil Bellamy. Now he IS a pig. If a man was hated around these parts then it's him. Colin Smith. Don't see much of him. He's related to Martyn somehow but seems on the level though. Doesn't seem to get on with the Martyn side of his family. Richard Parr. Dennis Bolsover. Dangerfield, forget his first name. I think he's an inspector of some description. I can't think of any others. I am not sure of their involvement with the Martyn clan but that's who I suspect."

"Nah. Never heard of any of them."

Carew made a mental note of the names. Bellamy. He knew that name of course. He wondered if Bellamy had recognised him after all these years. Would it compromise his plan if Bellamy did? Carew decided not to think too deeply about it right at that moment. After all, he was in conversation with Pete. If he went into thinking mode it would appear rude.

The men exchanged pleasantries about the weather and other things over breakfast cereal and tea.

Overhead an Air Force jet roared on its journey to R.A.F Collingsmote. Casually, they both looked out of the window to see if they could spot the jet.

They couldn't.

***

Martyn was not a thinking man. His pleasures were sadomasochism, the military and mind numbing reality TV shows. He was a villain. A small time racketeer in the town. He had dubious connections in the city. He sold class 'A' drugs, usually with the street name 'Krok', via his runners on the Brockwell estate in the city nearby. The police had visited him on several occasions but could not pin anything on him. It was no secret in the town that one of the coppers was of Martyn's family. This was Colin Smith, Smiffy. Not that they got on, but there is always the fear that blood is thicker than water. Some believed that Martyn had something on certain police officers that could get them prison time. Martyn was glad there was at least one bent copper in town. He knew that every man has his price and these twats were cheap. With the exception of cousin Smiffy and DC Andrew Dangerfield, he'd never met a good one.

Case in point was PC. Phil Chadburn Bellamy. There was the joke that he was a PC. and his initials were also PC. He was therefore P.C.P.C Bee.

Bellamy was a copper that brought Krok from Martyn on a regular basis. What Bellamy didn't realise was that Martyn had filmed, stored each one of those dealings and filed them secretly away. This was security, in case Bellamy tried to arrest him in the future.

It was Monday, mid day. Bellamy was off duty but still in his sweaty police uniform.

He walked behind the Martyn home. He peered across the immaculately kept lawn. There, stood the large Victorian style greenhouse. The grass glistened with moisture from the last shower of rain this morning. He walked over the hexagonal stepping stones that were carefully inlaid into the lawn. As he reached the greenhouse he heard Martyn invite him in. Not aware that the hidden camera in the greenhouse would be filming, he strode over to Martyn.

Martyn was reclining in a white wicker chair. The chair was merely a prop to maintain a Victoriana feel in the humid greenhouse. Bellamy thought it may not be the greatest of ideas to keep the chair within the humidity of the greenhouse. However, the Martyn family had plenty of money. Even expensive items were just 'throw away' trinkets in their opinion.

There were plants of many varieties and beautiful flowers within. Bellamy had no idea what the plants were, just that the place was clammy. There was a musty, earthy smell in there too, unsurprisingly.

Bellamy removed his police cap and rubbed his skinhead scalp to remove perspiration. Some sweat dripped onto his yellow chest covering and ran onto his stab vest. A blue oblongular badge read 'Police'. Martyn preferred the term 'Pig-lice'.

"That'll be the usual fee then Mr P.C.P.C. Bee." Martyn looked up from his garish glossy magazine, "Next time it'll cost you a monkey more. Short supply my friend."

"Don't try to push me, Martyn!" Bellamy was using his patronizing voice. He thought that because he wore the police uniform it would be a symbol of authority and instill fear. It was an arrogant delusion. Bellamy still thought it was a price bargaining tool. "I may be forced to..."

"Forced to what, Bell end? Take my sheep up the bum?" Martyn interrupted.

"I'm a copper, Martyn. Don't try and con me with your fake price rise."

Bellamy was angry. This was the third price rise in six months. He was a cop and should be given preferential treatment. He was not a public servant as they said. To Bellamy the police were more than that, and the people should serve the police. Police were superior and should be allowed to do as they please. That's why he joined the force after all. He lied on his application about being a racist bigot. Yes, he HAD been involved in racist groups but they weren't to know that.

It didn't occur to him that Martyn must either be really stupid, brazen or up to something, to be dealing from his own home.

"I don't care if you're the bloody Pope, Bell end. I've got enough naughty evidence on you to put you away for a long time." Martyn rose slowly and looked Bellamy in the eyes. A smile played across his lips. It was the kind of smile a shark would give you if you dipped your toes into the water. Except, this shark had stubble on his flaky skinned face.

After a menacing pause Martyn continued, "Watch my lips. They don't like bent pigs in the pokey, mate. You'll be some big bloke called Glenda's bitch before you get splattered and diced in the cell. Get me? Like cock up the arse do you?"

Martyn made a duck bill shape with his hand, thumb under forefinger. He pointed it at Bellamy and mimicked it talking.

"This is what you're doing," Martyn mocked. Then he held the 'bill' tightly closed and continued, "And this is what I want you to do!"

Bellamy reluctantly held his tongue. How dare he speak to one of 'Britain's finest' in such a disrespectful manner? This corrupt copper was as arrogant as Martyn but decided to be quiet. After all it was refraining from talking that maintained the secrecy that had protected him and his lifestyle so far in his 38 years. It would surely only be a matter of time before their clash would end in tears.

A tatty buff envelope containing money was handed to Martyn. Martyn held it between thumb and forefinger at arms length as if it was disgusting. His face showed his mock disgust. The envelope was not sealed and Martyn casually opened the flap. He counted the money. Notes. Some used and some crisp.

"That's only just right, Bell end." Martyn handed a small packet to Bellamy. Bellamy grunted. He thrust the packet into his trouser pocket, turned abruptly and walked away.

"Thank you, Mr Martyn," he said in a monotone, "I might be back depending on the asking price. Good day, sir."

"You'll be back. Need a straw with that?"

Martyn gave a wry smirk and then sat down in the fine wicker chair.

"What a twat," he exclaimed just loudly enough for Bellamy to hear.

As he walked away, Bellamy was thinking about how he might get back at Martyn one day. One thing was puzzling him though. Just what had Martyn got over him? Bellamy shook his head thinking that there was nothing. As well as arrogance, Bellamy lived in his own delusion of being invincible. As he pondered these things, Martyn was watching him leave the grounds of the house. He heard Bellamy fart.

Smiling, Martyn went to the small brick room behind the greenhouse to where his laptop was laid. It was at an angle on a large desk. He saved the 'flv' file of the latest transaction with Bellamy as he laughed under his breath.

Police corruption was a wonderful thing for Martyn. He pondered how all the police must be corrupt as they're complicit mutually. If there were any good coppers, they would never speak up against the bad coppers. The fact that they didn't, made them all just as guilty as each other. This was a view Martyn held without considering the complexities of the matter further. It was a simplistic and naive view and was typical of Martyn's mind set.

The tall trees rustled in the breeze with their tops swaying gracefully.

Bellamy climbed into his own private car and drove away. It was beginning to rain again although being warm outside. He opened the widow on the drivers side of the car. Softly, he felt the odd spit of rain on his face but it was not as uncomfortable as the warmth inside the car.

From the bungalow not far from the lake on Collingsmote Lane, Mrs Banyard was looking out of her kitchen window.

Despite her age she was determined not to be a frump. No housecoat or deep brown coggled nylon dresses for her. She had dyed auburn bobbed hair and owned a functional yet trendy wardrobe.

She watched as Bellamy drove past. How could she not look with disdain upon this man? It was well known that he was a bully and used his uniform to abuse power. She thought his mother was a strange person. She had once invited Mrs Banyard to a séance. Mrs Banyard being a strict

Christian had declined. She preferred the small congregation of St Matthew's church and the kindly ways of the Reverend John Cruickshank and his wife.

St Matthew's church was built to serve the railway workers in 1842. It looked much older though. It was an Anglican church holding to some Catholic traditions. Mr and Mrs Banyard were regular in worship each Sunday. Some Sundays the service was visited by a Pentecostal Christian gospel band. The service was always more liberal at those times. Mrs Fiona Banyard enjoyed reciting the Apostles creed. "I believe," she would say with gusto. She had the privilege of taking the offertory around during the middle hymn.

Mr Sid Banyard had been a manual labourer before he retired. His calloused hands made the hymn book appear to be a fragile thing as he held it.

The Banyards had been married since 1959. They had met when Mr Banyard was stationed in Kent during the war. Fiona Silver worked in the N.A.A.F.I. They joked that the way to a man's heart is through his stomach and without the N.A.A.F.I. there would have been no wedding. Her brother Pete Silver was there but was too young to remember the wedding at St Matthews.

The likes of Bellamy and Martyn were never seen at the church unless they were duty bound to attend by what Sid termed 'Hatches, Matches and Dispatches'. The last time Martyn was seen at the church was years ago for the funeral of his mother.

Fiona always believed that divine justice would be delivered to those 'Martyn' men. After all they had desecrated Holy soil with their presence on church grounds.

What scum these families were. Sodom and Gomorrah all over again.

Then there were the rumours about Doris Bellamy stealing clothes from washing lines at night. Of course with a corrupt copper as a son she was bound to get away with it. Everyone knew she was a shoplifter and had probably been a prostitute in her younger days. Surely it was well known that she had an incestuous relationship with her illegitimate son. Mrs Banyard's imagination was running away with fanciful negativity about Doris Bellamy and her pervert of a son.

It was Bellamy that had bullied their son relentlessly at school. Even when she had approached the headmaster nothing had been done about it. Jimmy Banyard was gay and now lived in London with his older partner Graham. Graham was a hairdresser and Jimmy was a nurse for a mental health establishment. Mrs Barnyard totally blamed Bellamy for Jimmy leaving and perhaps even for his chosen lifestyle. It was a lifestyle the Banyards would never discuss. No matter what his choices were, he was still their son whom they loved. Maybe her worship would move the Lord to work a miracle over Jimmy and change him.

18

Bellamy casually glanced at the Banyard bungalow as he drove.

How brazen Martyn was to sell krok from his own home Bellamy thought. However, this would be a good snort for the evening. Hopefully it wasn't cut too liberally with crap. Bellamy made the short drive home to where he lived with his ageing mother. He had never been married or partnered up. His taste was not for human females or males. Under the guise of a police officer, he knew he could get away with anything he wanted to if he gave the right threats to the right people.

A visit to farmer Roy Burns, with false evidence and the threat to plant it on his daughter Debbie, would provide him access into the sheep pen for half an hour or so. Nothing would be said. However, farmer Burns believed that Bellamy and his corrupt copper friends could fit his daughter up. She had been trouble for narcotics sales at University. He feared that she might face a stretch in prison, or at least heavy fines and maybe community service. This could ruin her because she had worked to improve her life. Now she had secured a good job at Warren, Smethwick and Weirdbottom solicitors.

Burns often thought about what a fucking coward he must be not to report the local police force to the higher authorities. Yet he knew that even independent police investigations were a joke.
'Oh, we're the police and we've just investigated ourselves. Guess what? We're not guilty.' Surprise, surprise!

Smug bastards. Could he even trust Dangerfield? Somehow he felt he might be able to but it was still a big risk.

Burns felt awful about himself not fighting back against this perverted corrupt filth. He was trapped by guilt on the one hand, and protecting his daughter from being fitted up unjustly by dishonest police officers on the other. He mused ironically, 'On the other hand I have four fingers and a thumb.'

There had been times when Burns had looked in his gun cabinet and wondered which of his fine rifles would be the best to shoot Bellamy with. Was it worth it if he got caught? Would he feel so guilty that he would give himself up? He hated Bellamy and longed for a day to be rid of him and his crooked influence. The prospects of seeing the back of Bellamy seemed bleak.

Bellamy strode into his home. It was a foul smelling dump but he didn't notice the stench. His mother stood slightly hunched in the dimly lit kitchen doorway. She smiled at him with her brown teeth. She was in expectation of what was to come. He tossed the small package onto the table. After farting, he went to his small room to change out of his uniform. He put on a maroon hand knitted sweater then pulled on some stained track suit bottoms. He farted again. He laughed. Then lumbered back down the stairs. He went to the kitchen where his mother had made lines of powder on the Formica table top.

Without speaking a word to each other they began to snort the Krok into their nostrils with plastic tubes. After a few seconds Bellamy felt invincible. He left his mother who was passed out and lying hunched over the table.

Bellamy only remembered waking up the next day groggy but ready for another day policing. He got ready and drove to work. He didn't reach the station.

Chapter 3
Tuesday

Carew casually looked at his phone and it was fully charged.

There was a spider crawling above him on the ceiling in the shed where he lay. Although the camp bed was not the most comfortable to sleep on, it was better than a hard floor. Pete had said he could stay a little longer as he lacked company these days.

Carew was in no hurry to move on. He had things to attend to that he was not revealing to anyone just yet, but it had to do with Moira. She knew and didn't approve but realized there was no stopping Carew.

He put the phone into his kit bag. There was no signal at the moment and no Wi-Fi to connect to either. The signals were very intermittent. The phone seemed useless apart from being an alarm clock. He didn't have any music stored on it. Instead, he usually listened to music from the Internet. Old dub reggae was his favourite along with some rock. In truth he had a very wide musical taste.

He could hear the rain splattering sporadically onto the shed. There was little sign of it as the shower was not falling onto the window directly. However, he could see the rain as it fell from a direction behind the shed. As Amy had once said, "It's only spitting in the puddles."

He remembered one particular day that he met Amy. They'd arranged to go to a local art exhibition at the museum. Entry was free. Carew waited on the corner of Pelham Road for Amy to arrive on the bus. As the bus approached he saw her sitting on the top deck smiling at him from the front of that orange vehicle. He watched as she rose from the seat and made her way to the steps for the lower deck and exit.

She seemed to swing from the bus then strode over to meet him. He gave her a friendly hug. As they embraced their eyes met. The language was unspoken and without hesitation they kissed full on the lips. It lingered.

Carew looked at Amy and apologised for being out of line. Amy just held on to him and moved in for another kiss. He didn't recall much of the exhibition and in truth, neither did Amy but they held hands throughout.

The memory was sweet and also sad. A familiar loneliness came over him.

From the shed window he looked toward the bushes on his right and saw more large hogweed growing. It diverted his melancholy thoughts.

He wondered why he hadn't seen any neighbours in the short row of houses but wasn't going to question it for now. Perhaps it was nothing. Maybe the neighbours moved around when Carew didn't. Timing maybe.

Carew took his bottled water and drank. Then he ate a cereal bar as he sat in the shed getting his mental bearings.

He thought about the meal he'd eaten in the town yesterday. He smiled. The food reminded him of the time his father had cooked for the family when his mother was in hospital. Carew was 14 at the time. He remembered being surprised at what a good cook his father was. His mother died two nights later in hospital quite unexpectedly. Carew bit his lip as he remembered. Was there no end to this sadness?

It was time for his exercise regime. Carew limbered up and then began with 60 push ups. Then he proceeded to do his regular 'cardio' routine for at least 15 minutes.

The spider had moved to the corner of the ceiling.

Afterwards, Pete came out to invite Carew in for breakfast and the usual benign chit chat.

Carew was a secretive man, yet he did reveal to Pete that he'd worked on building sites, spent time in the military and then did some mercenary soldiering. Not in that exact order though. He had instigated the conversation to find out more about Pete's son Nigel. Carew was told that Pete's deceased wife was from the Philippines, so Nigel had a slight Eurasian look. That was the reason Nigel had been a target of that bigot Bellamy, Pete revealed. Racism.

Pete told Carew that Nigel would be home on leave soon. Pete was preparing a bedroom for him.

"I had a good mate when I was a soldier. His name was Nigel too. We called him Nidge," Carew revealed. Then he thought he'd said too much and changed the subject to football.

Carew had decided to go to the nearest shop to buy milk for Pete, as promised. He must check out the hogweed too. If this was indeed Heracleum

21

mantegazzianum, then it may be a useful and natural weapon if administered correctly.

Carew began singing to himself, an old reggae song he remembered.

'Lick shot. Boomshot. Boom boom shot.
Police brutality, in dis ya society.
Boomshot, boomshot.
A wah me seh.
Mash Babylon to rasclaat.'

He walked toward Collingsmote Lane to buy milk from the post office cum convenience store. It was easier than walking the distance to the town. He may walk into town later, as yet he hasn't decided. When he reached the the corner that led to the lane he stopped. Ahead of him he saw the church with the vicarage in front of it, slightly to the left. To his right was the lake and just across the road, before the lake, was the bungalow where Mr and Mrs Banyard lived. He could see in the distance the bent sign post with the graffiti on. Pete had mentioned that his sister, Mrs Banyard, lived in the bungalow opposite to where Carew stood. Carew made a left turn toward the shop.

It began to rain heavily. Carew cursed under his breath as he lifted the hood on his jacket over his now wet hair.

He recalled how a sudden downpour of rain had caught him and Amy unawares during a country walk. Amy had shrieked with laughter as they both ran for cover into a small barn in a nearby field. They both fell onto the hay laughing. They embraced and kissed with passion whilst they grasped each other with gentleness. Carew began to fondle her breast. Her nipple became hard. Lifting up her sweater and moving her bra cup out of the way he began to lick and suck the nipple. Her cold hand found its way down his trouser front and began to arouse his warm penis. At first he flinched at the coldness of her slender fingers but gradually he surrendered willingly to the arousal.

They made love in the hay with Amy on top of Carew. Passionate yet loving. Unselfish and yielding. The union of penis in vagina was a perfect fit. She pulled hard on his hair as she shouted in orgasm. Carew's sperm shot like a jet inside her. She relaxed and lay on top of him. They kissed tenderly as his penis began to lose its hardness and flop out of her vagina. Semen dribbled over Carew's pubic hair and he could smell the faint, sweet aroma of her body.

"I love you Amy," admitted Carew as he stroked her hair. Amy smiled appreciatively yet didn't reply. Carew wondered why she didn't reciprocate and the thought nagged at him.

The rain stopped and they continued their country walk.

Carew sighed as he recalled that day.

***

The Reverend John Cruickshank sat in his office as his wife Mona tended to her potted plants in the conservatory of the Vicarage.

He had worked in a bank before his ordination. He thought the vows of celibacy, that some churches held to, were totally a matter on conscience. A personal choice he felt, they had no real biblical basis let alone relevance in today's society. It seemed that when the Apostle Paul had made the comment about not getting married, that some overzealous church leaders had taken it too seriously. After all, as far as it was known, Paul was himself married.

John was working on his sermon for Sunday. What would he choose? He knew that if he were to deliver a message to boost attendance at the church it would be wasted words. Those that had strayed from worship would not be there anyway.

The Martyn family and the rather strange Bellamy pair would certainly benefit from a life dedicated to the Lord. All they had to do was accept Jesus for salvation. As it was, they had chosen another path with a terrible final destination: Hell! Cruickshank had no fixed concept of what 'Hell' was but he hoped it was not eternal torment as this raised so many ethical and moral questions about the personality of the Lord. In the parable of 'the rich man and Lazarus', Hell was illustrated as a fantasy only, he believed. Cruickshank thought 'Hell' simply to be a place alienated from the Lord and maybe, just maybe, there would be a road to redemption to Him.

He had decided on an encouraging piece from the gospel of John chapter 9. "Jesus heals" he would call it. Then he would link in the dangers of sin and how Jesus saves.

As if dazed, he peered outside for a while. It looked like it might rain soon and quite heavily too. The outside world looked very drab. He observed a figure walking down the road toward the Post Office. He recalled seeing that same figure once before, walking into the town late on Sunday. It was Carew but Cruickshank didn't know him.

He recalled that they needed some more teabags for the refreshments for after Sunday service.

"What time you want to go shopping, darling?" he asked Mona.
"Well, anytime you like. Get it over with. Let's just wait. Looks like there's going to be a heavy downpour any minute now. So, when the rain eases."

She thought about wet rain soaked bags of shopping dripping all over the tiled kitchen floor. That would never do.
"Don't let me forget the tea bags for Sunday. You know how it is, dear, always forgetting the one thing you went for. You buy everything in the shop apart from very thing you want."

"Okay dear."

Mona watered the small plant. Her hands felt clammy in the bright yellow 'rubber' gloves she was wearing.

"I saw Mrs Bellamy in the town yesterday."

"Poor you! Is she coming Sunday for worship?"

"I sincerely doubt it dear. The woman is a pagan. A worshipper of Lucifer. She smells awful. Extreme body odour. I don't wish to judge, having just said judgmental things, but YUK!" Then she tittered to herself, shaking her head.

"I wonder about her and her son. Do you think they.....?" He tailed off too afraid to carry on with his question.

"Oh, John. Don't say it. I admit I've thought that too though."

He looked out of the window again at the dull day. He saw the pylons crossing the countryside from the outskirts of the town. A bird swooped into view and then flew behind the shed. Cruickshank put on his half moon reading glasses and returned to his sermon preparation.

The grandfather clock chimed the hour.

After the storm, John and Mona left the Vicarage for the supermarket in their car. Mona placed the recyclable shopping bags inside the largest one. Casually she tossed them onto the back seat as they drove out of Church lane.

***

Carew entered the Post Office. As he opened the door, a small brass bell above it rang. It was traditional, Carew observed.

He went to the fridge to get milk. A middle aged Indian man came to the counter. Raj Kumar had been born in India. His family had moved to London in the 1960's. Raj had a Cockney accent interlaced with a slight Indian twang. He greeted Carew. Carew acknowledged and made his purchase.

Raj asked, "How are you enjoying the weather?"

Carew smiled. "I wouldn't associate the weather with enjoyment. Would you believe I had a shower before I came out? I dunno."

"Nice weather for ducks as they say. At least its stopped raining now. A bit of sunshine too."

On his way out of the shop he felt his phone vibrate in his pocket. He looked at it and saw that a text message had found its way to him at last.

It was from Moira and simply read: 'Any news yet? X'

Carew smirked and typed back: 'Better than expected X' Carew inserted a smiley face in the return text.

***

At around 7:30pm someone found Bellamy's car half submerged in Barnow lake on the outskirts of the town. The rear of the car was just visible, slightly above the water. However, after the police had arranged for photographs to be taken they had also arranged for the vehicle to be removed. It had been established there was no body or bodies in the car. The seat belts were not fastened or cut. The doors were shut and the driver's side window was half opened. The window may well have been down due to the weather. Although it had been raining it had been warm. Of course the window may have been down to ensure water flooded the car as it sank. That left the question as to why all the windows were not down if that was the case.

The police had started searching for Bellamy. He had not responded on his radio.

When his mother was told about the car and that her son seemed to be missing, she simply leaned on her doorway and lit a cigarette. Doris Bellamy seemed emotionless. She decided to consult the tarot cards and hope the reading was favorable. She was convinced her son was safe in one form or another.

The police had been asking passers by if they had noticed anything that might be clues to the sunken car. There were no leads and no CCTV in the town to view.

Had Bellamy been in an accident or was this deliberate in some way? There was no sign of a body in the lake. The frogman investigating only found the usual detritus and the obligatory shopping trolley

The investigating officer Detective Inspector Andrew Dangerfield, looked at the scene. With his customary droopy look and pointing to the car he quipped, "Looks to me like the engine is flooded."

There were no laughs. His colleagues simply looked puzzled.

No one notice a figure dressed in black, with a black full faced balaclava observing the scene. The figure was laid flat on the felt roof of a garage and looking through green 60X50 army binoculars.

Chapter 4

Some days prior, Mike Rolph confronted his girlfriend in the living room of their flat. She was a short chubby woman with short bobbed blonde hair.

He leered at her with his weasel face as he walked in.

"So what's all this about you being seen with Vic then?" His words were accusing and angry. His eyes were wide with rage. He strode toward her and grabbed her arm. She stumbled backward and bashed her leg on the coffee table. A cup fell over spilling coffee on the surface. It dripped onto the carpet.

"I don't know where you got that," she pleaded, "I only saw him as we passed in town and he just said hello. That's all. We didn't even talk nor nothing. Honest."

"Oh yeah? You fucking him, Kay? You been fucking him?"

"No. No. Never. I only know him from school. That's all. I ain't fucked anyone. I never been near him. Honest, Mike!"

Suddenly he stopped in his tracks just as he raised his hand to slap her. He grimaced. He felt as if a sledge hammer had smashed him in the back of his head. He stepped back awkwardly. Eyes rolling, he fell into an armchair clasping his head. Rolph blacked out.

When the ambulance came, the medics confirmed he'd had some kind of a stroke. They said that Rolph was lucky it wasn't more serious than it potentially could have been.

Kay had mixed feelings about it. She knew full well that Rolph was a villain. She'd stood by him when he did a stretch in prison. He was also a brainless bully too.

On the one hand she thought she loved Rolph, yet on the other she was frightened by him. It seemed that when he made her feel like shit, that was when she needed him to make her feel better. It was a vicious cycle but one she couldn't break. She had seen her own father control her mother in much the same way. It was a weird comfort zone for her. It was a cause of much cognitive dissonance for her.

Each time Rolph confronted her, she would remember her childhood in Spalding, all those years ago. It seemed like a different life. Another person. Not Kay. Spalding seemed to her, like a dystopian place full of dismal buildings and unhappy people lining drab streets.

Tuesday Night

When Bellamy woke up he was tied to a chair in a darkened room. His mouth was taped shut with grey duct tape.

In front of him was a figure dressed in black with a full faced balaclava. The figure was sitting astride a chair and leaning on the back rest with their arms folded over it. They looked directly at Bellamy.

Bellamy struggled and grunted. The balaclava person just remained silent and rose casually from the chair.

The last thing Bellamy remembered before he woke up, was getting out of his car to investigate what appeared to be, the body of a person lying in the road near Collingsmote lane junction. He must have been knocked unconscious with a blow to the back of the head. Surely, this masked person in front of him had been the assailant that had crept up behind him, probably from behind the trees.

In frustration Bellamy growled loudly but could not speak because of the tape. A bubble of mucus formed under his left nostril and popped. He wriggled and struggled violently in the chair trying to free himself. His hands were tied behind him and his feet were bound to the chair legs.

The masked figure walked casually behind Bellamy. Bellamy twisted in his chair to follow the figures progress as far as it was possible. Then he followed with his eyes. The place was damp and featureless. It was an oblongular room, windowless, narrow and empty apart from two chairs, one of which Bellamy was seated on. Because there were no windows, Bellamy believed he may be situated below the ground. The only light came from a red low wattage bulb that was hanging from the ceiling behind Bellamy.

Bellamy was trying to work out who was behind the mask. His head hurt from the blow that evidently had knocked him out. The masked person paced annoyingly up and down the room.

Who would dare do this to a police officer?

From inside the black jacket the masked person took a pistol fitted with a silencer. Bellamy wriggled frantically trying to free himself. This was a life threatening situation and if he could just get free he would make this kidnapper pay.

The last thing Bellamy saw before the bullet tore through his brain was the masked person tug their balaclava off. As Bellamy looked upon the face his eyes widened in disbelief. Had his mouth not been taped up he would have exclaimed, "You!" in true cinema stereotype. Then the kill shot was fired.

The shot propelled Bellamy backwards still tied to the chair. As his corpse lay bleeding on the floor the unmasked person fired two more shots into the body. The figure then exited via the only door. Footsteps echoed as Bellamys killer walked up the concrete steps after turning the light off then gently closing the large red metal door.

***

As Carew got ready to bed down for a good night, he casually looked over to the house. He could see movement in the kitchen. He saw the silhouette of Pete moving around inside near the sink. The kitchen light formed a soft square on the ground outside of the house. The shadow of Pete seemed to dance over the ground like a macabre show.

As he idly watched Pete, he noticed that the upstairs bedroom light came on momentarily and then went off again. Carew thought it strange at first, but then thought it might be that Pete's son had arrived home on leave from the military at last. He noticed a car was parked on the side driveway of the house at the end of the terrace. He could just see the front of the vehicle poking out. Carew ignored it.

Lugubriously, Carew thought back to his parents as he lay down to sleep. The cycle of life was on his mind. Life, death and the inevitable end of everything. A book he had read a month ago had set his mind on a tangent of philosophical thought. He thought of his family.

His father, Fred Carew had been in the Marines during the war and stationed in Portsmouth before he was demobbed. He had many a tale to tell of his time there. When he returned home he met Joyce Lemmon at the Co-operative dairy. The Carew family had all worked at the Co-op over the years. Fred didn't know who his real father was. His stepfather Cyril, tended the horses that pulled the milk floats and bakery wagons. Fred's half brother Stanley, who didn't know who his real father was either, was a maintenance man in the dairy. Stanley only knew that his real father was an Italian.

Fred had been married before to Gwen Ashby and they had a son, George Carew. However, the divorce was very messy and he didn't see George again. Carew knew he had a brother but had only seen a grainy monochromatic photo of baby George. Carew and George were only a couple of years apart in age. He didn't know specifics because his father rarely, if ever, spoke about George. Carew suspected it was very painful for him and that may have been part of the reason he'd joined the Jehovah's witness cult. The cult appeared to offer all the answers to life. Maybe Fred felt that a higher power was needed to reunite him with George one day, in a magical place where everything would be put right.

Carew's mother was a very quiet woman. She'd been brought up as a Baptist but converted to the Jehovah's witness cult when she met Fred. The joke with Carew was that the milkman *was* his father. The Co-op dairy was where his parents met.

When Cyril Carew had first seen Gwen he said, "Bloody 'ell. You're a Lemmon."

It wasn't meant as an insult but Cyril could see, by her dark complexion, which family she belonged to. The Lemmons were a good natured family. All of them were very quiet. When Gwen was a pre teen, her brother Melvin had died in his cot, strangled by the chord attached to his dummy. It was a terrible accident but no one ever talked about it. Perhaps that was just the way tragedy was dealt with in those days.

Family history interested Carew. The fact that he had a brother somewhere intrigued him, so much so that he'd made enquiries of relatives and even searched on social networks. He didn't know which names to search under. An aunt had told him to look for either George Carew, or possibly George Jackson, if he'd taken his mother's new married name. Perhaps he was dead. He might be a millionaire or living in the gutter. Still the pull of blood drew Carew to have spates of obsessing over it from time to time.

He had been told many times that the 'JWs' were not a cult, but as far as control, intellectual dishonesty and leader veneration (whether individual or collective), they ticked all the cultish boxes. He had seen good people shunned by the cult members just because they simply didn't want to belong to the Jehovah's witness organisation. These people were not hell bent on destroying the organisation or getting a JW out of the cult. Mostly they just lived their lives and didn't even discuss religion. Still the leaders insisted that such ones must be vilified and shunned at all costs.

Then the gossip would start within the Kingdom halls (or 'king-dumb hells' as Carew referred to them). This was to reinforce that those that left must somehow be inherently evil. Carew had loved his parents but could not forgive them for raising him in such a mentally destructive excuse for a religion. Life inside the artificial religious corporation was depressing. Paedophiles were not reported to the police and they continued to abuse their victims. Carew wondered why this was all covered up by the leaders, until someone told him that it was simply because the corporation wanted to hide all the bad PR in order to attract more bums on seats. That way, the leaders and the money men in control kept their power and financial benefits.

A friend of Carew's once called the organisation, 'a filthy, disgusting cult!' Carew agreed. He had no idea of the scams that went on behind the scenes. This wasn't surprising because the rank and file members were like mushrooms, kept in the dark and fed shit.

Carew was angry at the way he'd been so suppressed as a child. He had no friends because he was only allowed to associate with other cult members and not always then, If they were deemed 'bad associations' or 'spiritually weak' then they must be shunned.

The rules of the cult were weird, very weird. You were told that you have a conscience and that is your guide. On the other hand, if you followed your conscience you would be hauled into a back room of the 'King-dumb Hell' and interrogated by some delusional elders who would judge you harshly in many cases.

Carew believed it was the mind control of the cult that had made him the way he was. He had a dark violent streak from years of having his authentic self suppressed by the guilt, fear and phobia he was subjected to. 'Carew is a fucking nobody' was exactly how the cult had made him feel so when Bellamy had said it to him it confirmed that feeling. But the cognitive dissonance was too much. He had thumped Bellamy when the emotional feedback exploded. Carew considered that the cult's thought reform or mind control, call it what you will, was the reason he had no conscience about brutally killing people he felt deserved it. Not just saying it but doing it. Carew had an inbuilt emotional detachment.

The cult was constantly begging for money in a crafty way. Surely if God was guiding them then they wouldn't need to beg. They ladled on the feeling of worthlessness until you felt forced to give them money or waste time door knocking. Door knocking was just 'busy work' with no real result. It simply prevented the JWs from thinking. Thinking is a dangerous thing for an average JW to engage in because it opens the mind to the shenanigans of the corporation. Especially for the cult leaders or 'Governing Body', because once a person opens their eyes they will cease to provide money to the corporation. Lack of money means that the corporation may be in danger of going bankrupt due to all the emerging paedophilia scandals and lawsuits. Surely, the gluttonous leaders could only provide hush money to protect paedophiles for so long until the well ran dry.

Carew recalled that one day his father had returned from an 'elders meeting' and with a stern face had said, "If Jehovah didn't offer me eternal life I'd still worship and obey him because he is worthy."

Carew thought that this was very strange. As he grew up, he became convinced that this 'Jehovah' was simply a made up character. 'Jehovah' was no more than a sock puppet from the corporation to promote their propaganda via 'appeal to authority'. 'Jehovah' was just a façade from behind which the leader or leaders of the 'filthy, disgusting cult' operated and spewed their lies. Anything the JW hierarchy said was not allowed to be questioned because it was believed that 'Jehovah' had spoken it via the leaders. How can you argue with God?

The leaders had it sorted. If they got caught out they claimed they were 'just imperfect men doing their best'. The rest of the time they had printed and proclaimed that they ALONE were 'Jehovah's mouthpiece'. Carew knew they couldn't have it both ways. The rank and file simply went along with it and continued to waste their lives and money on the cult.

As he grew up Carew remembered that if his father caught him slouching he'd be told, "Stand up straight. Stomach in. Chest out."

Fred Carew had some strange ideas about life and Carew wondered if it was because of the mind control from the cult.

War time and prior to the cult, Fred was stationed in Deal, Kent. Fred was on an assault course and the netting on his helmet had caught in barbed wire. His helmet lifted up and some barbed wire cut his head making it bleed. He was called to the medic. A senior officer asked that just before he was treated, that he borrow Fred to show the conscripts. Fred was told not to speak at all but to look down and play wounded.

The senior officer addressed the conscripts and said, "They're firing live ammo above your heads so keep down." He pointed to Fred and said, "This man looked up and see what happened to him!"

Carew's father said that the conscripts faces went 'as white as sheets'. They thought he'd been shot. Carew identified with this aspect of military humour. Brutal, but an effective teaching tool.

When Fred Carew was a boy he had some homework to complete. It consisted of scrambled words. There was one he couldn't get. The clue was: 'There once lived a wise old........'

The idea was to rearrange the letters E.G.S.A. to spell the answer. Fred decided to ask his aunt who owned the local sweet shop. She gave him an answer. Fred was called to the front of the class as the teacher asked,

"Carew. What is this? There once lived a wise old what? G.E.S.A? Geyser?"

Carew smiled to himself. Now he was free of the cult but the price had been very high. All those people he considered were friends and family now shunned him. This gave him a deep mistrust of people and he always wondered how conditional their love for him really was. If his friends obeyed without question, the rules from some suits in Brooklyn rather than rely upon their higher human nature, then they were not worthy of being called 'friends'.

Carew had joined the military and the cult members saw this as evil. To serve your country rather than serve some gluttonous suits in Brooklyn that protected paedophiles was, to the cult members, unacceptable. They didn't mind reaping the benefits of living in a free country and using it to the full, scrounging benefits, but to actually contribute anything of abiding worth was anathema to them. The corporation forbade its members from contributing to charities in order to have the money for the suits in Brooklyn. The corporation was rotten to the very core, he concluded.

Carew's mother was so quiet you'd never know she was even in the room. She was not keen on ornaments and pictures on the wall. This was not a religious quirk but she just thought it cut down on cleaning. Carew thought this was fair enough, but often he had found the home of his childhood appeared clinical and austere.

Chapter 5
Wednesday

Dangerfield sat alone in his office trying to piece together the whereabouts of Bellamy from the scant information he'd gathered so far. If you didn't know him better, you'd be forgiven for thinking that Andrew Dangerfield was a grumpy old sod.

Dangerfield was a greying thin faced man who stood 6 feet tall. He had sad watery eyes and an aquiline nose. His trademark was a baggy grey herringbone tweed coat that his wife thought should have been thrown out years ago.

His coat was hanging on the upright metal coat stand behind him, near his office door. Protruding from the pocket was a grubby blue bobble hat. The bobble had fallen off a long time ago somewhere in Cromer.

The sunlight shone through the slats in the blinds making stripes of light over his desk. An electric fan oscillated to and fro on top of the green metal filing cabinet.

When the fan swept its breath across the desk, a paper document slightly lifted itself in the almost antique wire filing tray. The papers flapped as if trying to take off and fly. Then they relaxed back until the next waft of the fan made its way over the desk. The brown tipped spider plant jostled its fronds in the fan gusts. Dangerfield hardly noticed it as he stared at his dim monitor screen. He typed his notes about Bellamy, ready to assign it to the recycle bin if Bellamy strode in. If Bellamy didn't appear he would keep the file. He was preparing in advance should Bellamy be found dead.

Although it was early days in terms of his disappearance, he realised that Bellamy was very unpopular. It was possible that someone had taken revenge on the copper. It seemed very unlikely, given his repugnant personality, that he would have 'gone walkabout' or 'jumped off his own wallet', thought Dangerfield.

Dangerfield looked at the silver framed photograph of his wife and two daughters. The photo had been taken in a studio in Cromer. The 'three belles' were his term of endearment for them. His wife Esme was French with a part Italian ancestry. Their youngest daughter, Miriam, was born on April fools day. This became a standing joke. Vanda was the eldest and was quite an inward person. She had the same face for happy as she did for sad. Dangerfield was sure that even experts in body language wouldn't be able to read her.

Each year the family would take a weeks break at the seaside. Cromer was their usual destination. It held a strange sentimental value for Dangerfield but he didn't know why.

He recalled talking to Detective Colin Smith, who was the nearest he had to a best friend, about the virtues of Cromer when Smith had asked him about why he didn't go somewhere more exotic.

"Cromer. Famous for its crabs," he had replied. "I'm not a fan of crab meat though. I have some maudlin memories of Cromer. That's the place to get decent fish and chips if ever there was one. Esme and me have our favourite place to get 'chippies' too. I'm not keen on fish and chips so much these days. Not now they've changed the bloody cooking oil. Only, from certain places they aren't too bad. Cromer. Oh, yeah. That's where. Hunstanton too, Smiffy."

On reflection it wasn't really an answer but it seemed to be sufficient at the time.

Dangerfield rose from his desk. He flicked the 'ctrl', 'alt' and 'delete' buttons on his keyboard to lock his terminal. He stretched his arms and yawned. Then he walked out of his small office and down the corridor to the vending machine, all the time he scratching his left buttock.

Colin Smith was a portly man with protruding ears and a cheeky glint in his eye. He had two failed marriages with no children. Currently he was dating an older woman from Collingsmote.

Colin Smith, Smiffy, was rocking the snack machine backward and forward, bumping it violently on its stand. The packet of crisps he had requested had got stuck when they fell from the top of their shelf in the machine. As they had fallen they had become wedged horizontally between the shelving and the glass. After several rocks they fell into the bottom compartment where he could get them. As a bonus, a bar of chocolate became dislodged and fell too. Smiffy looked at Dangerfield and grinned with delight.

"I hope you're gonna pay for that choccy, Smiffy," quipped Dangerfield, "Or I'll have to tell the police."

He winked at Smiffy who retorted with a smug look but in good humour; "Never heard that one before. Its as bad as the amount of times traffic wardens hear 'book em Danno'!"

Dangerfield laughed and replied, "I would get used to it, mate. You'll be hearing it for a long time to come yet."

Dangerfield got a coffee, white with sugar, from the adjacent vending machine. It came in a buff plastic cup that was a little too soft and pliable for his liking.

"Heard from Bellamy, Smiffy?"
"Not a bleedin' peep. I think he's absconded to a sheep farm in New Zealand, Danger boy!"

Dangerfield blew on his coffee then slowly looked up at Smiffy, narrowed his eyes and grimaced.
"Do you think that's true? You know, about him and sheep?"
"Er, it's common knowledge, Danger boy, common knowledge. Farmer Burns might tell you if he dare speak. Seems old Bellamy has some hold over Burnsy and goes to the farm for secret satisfaction."
"Bloody Norah. I know Bellamy is a bit strange, but sheep? Fuck me. On second thoughts, no fucking of any sort."

Dangerfield paused briefly and looked Smiffy in the eyes, "Smiffy, I was thinking of visiting that con David Martyn. So, I might just go and have a word with Burns after. Rule him out or in, you know. I've got a gut feeling we're not likely to see Bellamy again. I think he had too many enemies, one too many and someone got him."

"Fair enough but don't expect much." As Smiffy walked away he remarked, "Oh, and I get dibs on Bellamy's coat. I need a new tent for camping."

"Harsh," replied Dangerfield, "Harsh, harsh, harsh. You are a wicked old bugger!"

***

First, Dangerfield visited the Martyn residence. A reticent Martyn had answered the door in a brown silken night gown. As he stood in the entrance, Dangerfield asked Martyn if he had any information about the whereabouts of Bellamy. He explained that this was because he'd been seen leaving the Martyn home albeit Monday.

Dangerfield had been informed that Bellamy and Martyn were never on the best of terms. Bellamy had even told his fellow coppers that often enough. Dangerfield needed to evaluate Martyn for future reference perhaps.

Although the whereabouts of Bellamy hadn't been established, Dangerfield knew that people are creatures of habit. Bellamy especially so because he virtually did the same things and went to the same places as regular as clockwork. Dangerfield maintained and admitted that he had a gut feeling that Bellamy had been the victim of foul play.

Martyn played it cool and evasive not giving anything away. He claimed that he and Bellamy were old friends and had just paid a social visit. Dangerfield looked at Martyn with his dead pan face. He thanked him and left. "Lying bastard" he muttered as his feet crunched over the gravel drive. Martyn had closed the door and didn't hear.

Dangerfield had not drawn a total blank. He noticed that Martyn kept looking away from his attempted eye contact. Instead, Martyn would look up, cover his nose with his index finger and obscure his mouth from sight with the hand. Dangerfield noticed the micro expressions as he spoke, but it wasn't enough to accuse him of anything other than lying about his friendship with Bellamy.

Dangerfield sat in his car for a few moments to collect his thoughts. Then he drove to the Burns place.

Burns was nowhere to be found. There was no answer at the farmhouse nor around the farm. The farmyard was bereft of human life.

The familiar pungent aromas of a farm met Dangerfield's nostrils. He was glad his car had a new air freshener hanging from the rear view mirror. His shoes were caked in mud. He hoped it was mud. Dangerfield decided to drive back to the police station and try later.

His car bounced along hitting the potholes in the farmyard track and splashing in the muddy puddles.

'Bugger. Cost a bloody fortune in car washes,' he thought.

Back at the police station he went to the vending machine after visiting the toilet. There was a coin in the change compartment which he removed.

'There is a god.' He said in an ironic undertone and pressed the buttons for a coffee. Another flimsy cup was dispensed.

***

Carew finished his energy bar as he walked into town. The wrapper from the bar was tossed into a litter bin on the side of a lamp post. He walked down Church lane and made his way over to the Martyn residence to the east side. It was on the other side of the village. His face was tense and his nostrils flared. He wanted to see the Martyn residence but wasn't going to go at night and appear suspicious. However, he considered a daytime reconnoiter would be less conspicuous. He would just be a passerby to anyone looking.

Dangerfield turned to Carew's right from the driveway of Martyn's house. He drove by without noticing Carew. Carew made a mental note of the car and it's driver. It wasn't a police car but he could recognise a cop when he saw one.

He thrust his hand into his pocket and felt the small woodcarving with his thumb. He bit the inside of his lip. He was feeling anxious even though his anxiety may be unfounded. He wondered if Martyn would recognize him if he came out and saw Carew in the distance. He knew that Martyn would remember him from the fight.

He remembered that same altercation he had with Martyn on Sunday. It was just plain luck that it had happened because it was Dave Martyn he'd been looking for. It couldn't have been a more opportune meeting. Of course, Martyn didn't know why Carew was in Barnowby. If Pete hadn't told Carew the name, he wouldn't have been in a position to investigate Martyn further otherwise. It was perfect synchronicity!

There was a green park bench adjacent to the driveway. Carew decided to sit there for a while as he observed the house through the rustling trees. Over to his left was a park cum playground. It had traditional wrought iron railings around it and an ornate iron archway leading out onto the street. Opposite the park was a row of houses.

He might get nothing from this vigil but without trying he wouldn't know. It was something he felt the need to do. He had the time so may as well use it.

There was nothing happening, but what did Carew expect? After all, this was real life not fantasy or a film full of fast paced action.

Carew noticed a top range Porche 911 parked in the drive. It was next to the white van that Martyn and the two Mikes had used on Sunday. He observed the large Victorian style greenhouse that was partly visible behind the home of Martyn. There was a line of tall trees behind. Carew decided to see if they lined an accessible road. After about thirty minutes he rose from the bench. After sitting there his hip ached. Carew walked casually down the road to see if there was a turning leading behind the greenhouse.

"Oh snap," he exclaimed. He saw the beaten track behind the tall trees.

He walked along the track his feet slipping on the muddy ground. Small flies danced and darted around him. He swiped at them vigorously. To his right was a small stream and a field with crops growing in it. In the distance he could see a farm house, varied sheds and a silo. He saw Dangerfield driving away from the farmhouse slowly as if he had been searching for someone or something. He gave a slight smile to himself.

When Carew came to the end of the lane there was a gate with a sty fence next to it. It led to another muddy track alongside more fields. Beyond the fields he saw the traveler camp. There was another track quite overgrown that led to the rear of the Martyn home. Carew decided he'd seen all he needed to and turned back. He casually looked through the line of trees at the Martyn residence. He tried not to appear casual and not as if he was spying. Carew didn't know if he was being observed, either by CCTV cameras or human eyes. There was no evidence of CCTV, just a yellow alarm box on the side of the house.

Satisfied that he'd seen all he needed to see he walked back toward the town. He could smell the alluring aroma of cooking coming from one of the old terraced houses that faced the park. It made him feel hungry. This was West Indian cooking and very familiar to Carew.

***

Inside the house, Marcia Legister glanced at Carew walking by and without giving him any attention carried on making her clap hand roti. She was dancing from time to time to the CD she had playing.

The roti was made from a recipe her mother had handed down from her West Indian tradition. Just flour, water, a pinch of salt and oil. Flattened out very fine in her hands, then dropped into a frying pan that had no oil in it. The oil was in the dough. She was preparing dinner for her family and also for the visit of uncle Granville.

The mutton was cooking nicely in the old stained aluminum dutch pot. She gazed from the kitchen window to the park across the road. A blonde woman in a white trilby hat and shiny pink air wear boots was walking her two black dogs. Marcia smiled. It looked as if the dogs were pulling the woman along. 'Who is walking who?' Marcia whispered to herself.

Marcia was a short yet petite girl. Short black curly hair with red high lights. She kept a tube of lip balm on her all the time to prevent dry lips.

Marcia's children were still at school. Their uniform entailed a purple blazer with green piping around the edges. 'Yukky!' she called it. She'd dropped Devonn and Laquisha outside Barnow school every morning in the family car.

Yesterday she had driven to the city to buy foodstuffs that were not available in the town. She needed a packet of gungo peas for one thing. Normally she would use kidney beans or black eyed peas, but she knew that her uncle had a preference for gungo peas in his 'rice and peas'. A nice yellow yam, some cho cho among other things, were on the shopping list. Her uncle didn't eat plantain though as he thought it was 'too heavy on the belly and took a week to digest.'

Admittedly she wasn't using all the shopping today but most of it could keep for the following Saturday. Maybe she'd make 'Saturday soup' that would include 'spinners' and 'sinkers' dumplings.

During the week of course, it was food like pizza, corned beef or sausages for dinner. The weekend was for traditional food.

As she drove along the main road she noticed police activity around Barnow lake to her right. She saw that a car had been dragged from the waters. It had yellow and black striped hazard tape staked around it. She'd seen the car before.

Marcia had hoped that she was not high profile in the town. She tried to avoid contact with PC Bellamy which was a high hope considering she was of Afro Caribbean origin and he was a total bigot.

She did recall that Bellamy had arrested Ralston a few times though. Bellamy could never make his outrageous charges stick. She recalled how Devonn had been stopped and searched on his way home from school by Bellamy. That was one of the reasons she dropped the children off at school and picked them up after.

As she looked back she suddenly noticed that she was heading toward a concrete bollard at the roadside. She swiftly corrected her steering with a jerking motion. A momentary lapse of concentration almost caused an accident. She was shocked and her heart was beating like a jack hammer in her chest. She cursed, "Bumboclaat!"

A squirrel darted from the trees and across the road in front of her. Marcia hardly noticed it as she recovered from the shock of nearly scraping the family car on the bollard.

Marcia's father Lloyd (Lloydie) Collins, was British born of Jamaican origin. His parents had arrived in London on the Windrush.

The Empire Windrush was originally a German cruise boat that had brought upward of 500 Jamaican immigrants to Britain in June 1948. They brought with them rich and gorgeous traditions that would assimilate into Britain and then become diluted along the way, thought Marcia.

Her mother, Hortense Henry, was also British born, not of Jamaican origin but her parents were from St Vincent. Lloyd called her 'smallie' because she was from a smaller island than Jamaica. This was a nick name she didn't like but tolerated. Many a Jamaican and Vincention had come to blows over this term.

Marcia always looked forward to her uncle visiting with auntie Rose. Uncle always wore that same black leather cap with the red, gold and green banding. When he sat down he would take it off, put it on his knee and say in his gravelly voice, "A me kneecap dat."

He would tell his tales of his life and one particular tale was her favourite. No matter how often she heard the tale, Marcia still found it funny.

As a teenager, her uncle had lived in an overcrowded house in Ladbroke Grove where family, including cousins, lived too. Of course the term 'cousin' in West Indian culture was used loosely. It could mean just close friends that were not blood relative or related by marriage.

His 'cousin' Manley (Manman), worked on the railway as a maintenance man. He wore black ex army boots for work. Every evening he would leave them under the rickety wooden chair next to the kitchen window. After several very generous slugs of white rum and coke, Manley would retire to bed for the night. In the morning he slowly descended the stairs bleary eyed. Then he would get ready to go to work.

Uncle decided that on the morning of April the 1st, he would play a practical joke on Manman.

The night before the 1st he had carefully removed the bootlaces from Manman's boots. Manman had shambled off to bed in a stupor.

He replaced the laces with two liquorish laces that he had purchased from the market that day.

The next morning Manman stumbled down the stairs hung over from his imbibing rum the previous night. Uncle sat at the kitchen table eating his avocado for breakfast. He was waiting for the moment that Manman put his boots on.

Sure enough Manman did put on his boots without even noticing the liquorish laces. He pulled on the laces of his left boot to tighten them. The laces stretched and stretched. For a while he was wondering what was wrong with those laces. Manman's expression was one of total disbelief.

He'd uttered some profanities in Jamaican patios and looked at Uncle, who by this time was in fits of laughter.

Uncle had always ended the story by saying, "Boy. If only we had camcorders back way. I could have been rich from all the repeats on them TV clip shows. Bwoy, I tell ya!"

It seemed like a routine now but Marcia would still have to ask, "What happened to the liquorish laces, Uncle?"

The reply was always the same. "We ate them. Times were hard, man. Waste not want not, gyal."

Marcia continued to cook the food for the visit, smiling to herself as she did so. There would likely be a house full of relatives all in good spirits. They would be allowed to enter the special room that was set aside for visitors only. It was a room where the best ornaments and furniture were kept. Marcia realised that this was not such a popular tradition amongst the younger West Indians now, but it was a tradition she loved. It made her feel safe. She took out her lip balm and applied it to her mouth like lipstick. 'Pop, pop, pop,' she said to make the balm spread evenly on her lips.

Her other half Ralston, who was born in Jamaica then moved to London with his parents as a child, would provide the music for the get together. He had been a DJ for a London reggae sound system in the late 1970's to early 1980's. He still performed at the odd function as Jah Vital. 'Me Vital, me ital you nah get fright ya. Dis ya one a fresh from the J.A. capital!' He would shout over the music as the 'dub plate' started. It was his trademark. He no longer had dreadlocks or a beard but he still wore his red, gold and green beaver hat.

Ralston's nickname was 'Frenchman'. This was given to him as a child. He would run into the yard at their home in May Pen Jamaica, to watch the bus go by. The driver was Mr French. Hence Ralston was given the nick name based on the bus driver's name.

No such names were attributed to Marcia's children. That was one quaint tradition that was finished with in the Legister household.

Ralston worked in the nearby city as a store manager selling electrical goods. Marcia was a housewife and plaited hair for private customers. She didn't charge much and was quite popular for it within the Afro-Caribbean community.

Carew walked by and vaguely heard the reggae music. He recognised it immediately as 'Dutty Babylon' by the Jamdung Steppers.

Carew sang along quietly, 'Babylon. Dutty, dutty, dutty Babylon.' He knew the words meant that the police were dirty. The music relaxed him and eased his mood somewhat. He recalled the last time he'd heard that song it was at a reggae sound clash in the city some years ago. He couldn't quite remember the name of the sound system. Was it something like Jah Virus?

***

To look at Carew you'd think he was just your average Caucasian U.K. native. However, his grandfather was a cricket player from Barbados. Unless he told you otherwise, you would never know there was anything other than white European in Carew's blood.

He sang as he walked:
'Lick shot. Boomshot. Boom boom shot
Police brutality, in dis ya society
Boomshot boomshot
A wah me seh
Mash Babylon to rasclaat.'

He fondled the small woodcarving in his pocket again. The gift from Moira had much sentimental value to him.

He thought about Moira and the reason he'd searched for Martyn.

Moira's Destruction

It was the day Moira was found in the street. She was slumped like a rag doll in a grotty car park at 2:00am on an Sunday morning after a drink at the club Paradigm. The police thought she was just drunk, but she had only had one drink all night. She had been in conversation with a man that looked like a Toby jug covered in grease. He revolted her with his self confident manner and flaky skin. She tried to avoid him but he persisted in following her and talking. Her friends, Jayne and Simone, thought she wanted to chat to the man alone. They seemed to know each other. Jayne had dragged Simone away from Moira and the man.

Moira had sipped at her Southern Comfort and after a while the room seemed to swirl. The music reverberated through her head sounding like a train in a tunnel. She didn't seem to remember anything apart from being found at the car park in Corban Road, in the city. The police were told she was seen leaving the club with a stocky individual so they took little interest even though it was the heinous crime of rape. They assumed it was her choice to be with the man.

She couldn't quite remember with any clarity, what had happened. The whole thing was too traumatic. Martyn had led her struggling in his strong grip. Threats of being stabbed with the switchblade he held at her side, made her comply with him. They went to his van in the virtually empty car park. He opened the rear doors and bundled her onto the mattress inside. Breathing rapidly and wild eyed he pointed the blade at her throat. He clambered in and switched on a dim light. Moira begged him to stop. Pleading. Crying. He slapped her face.

"Shut the fuck up you bitch," he snarled with a malicious smile.

He grabbed her throat and applied pressure. He decided not to leave bruises so let go. He put packing tape over her mouth. A punch to her stomach made her double up. Her right shoe fell off and her handbag chain became wrapped around her elbow. Her eyes rolled in confusion.

He pulled down his trousers quickly. He wore no underwear. His small penis was hard.

With gritted teeth he violently ripped off the red thongs from under her short dress. In a frenzy of lust he mounted her. He slid his hard penis into her hairy vagina. It made him sore.

"Fucking dry, you slut," he growled.

Hastily he spat onto his erection several times to lubricate it, then thrust hard inside her. He pounded away on top of her for less than one minute. He squeezed her breasts while constantly muttering, "Mummy, mummy." Finally he lifted up her legs, shoved his member into her rectum and ejaculated thick yellowy sperm up her arse.

"One up the bum, no harm done," he hissed through gritted teeth.

Martyn sniffed the crotch of the severed thongs then licked the gusset. Slowly he wound the thongs around his testicles then rubbed it on his now limp penis. As he became slightly erect he pushed his index finger up her rectum. There was a slight browning of excrement on his finger. He sniffed it then put the finger in his mouth and sucked it off relishing the taste.

"Mmmm, good shit," he breathed.

He tied the thongs tightly around his testicles and hilt of his semi erect penis. The pressure made him hard again. He scrambled onto a gagged and dazed Moira and pushed up inside her a few more times before stopping.

He put his head to her crotch then sucked at her pubic hair. He clenched his teeth over the hairs and pulled out some strands and swallowed them down with bottled water. One pubic hair was lodged between his front teeth at the top, but he ignored it.

Martyn wiped his penis on the tissue that he kept in his jacket pocket. He untied the thongs and placed them into a small plastic box that he called his 'trophy box'. It was attached to the inside of the left rear door. From a compartment in the box he pulled out a small pin. The pin was from the packaging of a shirt he purchased some years ago.

Slowly he inserted the pin into his own left testicle uttering a high pitched wailing sound as he did so. Swiftly he pulled the pin out and jammed it hard under Moira's toenail and left it there. Even in her stupor she squirmed and although her mouth was taped she tried to scream. A bubble of snot formed under her right nostril.

"Always the snot," Martyn remarked.

A small amount of blood dripped from her slightly torn rectum, it mixed with the yellowy sperm and formed an orange mess.

He wiped the mess away and cleaned Moira's crotch as he cried real tears. He'd been determined not to bruise her but now she had been brutalized anyway so a little more punishment was in order he thought. No turning back now.

"Look what you made me do you fucking cow. You bastard bitch. You piece of slutty shit. Cunting fucker!" Martyn was shouting with more tears in his eyes. He was clenching and unclenching his fists. He thumped himself on the head several times as his face contorted.

Roughly he turned Moira over and rabbit punched her viciously several times in the kidneys then he pushed the pin all the way in under her toenail twisting and stirring it as he did so. He pulled it out, sucked the moisture from it and threw it onto the mattress. All the time he was saying in an undertone, "Matris, ego operor non have connubialis intercourse per men!"

Martyn wasn't sure if the Latin was correct but he didn't care.

He replaced his trousers and a small wet patch began to form visibly around the crotch from his still wet penis.

He opened Moira's handbag and rummaged around until he found a tube of crimson lipstick. He puckered his trembling lips and smeared it on. He put the lipstick in his pocket.

He was breathing heavily. Martyn kicked the rear doors open. He climbed out of the van. He looked around to see if anyone was there. He knew there was no CCTV. He pulled Moira out by her feet. Her left shoe fell to the ground into a puddle.

Violently he ripped the tape from her mouth and screwed it up then flung it over the rear wall. A passenger train went by just at that moment somewhere beyond the wall. He dragged Moira to the corner of the lonely car park and shoved her forward against the yellow plastic box that contained rock salt. He laughed after punching her in the stomach. Five more punches to the kidneys and the he left. His van sped off down toward the dock area.

Blood trickled down her inside leg from her torn rectum and dripped from her foot onto the wet ground. The torrential rain washed it away an hour later.

Chapter 6

Moira had spoken to the copper that was called to the scene. It was a PC Bellamy.

"I went out with my friends. On a usual night I can consume lots of alcohol get drunk, then the morning after feel a little groggy. I only recall having one drink. But this time I didn't feel right. I am in pain all over my torso. I did feel totally zoned out and paranoid. I've never done drugs. This was on Sunday and I still don't feel right, dazed, confused and being really anxious at times and also forgetting things I've done just minutes ago. Was my drink spiked with date rape drugs?"

Bellamy had told her that she'd just got drunk, gone to the car park with her one night stand and that was that. He wouldn't take the matter further. He refused to make any note of her pain or injuries. How could he? He thought. It was Martyn, supplier of his addiction. Bellamy scared her. She didn't want to discuss anything with him.

Moira couldn't talk about the pain or the vague snatches of the ordeal that flashed through her mind briefly. She became withdrawn. Carew was out of the city that week with her brother Frank. She was alone and in paralyzing fear.

A week later after constantly crying, she had attempted suicide by ingesting pills and a large quantity of alcohol.

When Frank and Carew returned they asked Moira why the police wouldn't take any action or involve forensics. No answer was provided.

She became agitated and just wanted the subject left alone. In total frustration they complied with her wishes, for now.

Carew was at her hospital bedside. Moira slept after having her stomach pumped. She lay there, pale and fragile looking. Carew would speak to her when she was strong enough so that the matter could actually be pursued by the police. He thought it would be prudent of the police to assign a female officer to assist Moira. It was obvious that the pig that had interviewed her earlier was a complete incompetent dickhead. Perhaps the pig was hiding something.

He watched the monotonous dripping of, what he believed to be, a nutritional fluid passing into the tube leading to the 'Peripheral cannula' that was stabbed into Moira's hand.

Carew felt helpless. He felt the need to get resolve or revenge. He remembered his Father used an expression for this kind of frustration. "I feel like a caged tiger."

He also remembered a song that inspired him to seek vengeance:

'Lick shot. Boomshot. Boom boom shot
Police brutality, in dis ya society
Boomshot boomshot
A wah me seh
Mash Babylon to rasclaat.'

Carew smiled ironically and thought, 'Boomshot. Bum Shit."

After several conversations with Moira it was obvious that she was too frightened to take the matter any further. Even though the original copper she spoke to had been posted back to his home town of Barnowby, she still resisted.

After several more weeks Carew decided it was time to get his revenge. The 'caged tiger' was bursting forth. He had to use all his contacts and skills to accomplish this. Carew knew some pretty dodgy characters who owed him favours. Now it was time to collect.

***

It was at the Club Paradigm that he went to meet Harry 'Chorry' Jones. Thick set, jet black gelled hair swept back, Harry worked in security at the club. He was a traveller. Chorry lived on the traveller site on the outskirts of Barnowby just a few miles away. A 'chorry' was a word for a blade or knife. He said it was a Romany word. Carew believed him.

In the cramped, dusty and musty smelling security room, Harry found the CCTV recording for the night in question. There were several cameras placed inside and around the club so the task was arduous.

"Bingo, ya bastard!" Carew said as he saw Moira approached by a man. As they watched the CCTV recording, they saw him casually distract Moira's attention and slip something into her drink.

"Any idea who that is?"
"Ain't got a clue," said Harry. He paused then continued, "I know he lives in Barnowby though. Drives a flash car."

"Can I get a still of his mugshot printed?"

"Yeah, sure. Give us a few minutes and I'll have it ready for you, Carew."

Harry sat in a chair clicking away on an old looking computer terminal. Then the printer whirred and a small black and white picture in the middle of A4 paper emerged.

Here was a good full face of the man that Carew would discover was Dave Martyn.

"If the coppers won't do anything about this bastard rapist, then I fucking well will, Harry!"

"You want to use traveller justice. Bang him on the head. Put him in a van, then take him to a field in the middle of nowhere, miles from anywhere. Make sure he's gagged and bound. Then break a few bones. Smash his shins to pieces. Take off his chockers…er…shoes, then cut his feet up with a chorry so he can't walk. Job done. Job bloody done!"

Carew smiled. He already had some ideas about how he would deal with this. A memory of a man called Dan Payne crossed his mind.

All his life he'd felt like wimp but now it was time to redress the balance again. He wondered if it was more about his self worth or about avenging Moira. Maybe it didn't matter because he was driven by an urge he couldn't suppress. He also wondered if the balance could ever be redressed or was it all out of control now?

He wasn't sure if finding the Martyn residence would be beneficial but it was worth the effort. It may be useful for future reference if he needed to make a visit there.

***

On the local news it was briefly mentioned that Bellamy was missing and anyone with information could call the number they provided. People were 'urged' to come forward and talk to the police.

In the shop on Collingsmote lane, Carew saw the local paper on top of the counter next to the cash register.

"Bellamy missing is he?" Carew asked Mr Kumar.

"Yes. I hope he's gone forever. The amount of times he's been in here to harass me just because I'm the wrong colour skin is impossible to number. He is rude and threatening. He's a real racist. I think he's been trying to intimidate us so relentlessly that he's attempting to get us to leave Barnowby. Plenty of enemies that one."

"Racist is he? Can't stand those types."

"Oh indeed, sir. We think it was him that slashed the tyres on our car and put a brick through our window. Can't prove it, and how do you fight the

45

police by going to the police? My son had a bicycle and he stopped him and tried to say he'd been out stealing handbags on it. None of it was true but it caused us great pain."

"Doesn't sound very popular then. I recon he's been bumped off. Plenty of people to do it, ay?"

"He even arrested Ralston Legister a few times, on fake drug busts but each time Ralston could prove where he was and had nothing on him. Bellamy was warned by his superior officer, DCI Dangerfield, I believe, to stop the busts as it was making fools of the local constabulary."

"Ha. I don't think they needed Bellamy. The police are fools already, don't ya know?!"

They both laughed and Carew purchased the news paper and a few other items and left.

Again the song came to his mind and he sang:

'Lick shot. Boomshot. Boom boom shot
Police brutality, in dis ya society
Boomshot boomshot
A wah me seh
Mash Babylon to rasclaat.'

Chapter 7

Mrs Barnyard had heard the news about Bellamy and told Sid as they ate their meal. It was an oven baked lasagna. Lasagna was their favourite convenience food. For afters they had individual strawberry cheesecakes that she had found on special offer at the supermarket.

In the background, the TV was showing an Australian soap opera. Neither of them paid any attention to it. It was simply on because they tended to put the TV on and just leave it on. Perhaps it was a comfort thing but they really didn't know when asked why they left it on.

Sid had a mouthful of lasagna but still spoke. He gestured at the TV with his knife and declared, "You know when the telly is rubbish when the adverts are better than the actual programs they show."

Mrs Banyard reminded him not to speak with his mouth full.

"You're spitting your food everywhere," she remarked.

He smiled and remembered that she could be quite controlling at times. He even thought she was capable of sorting Bellamy out if she so desired.

The phone rang and Mrs Barnyard answered it. It was John Cruickshank asking about the flower arrangement for Sunday service.

"It's all in hand, John," she said with a smile.

"I was wondering what you make of the Bellamy thing, Fiona. Should we include him in our prayers?"

"Well, that isn't for me to say. If you want my view, it is best we leave the subject alone. You know my view. He's going straight to Hell when he dies. Might be there now."

"Yes, I get your point. You know we've had our run ins with him recently. That bother with the communion wine on the bike. Awful business. Tried to get me arrested for carrying the bottle in my jacket. The man is crazy. Of course it would never have washed. He is constantly being hauled over the coals by his superiors but they just let him carry on. It is blatant harassment. I think he has a grudge against a lot of us here, but the Lord knows why. Best leave it in the hands of our Lord."

"The man is a bigot. You know it has to do with you christening the Legister children. Well, that's my theory for what it may be worth, of course."

Mrs Barnyard recalled the evening their son Jimmy, was driving home along by Barnow lake. She really had no idea what had happened when Jimmy came home crying. It was because of Bellamy.

Jimmy saw the police car flash its headlights. Then the blue lights flashed. He pulled over to the side verge next to the sign for Barnowby. He remained seated as Bellamy waddled slowly over to him. Jimmy wound down his window and greeted Bellamy in a friendly tone. Bellamy gave him a filthy look. With a flash and before Nigel had time to react Bellamy had sprayed Jimmy in the face with pepper spray. As he held his face in his hands reeling from the sting, he heard a cracking of perspex. Bellamy smashed the off side headlight on Jimmy's car.

Bellamy returned and slowly spat words into Jimmy's ear, "Get your light fixed or I'll be pulling you over again. Keep your gob shut about this and remember, I don't want no pouftas in my town. So, you can fuck off, you queer!"

When Jimmy had recovered sufficiently he drove away. The wing of his car glanced the side of the sign post bending it.

Mrs Barnyard replaced the phone handset and sighed loudly. The reminder sickened her. Then she thought of Bellamy being killed, smiled at Sid and returned to her meal. The Lord certainly was a just God!

On the TV a comedian was saying, "First thing this morning, there was a tap on my door. Funny sense of humour my plumber has."

There was the obligatory canned laughter.

***

It was the day Rolph had decided to take his normal short walk. The walk was all part of his recuperation from the stoke. He was determined to be mobile. He'd been informed by the doctor that it was 'the sooner the better' for recovery that he became mobile.

It was also the day Bellamy had gone missing. He noticed the trees waving in the slight breeze at 9:15pm. There was a noise behind him like a footfall squelching in mud. He turned. There was nothing but the road and the usual scene. The illuminated church spire was further behind him. He was alone. Rolph grunted and fumbled for a cigarette. He patted about his shirt and trouser pockets to locate his lighter. Then he remembered he'd put it in the box with the cigarettes. How had he missed that? Probably Kay. Her bloody fault.

A figure in black with a black balaclava, hid behind an oak tree and watched as he walked. When Rolph reached the dry stone railway bridge he felt a tap on his shoulder. He turned. No one was there. He had not looked down. The figure had tapped his shoulder then squatted down. Looking directly in front he did not notice Balaclava move around his feet. When he turned to carry on walking the figure stood right in front of him. Rolph was shocked and stepped back but it was too late. A tiger blow flattened his throat. He fell to his knees choking, struggling to breath. His throat closed as the bruising began to swell. He clawed at the air wildly. The pain was excruciating as he suffocated. Just before he passed out he was dragged and pushed violently around the side of the bridge.

The Balaclava dragged Rolph's twitching body by the collar and down the damp screed to the railway line. The fly ash tumbled down the incline behind them as Balaclava heaved the body along. Rolph's trouser leg caught on a bramble leaving thorns and small quills embedded in the course cloth, along with a tiny tear.

His body was placed just inside the darkness of the tunnel.

Just as the New Street train thundered around the corner in the tunnel, Balaclava fired a flare that burst with a brilliant blinding pink flash. The train driver, who was by mere coincidence also surnamed Rolph but no relation the Barnowby Rolph, was momentarily distracted by the flashing pyrotechnic burst over to his upper right view.

Reg (Chimpy) Rolph shook his head and blurted, "Blimey, is it bloody fireworks night?"

He then popped a nicotine lozenge into his mouth and gave the matter no second thought. Instead his thought went to his local football team. He wondered whether his five year old son would ever play for them when he was old enough.

It was sufficient for him not to notice Rolph's body on the cold rails before him. Balaclava's ploy had worked, as bizarre as it seemed. Make a distraction to leave an element of doubt about Rolphs death. Had he been hit when alive? When? Balaclava realised that the flare may come in to question, but by the time they were looking for clues they would be few and far between. That is even if they did suspect foul play. It seemed complicated, but if there was doubt, then surely the other villains in the town would begin to take notice. Perhaps they would fear for their lives, if they made the connections right. It was high time to take matters into one's own hands.

The train sped over Rolph slicing him into bloody pieces under the wheels. His head rolled and bounced into the bushes. The balaclava clad figure watched from behind the gap in the fence next to the bridge. Then disappeared into the copse adjacent.

***

Pete told Carew about his sister, out of nothing more than idle chatter. They sat in Pete's living room. It was decorated in purple, maroon and yellow wallpaper. There was a garish carpet in similar colours. The room was quasi modern in feel with some 'eclectic funk' from no particular era. Carew particularly liked the Voodoo mask that hung to the right of the mantel. It reminded him of the woodcarving that Moira had gifted to him. In fact, it was almost identical apart from the size.

"Banyard," said Carew. "I know that name. There was a Jimmy Banyard, nice lad, in the same school as me. Can't remember if he was a year above, below or the same though. It is just a vague memory."

Pete raised his eyebrows in pleasant surprise. "Jimmy, yes, that's my nephew. So you were at Walton School. Did you live in the town?"

"Yes, Walton Wankers they called us. And no. I lived out of town but my Dad was lived in Collingsmote after the war. He gave me a lift to school of a day. Surprised I don't recall the Martyn mob."

"I think they would have gone to Lincoln Road school because of the location they in lived in at the time. Nigel used to get a lot of grief from Bellamy you know."

"Didn't we all, at that school. My gut feeling Pete," said Carew as he looked intensely at Pete making eye contact, "Bellamy has been topped!"

Pete looked uneasy. He took a deep breath then sat back in his armchair relaxing.

Carew suspected that Pete knew more than he was saying but continued, "Rolph's death seems a tad suspicious. I recon someone or ones, are going to be picking off the scum around here."

"Oh, I don't know, Carew. Sounds a bit like fiction. This is real life not television, ay."

"We shall find out soon enough." Carew changed tack, "Oh, Pete. Have you got a plastic carrier bag I can have?"

Pete complied with the request.

"ASDA or Tesco?" Pete asked with a laugh.

Carew gave a big grin, looked at the ceiling then replied, "Aldi!"

***

It was overcast outside and Carew wasn't sure if it would rain or not. He thought he'd felt a spot on his cheek but couldn't be sure. He was a long way down Collingsmote Lane and had turned off into a small nameless track.

He put his leather gloves on and walked into the thick of the bracken where the hogweed grew, near the stream. The weeds seemed to tower above him. From his travel bag he took a folding knife and using it with care, cut stems of hogweed. He placed them in the carrier bag Pete had provided.

"Perfect amundo!" whispered Carew to himself.

He tossed the tops of the plant into the stream and watched as they floated away, slowly and gracefully.

When he had collected a large bundle he removed his gloves so that they turned inside out. He made sure that the hogweed sap would not make contact with his skin. He didn't want the pain of the purple rash it brought.

Back in the shed he placed his travel bag down on the floor and the bag of hogweed stems on the small table next to his bed.

He laid out a pair of yellow 'rubber' gloves on the table along with two small hollow rods and fifteen hypodermic darts that would fit into the rods. They were part of a blowpipe weapon that Carew was assembling. A pestle and mortar that he had found in the shed, was placed next to the items.

It seemed like hours that Carew worked on the hogweed stems to extract the sap for his tiny darts. He knew the darts were probably totally unnecessary. However, he knew they could cause his quarry discomfort for a start. It was all part of Carew's plan, not that you could call it that as it was constantly changing. In reality, Carew hadn't made any real plans. He was just winging it as he went. There was a cruel streak in Carew that made him want to use the hogweed sap rather than a direct knock out.

The hogweed had given Carew the idea to inflict pain onto Martyn. Yes. It was no secret shared between Moira, Frank and Carew that revenge was the reason he had entered Barnowby, on a lead from Harry 'the Chorry' Jones. It had just been pure chance that he'd been approached by Moira's rapist for an altercation and that Carew had been able to identify him straight away.

Then there was the stroke of luck that Pete came over to assist him and give him lodgings for a few days. How odd that after all these years of mental torment he finds out the whereabouts of Phil Bellamy who was hopefully deceased by now.

Then there was the death of Rolph, one of Martyn's goons and how strange that was. Why now? Was it more mere coincidence?

One thing Carew was certain of was that he had to get to Martyn before anyone else did. He had to make Martyn suffer to the extreme before he put him out of every one's misery. Carew was clenching his teeth at the very thought of revenge.

Carew worked on his 'plan' alone in the shed.

He heard two jets from Collingsmote base, fly over and fade away into the distance as the sound of birds chirping returned to his ears.

***

Outside the greenhouse at the Martyn home, Mike Kitter, Kitter the cutter, held the Bowie knife by the handle and admired the pristine, gleaming blade. This was the implement he intended to use to 'slice'n'dice' Pete Silver's strangely familiar guest. Where had he seen him before? Kitter knew he needed to catch Carew off guard, possibly from behind. He'd seen how Martyn had been beaten on Sunday evening which indicated that this guy was no push over. Martyn himself was a highly respected fighter who had received private tuition.

He smiled his vile toothy smile as he threw the knife toward a tree at the bottom of Martyn's garden. It hit dead center in the circular patch where a branch had been lopped away some years previously.

Martyn was wearing his usual blue suit. He stood, watched as Kitter retrieved the knife and walk back to where he had been standing.

"Oi. Mike," called Martyn rubbing his stubble, "Come 'ere for me."

Kitter immediately jogged over to Martyn like a dog to it's master.

"It's about 'other Mike'. I just got some news. Bad news. They found his body in bits down the bank near the tunnel."

Kitter's smarmy smile turned to a look of disbelief. He put his knife into the holster and placed it in the back pocked of his faded blue jeans.

"What the fuck?" he spat. There was a pause as Martyn looked at him with a serious expression. Kitter continued, "What? Was it an accident? Murder? What did they say?"

Kitter felt the shock of the news set in. He felt a confusion of emotions.

Martyn broke the stony silence, "We know he'd been ill after that stroke thingy. He could have fallen down the bank and fell on the line. I feel a bit suspicious coz old Bell end has gone missing. I ain't normally doubtful but we gotta be fuckin' careful. We've got a few bastards that we've pissed off. Look at it like this; With Bellamy gone, then so's our protection from the pigs. I know I wound old Bell end up but that sheep shagger was our ultimate weapon. Might just be me but I got a sort of feeling we're in for some fun."

"Do you recon it's Silver and his new mate?"

"Dunno. I think that bastard Silver is in this somehow. As for his mate, that face, seen it before."

"Yeah. Me too but I can't place the fucker. Right. We need to get the cunt and soon. Tonight we go over to the Silver place and….."

Martyn cut in and spat vehemently, "Oi. Shut your fucking 'ead Mike. We'll do what I say and when I say it. Don't fuckin' tell ME what to do. Okay?"

As Martyn's eyes blazed, Kitter held his hands up in apology. "Sorry, Boss, sorry. Just eager y'know," he said.

"You and me might benefit from a visit to the Silver place but from a distance at first. I said I'd get Silver one day and I've been putting it off. Now we can get two turds with one stone. We just gotta case the joint first coz there's no sense in bursting in there and they're both out at the nancy boys nudist club reunion. AND…….even if they ARE there we need to know when the coast is clear you twat."

Suddenly Martyn's face changed. He felt his face with his hand. He looked shocked.

"You okay, boss?" Kitter asked stepping back.

Martyn shook his head as if dazed. Then he looked at Kitter strangely and said, "I'll let you know."

"Yes, boss. Got it!"

Chapter 8

Dangerfield felt nauseous as he examined the area where Rolph had been mutilated. He remarked with his usual dead pan face and dry sense of humour, 'Where Rolph had been chuffed to bits.'

He pouted his lips in disdain as he surveyed the scene. Dangerfield walked and peered at the screed and fly ash incline and the track. He looked for any signs of activity. His boots crunched over the fly ash as he walked along the track side. In places, he would slip and have difficulty balancing as he trudged in the deep fly ash.

It had been raining during the night. Quite torrential rain too. There really wasn't much to see. No sign of a scuffle. Nothing apart from a small piece of fabric that matched Rolph's trousers caught in brambles at the top of the incline that led down to the track. That in itself meant nothing because brambles DO tear clothes. The fly ash and screed made it impossible to find any footprints.

Several train drivers had been interviewed. These were the drivers that would have driven the route around the time it was believed Rolph had died. All their trains had been examined.

It was Chimpy Rolph's train that had the evidence of the mutilation of Mike Rolph splattered over it. It had been established that they were not relatives despite the same surname. Dangerfield was very interested by the information about the 'pink flare' after he had read through all the notes in the on line report.

"Pink bloody flares. Sounds more like a fashion statement," Dangerfield said to Smiffy.
"What do make of it Danger boy?" Smiffy looked serious.
"Well to be honest Smiffy, I have a funny feeling it wasn't just because matey had had another dodgy turn again or just decided to slide down the bank and jump under the bloody orient express. Rolph had form. And as a result he had enemies. Can't rule out foul play, Smiffy."
"Yeah. The whole town knows about him being an old lag. Didn't he used to run that seedy club on Empire Road back in the day?"
"Oh that shit hole. I remember it. The Pink Bottle wasn't it?"
"Leather bottle."
"Not The Pink Bottle then?"
"Nope."
"Blue Bottle?"
"Not even close."
"Bugger."

***

Mona Cruickshank looked into the garage at the car and motorbikes. The trials bike was one that only John used. He rode it once in a blue moon. The garage contained old paint tins that needed throwing away as some of the paint was rock hard by now. There were cobwebs festooning the place. It had a strangely pleasant aroma of oil in there though.

The window had a crack diagonally across it but it wasn't bad enough to require repairing. This was a typical garage, she thought. Thank the Lord that they weren't poor or living in a hell hole. Yes, there were some odd people in Barnowby, but on the whole things were good.

She walked over to the old kitchen unit that was now used as a storage cupboard. She thought back to when it was in the vicarage. The unit had been removed but not destroyed, when the kitchen was renovated. It was the day that John had been rushed to hospital writhing in agony from appendicitis. In those days they didn't use keyhole surgery and he had to have a large cut across the groin. He was in bed and resting for weeks.

Mona opened the cupboard and looked at the old pots and pans that were in there. She decided that as they'd been in there so long, they had no use for the Cruickshanks anymore. With a little spit and polish they would be good for the church jumble sale. There was an ASDA carrier bag tightly wrapped up. Mona couldn't remember what was in it so opened it after using a hand brush, dusting off the large spider.

The package was soft. Inside was a black woollen military balaclava. She smiled to herself as she recalled her days learning martial arts. The class was hosted by a mysterious man by the name of Powers. Captain Powers. She knew nothing more about him apart from the fact that he tutored a private student on a one to one basis. However, the lessons seemed sporadic and Powers was heard to complain that the student was very unreliable. That was about all Powers was ever heard to say that was considered a personal viewpoint. He was a hard man and his eyes were dead in their sockets almost. She had heard the name Tom Eccleston bandied about. He seemed to wear a face covering. Perhaps Eccleston was disfigured or something she thought. Whatever the case was he didn't seem to have any concept of time according to Powers.

Wrapped up in the balaclava were a set of martial arts throwing knives that she remembered with fondness. She picked two of them up and swivelled to face the grubby dartboard to her left. Mona whispered 'Double top.'

She threw the first knife and it stuck into the double top on the board. Then she looked away and thought, 'eight.' Then she threw the second knife. There was a twanging sound as it hit the wire next to the bulls eye. The knife clattered across the floor. Mona laughed to herself and thought, 'You can't win 'em all!'

She picked up the knife and walked to the dart board to retrieve the other knife. With a sigh of nostalgia she wrapped the balaclava up with the knives and placed them back into the cupboard.

***

Some years ago Captain Powers dressed in a black silk Shaolin type suit, would wait in his gym. He called it a gym as the term Dojo seemed rather limited to a specific martial art to him. Powers specialised in unarmed combat by any means. It was the person, not the style that won the battle he thought. He'd seen various schools of combat compete with each other. This had convinced him that skill won the fight.

Powers sat with his back to the large mirror and his head bowed yet looking straight ahead. He was a secretive man and no one really ever got close to him. None of his associates were sure if he had a partner, was married, was celibate, gay or just darned weird. This was how he liked it. When confronted in the street to complete a survey or donate money he just gave a maniacal stare and walked away. Usually the person with the clipboard would feel intimidated by this large stubbly battle scarred man.

Rain fell on the roof of the Dojo and bounced off the fan light with no perceptible rhythm. The usual students had all left. There was one chatty lad who bored him with his theories about martial arts. He was always the last to leave. Powers was well aware that the students paid good money for lessons so he tolerated the inane babble with an insincere smile. As his old boss used to say, "They are your bread and butter." Powers was never rude or dismissive to students. Bad vibes would result in bad cash flow. One dissatisfied customer could put others off and that wasn't worth the hassle. 'The power of ten' it was called. At least there was a sortie up and coming soon with a mercenary troop. That would be good money but it was the action that appealed. Powers thrived on the battle. The adrenaline surges and the feeling of conquest over adversity was a prime mover to him.

Powers was waiting for a private student called Tom Eccleston. For some reason Eccleston insisted on wearing a mask. Sometimes it was a balaclava and sometimes a ninja mask. Either way he never once showed his face. Powers thought it very strange but then the money was good so best not to question. He thought he knew who Eccleston really was but as he paid good money it was not for Powers to question. Eccleston picked up the moves very well but his attendance at lessons was to say the least, hit and miss. There was an inexplicable viciousness about Eccleston too. He seemed to want to learn moves that would maim and kill rather than defend or disarm. Powers had asked him in an oblique manner if he wanted to be a soldier wondering if he would be interested in mercenary work. Eccleston had not really answered the question. Eccleston was very precise with throwing weapons. Shuriken was his forte. He could throw a shuriken star and hit the target practically with his eyes closed. It seemed as if he picked a shuriken star out of nowhere when he threw one. His sleight of hand was fantastic and even a veteran like Powers was impressed.

Eccleston always turned up dressed in black. It appeared he would arrive at the Dojo running from across the car park from out of a large wooded area. Powers gave it no more thought other than receiving payment. Perhaps he parked his car in the woods, got changed into his martial arts gear and entered via the wood. Who cared? Not Powers.

The rain stopped battering on the gym roof and the sun shone through the fanlight.

That was then. This is now.

***

Marcia's uncle and his car party arrived. He parked his car. It had plush leather interior and he took care of it. Having had a life of penury in his early years he now appreciated 'good tings' as he called them.

Marcia knew it was her uncle arriving as she could hear the music thumping from the vehicle. Sure enough he was wearing his usual cap as predicted. The passengers all filtered into the house with happy greetings. Lastly uncle came swaggering in swinging his car keys casually. There were already some friends and family in the house catching up and reminiscing over old times. Marcia hurried around getting drinks for the guests as they mingled.

"Cassava chip uncle?" she asked as he walked into the best room.
"Oh, thank Yuh darlin'." He winked. "Bloody foreign food."

They laughed heartily together. She took out her lip balm and applied it to her mouth like lipstick. 'Pop, pop, pop,' Marcia said.

Cheryl stood by the fireplace in the best room. She was a large blonde woman. She had a lip stud that didn't suit her. It looked more like a pimple above her lip but no one told her that, not even Andrew who was the 'other half'. They were not married. Andrew was Marcia's mixed race cousin. He was not able to attend the gathering due to business in the city. They had two dogs, miniature schnauzers named Mollie and Maddie. Although they were described as 'miniature' they were very well fed creatures.

Cheryl arrived later when it was getting dark outside and darkened more by the rainclouds. The couple had two children, Lee and Aimee. Cheryl had once been a short term girlfriend of Mike Kitter but that was years ago. He had stalked her. Eventually she had to obtain a restraining order to prevent him harassing her. She was edgy coming back to Barnowby in case she bumped into him. Inside the Legister house she felt safe though. The aroma of the food and the jollity distracted her from the pain she'd felt in Barnowby years before.

She realised she'd left her phone in her car so she casually strode out of the house. She rebuked herself for being so absent minded. 'A senior moment.' She mused. Her pink high heels clacked on the paving slabs and echoed in the night. The streetlamps cast their yellowy light across the damp street. The lush bushes moved slowly in the breeze. She stepped onto the street to gain access to the driver's side door of her vehicle. Cheryl heard a car slow down as she opened her own car door. It's headlights shone behind her. As she retrieved her phone and clicked her door shut the large black saloon car slowly pulled level with her. It's near side window whirred down and she beheld an all too familiar face leering at her. She was shocked. Her heart raced as fear gripped her throat.

"Hello princess," mocked the voice, "Come to visit me 'ave ya?" There was now a face to the voice. He lowered his light reactive shades halfway down his nose.

"Mike Kitter!" She gasped. "No. I'm at a friends house. Goodbye."

As she began to walk swiftly back to Marcia's house Kitter pulled up, got out of the car and strode up behind her.

There was a park opposite and it was dark. In her haste she didn't notice a silhouetted figure dart from behind the trees. She hurried her pace, stumbling and almost falling as she ran back to the house. Her high heels scraped loudly on the damp ground.

Kitter was right behind her with his arrogant smile. "Come 'ere Chez. Pappa Mike wants a word with you. I got something to put to you," he scoffed as he grabbed his crotch. Cheryl didn't see as he was behind her when she fled.

Suddenly, she felt his sweaty hand grab her upper arm roughly and grip tightly. She heard a sound as if Kitter had been strangled rapidly. She could only describe the sound as a guttural 'Hukk!' Kitter simultaneously released his grip. Cheryl didn't see or hear Balaclava run behind Kitter and in a lightening move wrap a thugee around his throat. The wire sliced into Kitter choking him. Balaclava dragged him behind Cheryl's car. Balaclava bundled Kitter into the rear of his own car. Kitter had left with the engine running. What a stroke of luck for Balaclava that Kitter had stopped the car when he had. It was next to where Balaclava was going to fire a shot through the car windscreen at him. But circumstances alter cases. No shots with the woman there on this usually empty street. Yes! Far, far better than planned.

Cheryl turned around and Kitter was nowhere in sight. At first she was afraid to look to see where he had gone and she ran a little further to the house. Finally she paused for what seemed an eternity on the pavement just outside Marcia's gate. Gingerly, she peered around to see if the coast was clear. Her heart thumped like a bass drum in her chest.

She saw Kitter's car accelerate past her, down the street, into the next road and toward the town. It wasn't Kitter driving though. It was a figure in a black balaclava wasn't it?. Kitter seemed to be reclining in the back seat with his shades askew on his nose. Not that Cheryl was in the right frame of mind to be objective, let alone observant.

She was unsure what to do. Maybe Kitter changed his mind and decided the joke was over. Yes! Surely that must be the explanation. She decided that she might talk to Andrew about it if later. Maybe not. For now she would return to the gathering and get her brain back together. She thought of Andrew, her children and the two schnauzers and it gave her comfort.

She didn't see the small specks of blood that had splattered on the back of her dress and some on her arm. Not big enough to notice unless examined as they blended in a macabre way with the pattern on her dress.

Standing in the park and watching from behind the children's slide was Carew. He melted into the darkness unseen and unnoticed.

When she went back into the house, Marcia asked her if she was okay. Cheryl confirmed she was fine and gradually relaxed as the fruit punch and reggae music soothed her.

***

Through the steel door and into the gloom of the oblongular room Balaclava carried the Body of Kitter over his shoulder in a fireman's lift. There was a rank smell in the room and the body of Bellamy lay where it had been left tied to the chair and fallen to the floor. Balaclava dumped the body of Kitter on to the floor with a sickening thud. As he fell, his face hit the leg on the chair that Bellamy was tied to. The impact knocked his rotting upper left incisor out. It skittered across the concrete floor and landed next to Bellamy's head. As an after thought, Balaclava searched through the pockets of Kitter's Crombie. After removing a wallet Balaclava thumbed through it with gloved hands. Then Balaclava took the bank notes out and kept them. Balaclava looked at the various cards with disdain and then tossed the faux leather wallet into the corner.

Pitch black returned to the room as the metal door slammed shut once again. Balaclava climbed the steps leaving the carnage.

***

Carew emerged from behind the iron arch of the park. The streetlight cast his shadow behind him. It was daunting yet majestic.

He had noted the direction the car had taken. Carew also recognised the moves and technique Balaclava used to dispatch Kitter.

His eyes glazed over as he recalled his days in the mercenary army. He thought of the training the platoon had endured prior to going into action. All forms of defence and offence in unarmed combat were used. The footwork used was very similar to that which Carew had learned from Captain Powers. Powers had been killed in action in the Congo. Carew was there when it happened.

He recalled they were all running through a small village with their machine guns at the ready. Taking cover as they went. Looking all around them. Alert and ready to respond like coiled springs at the first sign of trouble. A grenade had been thrown near them. Instinctively they fell to the hard ground as it exploded. Carew remembers it was as if he'd been lifted from the ground by a titanic wind. The blast lifted him horizontally and flung him backward. Sadly, Carew recalled being hit by the gruesome and hot minced parts of Powers. There was a shard of bone from Powers that shot like a dart and wedged into Carew's cheek. The scar was still there as a vile testament to the horrific death of a colleague.

He was sure that Balaclava was not unknown to him. The questions that tantalised him were; who hated Bellamy and the Martyn gang enough to bump them off? Was this someone Carew actually knew? If so, who was it? Carew would have this running around his mind until he found out.....and he had to!

Carew remembered his conversation with Pete about Nidge. Could it be him? Surely it wasn't Moira's brother Frank either. This was indeed a riddle. He was convinced that the assassin was a male by the musculature and movements made.

Carew decided it was time to stop obsessing over it and make his way back to Pete's. He sang:

'Lick shot. Boomshot. Boom boom shot
Police brutality, in dis ya society
Boomshot boomshot
A wah me seh
Mash Babylon to rasclaat.'

***

Carew lay in the dark on the camp bed in Pete's so called shed. His mind was racing about the assassin in the balaclava. He suspected that the body of Kitter wouldn't be found. He also surmised that Bellamy's corpse would be hidden in the same place as Kitter. Was it the same killer that had shoved Rolph under a train or had that been a genuine accident. It seemed like a different method of killing but perhaps it was planned that way.

Bellamy's car was in the lake. Why? The disappearance of Bellamy made the news as a result though. Did that mean that the body of Bellamy had been deposited nearby? Or had the car been driven to the lake after. Why had it been dumped in the lake? Was it to illustrate that Bellamy was dead? He wondered if Kitter's car would be found.

Then he decided it would be time to kill Martyn before he was beaten to it. Surely Martyn would be the next victim as there didn't seem to be anyone else left for the Balaclava to kill.

Carew smiled and thought, 'To kill a fucking turd.'

Chapter 9
Thursday

Martyn cursed as he tried yet again to call Kitter. He threw his mobile phone onto the grass just outside the greenhouse. His mind raced with thoughts of where Kitter could be. He tried not to think about the possibility of murder. Surely Rolph had simply had an accident. He'd probably had another stroke, fallen down the railway bank and stumbled onto the rails and been hit by the train. Bellamy? Surely not murder. There was no evidence although the car in the lake had seemed strange.

Perhaps it was time to get away from Barnowby for a while until he knew more. There was his father's summer refuge by the coast to escape to. He smiled to himself as he recalled how he'd faked his mother's accident there when he had actually killed her deliberately. Was this karma?

***

Carew held his head down for a moment and there was tightness in his throat. He heard the breeze rustling the bushes outside. It was the sight of the ambulance earlier that was driving past that reminded him of most painful event he'd ever experienced. Yet, although the pain was something he'd learnt to manage it still churned him up inside and he knew it would haunt him until the day he died.

They were driving to the hospital in Carew's sports car at about 9:30pm that freezing autumn evening. Nine months pregnant and Amy was having regular contractions. Her waters had broken and Carew had decided to drive to the Maternity unit himself rather than burden the Ambulance service. They had already named their unborn baby boy Curtis. Amy had a travel bag packed ready for her stay in the Mat unit. It was now a race against the clock to arrive on time. Carew applied pressure to the accelerator. The car sped up on the frosty road.

Amy gave a sudden cry of pain as a contraction hit. Carew glanced across to check her. He hadn't noticed that he was veering toward the wrong side of the road. He heard the blasting horn of an on coming lorry. When he turned back to look at the road, he saw the headlights of the articulated lorry barrelling toward them. He jerked the steering wheel to avoid a collision and to correct his lane position. He had miscalculated his position and, at the speed he was travelling, the sports car slewed wildly over the icy road. There was a violent slam as the passenger side of the car smashed into a lamp post. A cascade of shattered glass sprayed everywhere like a fierce hailstorm as the airbags exploded into life. The car skidded, rolled over and over, down the rocky bank and smashed onto a cycle path below.

There were brief snatches of memories. Voices saying, 'On the spinal board.' Flashing blue ambulance lights. Searing pain that had no location. A ceiling with white lights. Looking up at them, they passed overhead as he was pushed along on a stretcher. Voices of nurses as if echoing in the distance, yet the nurses were next to Carew. Blackness. Then the image of a Doctor examining him. A light flashed into his eyes making him see his own reflected, translucent veins. Blackness. Waking in delirium and seeing another ceiling pass by overhead. Lights and chaos.

Pain. Numbness. Waking just briefly. Blackness. Confusion. Nightmares. Heat. Dreams. Voices. Always distant echoing voices.

With a jolt, Carew woke up finally. He was in a strangely familiar place and yet he was confused. Carew was disorientated. There was a wide shaft of sunlight making an oblong shape on the wall. Carew saw the tiny dust particles float aimlessly in the beam. A wave of revulsion wracked his body and mind.

It was 4:15pm when he was informed that Amy and the unborn child hadn't survived. The Doctors had worked for hours trying to save them both but all to no avail.

Carew attended the funeral in a wheelchair.

The crematorium was surrounded by a carpet of red and gold autumnal leaves that had already fallen from the line of trees outside. The first frosts still hadn't thawed in the shadows. An icy wind blew through the garden of remembrance, but it was a different and less cruel and devastating wind than the one that blew through Carew's tortured soul.

Surely Catholic Hell was better than this life!

"Carew IS a fucking nobody!" He thought about it as he wept bitterly, so, so bitterly.

***

Dangerfield was leaning on the wall outside the police station and without any real interest, idly watching the traffic. He had the sleeves of his blue shirt rolled up in such a way that sometimes bending his elbows was not easy. It annoyed him slightly but not enough for him to correct it. His eyes were squinting in the sunlight. He held a cigarette near his mouth. He was thinking about Bellamy and Rolph when Smiffy came out to join him.

Cars went whizzing by on the main road near the Collingsmote South Interchange. The noise was only a mild distraction to Dangerfield.

Smiffy strode out into the car park with his hands in his pocket. Dangerfield didn't notice him until he spoke. "Looks like another one, Danger man."

Nonchalantly Dangerfield turned his head toward Smiffy.

"You speak in riddles," he smiled. "Another what?"

Smiffy opened his eyes wide and held his spread hands up in mock fear. "Another strange disappearance."
"Martyn, Kitter or miscellaneous?"
"Guess."
"Martyn."
"Nope. Kitter."
"Bugger." Dangerfield flicked his cigarette end away. "So how do we know he's not just gone to Chatteris for a week?"

"Car missing. Didn't ring his Mum yesterday evening like he does every night. He didn't turn up for his gun club meeting and he failed to turn up to meet his girlfriend, the one that used to be a bloke. Was meeting him. Er, or her at the Inn."

"Bugger me, Smiffy. How do you know all this? No. Don't answer that." He looked off into the distance then looked back at Smiffy. "I'm going to bore you now but in 2011 for example, there were 327,000 people went missing. I read a report that said we as cossers, spend 14% of our time looking for missing folks. Does that fat bastard Kitter fit the criteria? Such as, risk to the bloke? So, if it's out of character for him to fuck off then he's at risk.....having said that....he's over 18. Not being callous but why should I be interested in some petty thug like Kitter who goes walkabout?"

"Regular font of knowledge aren't you, Danger-man?"

"Danger-man? That's new. Sorry. Carry on."

"Where was I? Oh, yeah. Er...take Bellamy for instance. We all know he was a disgrace to the force but you could set your clock by him. A creature of habit. Obsessive almost. Then we find his car in the lake. Very out of character. I don't mean the car in the lake. Anyway. Did you ever notice how clean that thing was?"

"Oh, fuck yes. I purposely drove through a puddle to splash it just to annoy him once. So, are you connecting Bellamy with Kitter?"

"Yes." He paused. He looked at his shoes. Then he continued, "And Rolph."

Dangerfield decided to cut to the chase. "Motive?"

"Revenge."

"I'm listening."

"Bellamy was a bigot and a bully. There are plenty of people would like to see him out of the way. Right from memory....er....He bullied the Banyard boy, that Legister chap, there is a bloke up Collingsmote way that had a wife from the Phills, that Indian lad from the Post Office....um......and the stupid twat even had a go at the Reverend Cruickshank. Oh, and Farmer Burns....something very dodgy there."

"Any of that officially reported to us?"

"Some of it, but you know I have my sources."

"Bellamy certainly made folk afraid to come to us. I know about Cruickshank, dealt with that myself." Dangerfield lit another cigarette, gestured with it toward Smiffy then continued, "Okay. I don't doubt your sources...but.....why connect this with Martyn's cousins? I don't follow."

"Yeah, well this is a bit tenuous but hey ho, here we go. It's the psychology of revenge. I think someone wants to clean up this town. What the deeper motivation beyond that is, is a mystery to me....can only guess. The Martyn cousins are cunts quite honestly. Rolph and Kitter did time for robbery with a bladed instrument. Rolph was a woman beater. All three of the Martyn gang are all around thugs. Martyn himself is a fucking weirdo. He spent some time in Ranstead loony bin back in 1989. He's both sadist and masochist. Ever wondered why he lets those nettles grow near his greenhouse? Anyway, we think they were involved in the armed robbery on the security van at Collingsmote services......but......because of Bellamy's apparent blundering all evidence was compromised so there was no case in the end."

"So you're suggesting a vigilante? Hold on. Why would a man like Martyn get involved in robbery? He's pretty well off surely....No. Wait. I digress. He's a loony isn't he. Supposing there is a vigilante. I'm not saying there is, but just supposing. Revenge for what and who could it be? Do you think Bellamy was in Martyn's pocket?"

"That and others are the six squillion dollar questions, Danger-man!"

They continued talking on their way back into the station. They took their usual route to the coffee machine. Just before Dangerfield returned to his office he looked at Smiffy and asked with a laugh: "Oi. Hold on. What's this about Kitter with a girlfriend who used to be a bloke?"

Chapter 10

Carew decided to shower then go for a walk. Pete was nowhere to be seen. That was unusual. There were three dirty coffee cups on the kitchen table.

Kitter's car drove past Carew and headed toward the Martyn residence via the back road from Collingsmote Lane. Carew immediately saw that Balaclava was driving.

'Bloody hell, how blatant,' thought Carew. 'Whatever happened to night cover?'

The car approached the Martyn place via the Traveller camp and past a line of trees that would shield it from any CCTV or prying eyes. The car was driven onto the property from an overgrown rear entrance. It was a bright day. However, Carew wanted to see where Kitter's car was being driven to, although he could easily guess. He believed this was some kind of mind game that Balaclava was playing with Martyn. Carew could make it to the Martyn house by going over the field diagonally. The car couldn't.

Martyn was feeling edgy as he walked from the greenhouse area to the back door of his home. Looking in all directions as he went, he changed his walk to a jog.

Once inside, he locked the door to the house and ran to a place near the stairs. Martyn took a revolver from a metal box that was hidden in a recess behind a large original painting by a Parisian artist. He rotated the chamber of the American Colt Trooper and checked it was loaded with the .38 cartridges in all six chambers. He licked his lips.

Violently, he flung his jacket onto the floor. Then he took the holster out of the box and clipped it on over his shirt. The Colt sat snugly in the holster and made him feel invincible. Martyn licked his lips again.

Picking his jacket up as he went, he sprinted up the stairs to his bedroom. Hastily, he packed a suitcase with clothes and toiletries. On his bed were the tattered remains of the nettles he'd used in the night to thrash his own testicles. He decided to take some pins with him to pierce his testicles when he got bored, and a candle to drip burning wax on his nipples. Thoughtfully he packed a pair of nipple clamps and weights.

There was a sudden noise, like a thump outside. His heart started beating fast. He put a clammy hand on his Colt and gingerly edged to the door where the noise came from. His step mother's cat was standing beneath the window. He deduced it had just jumped off the windowsill. She hadn't been home in weeks and neither had his father. He missed his father. He wanted to shoot the cat but decided to kick it to death instead. The cat flinched but Martyn was lightening fast with his powerful kicks. Its entrails splattered the wall and carpet in the upstairs hallway. Finally he brought his booted heel down onto the creatures head and felt its skull shatter. A gelatinous eye spat from the crushed head. Laughing loudly, Martyn picked up the eye and swallowed it.

Martyn took his suitcase and sat on the stairs. Something made him look out of the hallway window. He saw a car smouldering on the large lawn to the right of his driveway. It was Kitter's. How long had that been alight? He wouldn't have seen it when he was coming from the greenhouse to the back door. Why hadn't he seen the fire or smoke?

"What the fucking hell? Bastard," he shouted aloud and ran to his room and locked the door. Martyn looked at his hands and noticed they had smuts on them from a fire. Then there was darkness.

Many minutes later Balaclava appeared from behind the husk of the car and stood watching. The long game was well underway after so long.

Carew edged his way down the lane and took position. From behind the line of trees to the rear of Martyn's greenhouse Carew crouched, observing through small field glasses.

"Bollocks," he spat, "No. no, no, no, no! This is my kill." Carew wondered why Balaclava had so brazenly appeared in full daylight at the Martyn place.

Carew decided to experiment. He cupped his hands and issued a shrill jungle communication call as used in his old mercenary platoon. Carew issued the fake bird call. Immediately Balaclava looked over toward Carew.

"Fuck. Knew it," muttered Carew. He realised that Balaclava had some kind of military understanding. Carew thought about standing up to be seen. He wasn't going to let Balaclava steal his kill.

Despite his urge to reveal himself Carew remained hidden. He didn't want to be recorded on any CCTV system that Martyn might have.

Balaclava stood legs astride and faced toward Carew. They were about 200 yards apart.

"Hey, Soldier boy," shouted Balaclava in warning. "This fucker's mine. Leave well alone."

Carew remained silent. He did not want to be identified visually or verbally for that matter.

Balaclava approached across the lawn with bold strides.

Carew huffed, got up and ran down the track to the sty. Having jumped over the sty, he looked for ground where he would be out of the line of sight of any possible CCTV or prying eyes. He had to make a swift choice. It was either the path to the side of Martyn's greenhouse, or toward the traveller camp. There was an incline to the left of the track to the traveller camp. This would provide the cover he required.

Carew could hear footsteps behind him and he spun around to face Balaclava. Balaclava threw a kick at Carew's bad hip and it connected. In pain, Carew stumbled back to provide space. He leant back on his hands and attempted a sweeping kick to knock Balaclava over. Balaclava jumped to avoid the trip and simultaneously threw a shuriken star at Carew's face. It glanced Carew's forehead as he dodged to miss it. Blood began to trickle into his eye. Carew sprang up aiming a rabbit punch directly at Balaclava's throat. He missed and caught Balaclava's chin. He felt a snap. It was either his finger breaking or spraining. Bloody right hand too. There was no time to worry about pain. Balaclava pulled out a Bowie knife from behind him. There were the sound of voices.

From behind Carew, a group of swarthy traveller road workers came walking toward them, down the track. Balaclava hesitated as Carew brought his knee up into Balaclava's testicles. Balaclava laughed as if either feeling no pain or enjoying it. Did Balaclava even have testicles? Then, with a heel palm blow to Carew's chin, knocked him out cold. As Carew blacked out he could hear his own heart beat. Ba boom, Ba boom. The words of a song echoed in his head and the music turned into reggae dub,

'Lick ick ick ick. Boom oom oom oom oom
Brutality ee ee ee ee
Shot ot ot ot ot ot
Seh seh seh seh seh
Babylon lon lon lon..........'

Balaclava re holstered the Bowie knife then fled down the track to disappear behind the Martyn house.

***

65

There was a light knock at the Dangerfield's office door. It opened slowly. Dangerfield sat hunched in his shabby chair with his head in one hand. He was holding a ballpoint pen with a chewed top. He recognised that knock.

"I hope you brought a coffee with you Smiffy," Dangerfield said without turning around.

"Something better than that for your perusal, Dangerous one."

Smiffy smiled as he plonked himself down on the mesh chair next to the desk. The fan was blowing its usual rhythm of frond wobbling annoyance across the 'in' tray. The same document in the tray rose and fell in the breeze.

"This about your favourite cousin Dave?"

"How did you know?" Smiffy wasn't surprised and his question had no real impetus.

Dangerfield made a cheerful grunt and looked as Smiffy slammed a USB memory stick onto the desk.

"Viola! Danger-man. Have a butchers at what's on here."

Dangerfield knew Smiffy of old. Smiffy had his underhand methods but he was a good cop and totally different to either his cousins or Bellamy.

Dangerfield had been pondering the connection, or lack of it, of Smiffy to Martyn. The two Mikes were cousins on Martyn's elusive father's side. Smiffy was from Martyn's mother's side of the family. He wasn't sure if there was anything significant there, given that Martyn had shown disdain for his mother's family. Then, there was the mother's death. Martyn had been there at the time but escaped the blaze.

Martyn seemed to be a class IV masochist with equal sadistic tendencies. There had been the unsolved rapes some years ago in the Collingsmote Viaduct area. Forensic science was nothing like it is now and the cases were left as 'unsolved'. Cruel, brutal and savage attacks were made on 4 women over time that the police were aware of. There had been a brief pause between the second and third attack. Without evidence of Martyn being involved, Dangerfield could not make any assumptions, but he still had that gut feeling that persisted.

He looked at his brief and historic:

Maggie Fairchild, 32. Body found under the viaduct. She had been raped and her left big toe had been mutilated with a pin.

Ruth Rutherford, 24. Reported her rape to the police. Her left big toe had been mutilated with a pin.

Amanda Pape, 26. Reported her rape to the police. Her left big toe had been mutilated with a pin.

Faye Lauren Jaracz, 19. Body found a mile from the viaduct. She had been raped and her left big toe had been mutilated with a pin.

The city A&E department treated 4 more females with similar toe injuries over a 3 year period. When questioned the alleged victims refused to talk.

All unsolved cases. Reports filed away.

What was the connection between Bellamy and Martyn. No one would say.

Casually Dangerfield inserted the red USB stick onto the PC port and waited.

After the usual rigmarole of selecting files, he clicked on the first one. It was an FLV file of a CCTV recording taken in Martyn's greenhouse. There, in the foreground, was Bellamy paying for and taking a package from Martyn. Although the sound quality was spotty it was audible.

Dangerfield held his head in both hands as he watched.

"You have got to be kidding me!" Dangerfield spat. "Why am I not surprised, Smiffy?"

They both watched more. Dangerfield asked if Smiffy had seen the recordings to which he replied, "Every one!"
"Bellamy was an addict?"
"Looks like it. I don't think he's shopping for his groceries, Danger-man."
"Where did you get this?"
"I went over to Martyn's. He didn't answer the door so I looked for him in the greenhouse. The door was unlocked so I went in. Obviously, I was concerned for his safety." Smiffy winked and Dangerfield gave a wry laugh.

He went on, "I couldn't find him so looked in the brick building at the back. What did I espy with my little eye? Something beginning with 'incriminating evidence'. This dongle thingy was bunged in the lappy on the table. The lappy on the table was still running and not password protected. I had a nosey on the basis that it is family business. No warrant. Strictly a family visit from his concerned cuz."
"Concerned cuz, indeed," Dangerfield mocked humorously. "Still. I don't get it. Do you think Martyn wanted someone to find this? I mean. No password. Laptop fired up. Place not locked. Something doesn't add up."
"He wasn't expecting me. So, unless he can see into the future, he may have either left it open in error or on purpose. Someone else left it open either accidentally or deliberately. Or, I'm just lucky and the gods are not conspiring against me."
"What do you reckon about the films of Bellamy, Smiffy?"

"Without forensics there's no evidence, but if I were to hazard a guess, I'd say Crack or some Coke derivative. What's that stuff on the street called? Kroc? That's what they're calling it on the Brockwell and around here too. If it is that it's bloody fatal stuff. Sorry, I digress. Hard to say but if it's Crack that probably explains Bellamy's aggression and his sweatiness."

Dangerfield looked at Smiffy with a thoughtful expression.

"This Krok muck. It's different to the Russian Krokodil or Croc. I wonder why they called it Krok when it sounds so much like the Ruskie stuff. Unoriginal. Sounds like the workings of the non academic mind. Where do you think Martyn gets it or makes it?"

"Dunno," replied Smiffy. "I wonder if Martyn and his ever diminishing crew, make it at his place. There's plenty of room at that gaff. Forensics said the Krok we think Martyn sells, is a derivative of heroin with some extra crap added. They gave some big names for the stuff but hey ho. All I know is, it isn't Krokodil."

"You know why the Ruskies call it Krokidil?"

"Coz it snaps?"

"No. It makes the skin look like a crocodile's skin. I've seen cases where some bloke had to have his foot amputated. It caused gangrene. When they don't get the chemical balance right the user's co-ordination goes to pot. No pun intended. If they go to blink their eye, they'll probably kick their leg out instead. Foul muck."

Dangerfield took a pen from his desk tidy. As he did so he caught the tip of the pen roughly on his monitor. The end broke off. The spring and cartridge flew out across his desk.

He looked at the empty pen top in his hand and muttered, "Bug-rakes!"

Dangerfield looked at Smiffy and continued, as if thinking aloud, "Oh, and Smiffy. And to what end would he, or anyone else for that matter, want us to find films of Bellamy buying Class A narcs? If that is what they are. Could be just sherbet. Probably Krok! In the words of the wise man; if you try to fail, and succeed, which have you done? You failed at failing."

Smiffy rolled his eyes.

"Droll." Then continued, "Well, Danger-man, I better keep out of this one. Conflict of interest and all that jazz."

"I getcha," Dangerfield paused. "Right. Coffee time and then I'm off out."

He winked and Smiffy knew exactly where he was heading to after coffee.

They walked to the vending machines. Smiffy looked thoughtful and asked slowly, "Better issue a warrant for Martyn's arrest for dealing that filth?"

"Yeah. Then you're implicated in this if you're not careful, Smiffster. All we have is some videos but no proof of what is in the packets Bellamy got."

Dangerfield looked sideways, "No. Hold the arrest for now. We'll play a waiting game on this one. Either the Balaclava will strike or Martyn will implicate himself somehow. Unethical I grant you, but I trust my gut on this one."

"Hope you're right, Danger dude. This could get very complicated for us."

"Trust me, lad. Trust me!"

Dangerfield thrust his hands firmly and deeply into his trouser pockets. There was a ripping sound in the right hand pocket. Then a clinking sound as a collection of coins fell from the bottom of his trouser leg and rolled around the floor.

Smiffy corpsed, then spat into uncontrollable laughter.

Dangerfield looked perplexed and said, "Why me? Bugger it!"

***

Dangerfield arrived at the Martyn house to see the burnt remains of Kitter's car on the lawn. The seats and steering wheel were blackened skeletons of metal and the upper body paintwork was gone. The windows were now just dollops of darkness. The window trims hung down like dying worms. Just a grey and black husk remained of the vehicle.

He decided not to approach the smouldering car but observe from a distance. He still wanted to be cautious.

There was the aroma of acrid smoke in the air. Dangerfield looked to see if he could ID the vehicle registration plates. The front plate hadn't melted. He hoped he would be able to contact base and establish if this was really Kitter's vehicle.

As he looked down toward the greenhouse he noticed an athletic dark clad figure jumping over the fence to the track beyond. He was sure the figure wore a balaclava.

The least he could do at the moment was to observe from a distance. However, he needed to drive out and around to where the track was and park at the end of it. He didn't want to get his car stuck down the track.

He parked opposite the recreation area just outside Marcia's house. Dangerfield decided not to ask for police backup yet. After all, the back up would have only consisted of Smiffy and probably another copper, if they could find one. This was only a small town cop shop.

It was a short walk to the park bench and then bearing left to the track. Dangerfield stood opposite the track and watched as Marcia stepped over the sty. 'My god. I hope she's not in danger,' he thought.

Awkwardly, he jogged down the track and stepped over the sty. There were two directions he could go in. One was to the side of the Martyn house and the other was toward the traveller camp. The out cropping bushes made it impossible to see which way Marcia had walked. Cursing to himself, he jogged to the side of the house thinking that the woman in front of him might not be heading toward the traveller site. He was wrong.

With a few choice words and panting wildly, as his chest began to feel like a blast furnace, Dangerfield headed the other way. As he reached the top of the grassy slope he could see Marcia talking to a bushy haired man. The man was wearing green army trousers and nothing black. This wasn't the Balaclava that had jumped over Martyn's bottom fence.

'Why do I bloody well bother?' thought Dangerfield, disappointed that balaclava was nowhere to be seen. Then again, that might be a good thing. He was certain that Balaclava was directly involved with the burning of Kitter's car.

The air smelled shitty like stagnant sewage. Flies were buzzing around and annoying Dangerfield.

Dangerfield strolled purposefully over to the crowd. There were traveller workmen, Marcia and the man with green trousers and bushy hair. He took his police badge from his pocked and held it up as he approached the group. He hoped that by showing his badge, it would cut down any polite chit chat and cut straight to the issue at hand.

He could see that Carew was bleeding from his lip and forehead. There was evidence of a scuffle by the dirt on him and a well placed army boot print on his bomber jacket above the hip. It was obvious that Marcia and the men had happened upon Carew and had been asking about his welfare.

"DI Dangerfield. I'm looking for the whereabouts of a figure in a balaclava who was heading this way. Any of you seen him?" he said.

Carew averted his eyes from Dangerfield's gaze. This spoke volumes to Dangerfield. This man knew something.

One of the travellers, Didlow Hinkins, pointed at Dangerfield and said, "That mush is a shanglo. Let's go. Can't trust a shanglo."

Another traveller said, "It's okay, Didlow. He's here to help Carew. Carew is a friend of cousin Chorry."

The tallest of the travellers said he hadn't seen a thing. They all wished Carew well, said they'd give his regards to Chorry and departed.

Marcia answered Dangerfield, "Haven't seen anything at all. Sorry."
"No need to be sorry er miss? Mrs? Ms?......."
"Oh, I'm Mrs Marcia Legister."

Dangerfield turned to the man and asked him what his name was.

"Everyone calls me Carew," Carew said.
"You had a fight with that balaclava chap didn't you Mr Carew?!"
Dangerfield was to the point.

Carew looked away from Dangerfield. He knew this man was very
astute and would know if he was being lied to.

"Lives could be at stake, Mr Carew," added Dangerfield. "And I would
advise you to take a different path today to wherever you're going, Mrs
Legister. I don't want to frighten you but there may be a madman on the
loose. Just for your own good, ay."

Carew admitted, "He's not, er, exactly what I'd call a madman and he
won't hurt Mrs Legister. Well, let's just say as long as she keeps well away.
Oh, verdammt! I sound like a German psychologist." He cleared his throat, "I
think I have a good idea who he is.
"Not exactly a madman? We'll rewind on that later. Do you have any
idea where he is going to?"
"Well, DI Dangerfield. This is hard to explain, and I can't say for sure
right now. Whether he's gone home or not I don't know. It depends what you
call home."
"Do you always talk in riddles, Mr Carew?"

Dangerfield didn't expect a reply. He looked at Carew's hand and it
was swelling. Carew mopped blood from his face with his hand.

"Your right hand, Mr Carew. I think you need A&E. Looks like it could
be broken. Your hand that is, not A&E."

Carew began to feel the pain in his hand as soon as Dangerfield
mentioned it.

"You could be right, sir. It is really beginning to hurt now."
"Follow me. I'll drop you off at A&E. On the way, if you tell me how and
where I can contact you. We need to talk. It's important."

Marcia was puzzled. Her phone rang and it was Ralston. He rang to
ask if the post had been because he was waiting for a DVD that the family
could watch together.

She returned home nonplussed about the whole Carew and
Dangerfield affair. She took out her lip balm and applied it to her mouth like

lipstick. 'Pop, pop, pop,' she whispered, to make the balm spread evenly on her lips.

Dangerfield and Carew had left in the car. Carew was feeling the usual uneasiness about being in a car.

***

The waiting time in A&E, at the city's hospital, was a 2 hour balance of boring and painful. Carew watched the wall mounted flat TV display screen repeat the same things over and over again with garish inane images. He saw the dangers of smoking, how to deal when someone had a stroke and general information about the hospital. His hand was really throbbing now. He rested it awkwardly in his lap. Carew was in no mood to read any of the glossy magazines that were scattered about on the chairs.

Opposite sat a man with stubble on his face, a bright chequered short sleeved shirt, camel coloured shorts and tattooed legs. He was chewing gum with his mouth open. This was a pet hate of Carew's and he always noticed it. There were a couple of teenage girls caked in makeup complaining about the waiting time. Carew watched as various characters were called into the consulting room. He saw others check in at the desk, give their details and then sit in the waiting area.

Finally a voice from behind. "Julian Carew?" It was Doctor Khan.

In consulting room C, Dr Khan asked Carew about his injury. Carew said he'd fallen over. Dr Khan wasn't convinced considering the gashes on Carew's face.

After being given pain killers he had to wait in a dim alcove for an x-ray. The x-ray machine looked gigantic. Both of the assistants wore white aprons. It was all over in a short time but now he had to await the results.

Purple and pink clouds scudded a dim sky. It was getting dark when he left the hospital. It had been confirmed that just one finger was fractured and only required a splint but no surgery. Dr Khan said the recovery time would be 4 weeks.

Carew felt tired so he decided not to travel all the way back to Pete's. He would go home as it was closer. After resting he could then think about Barnowby. Time wasn't running out if the Balaclava was the bastard he thought it was. Still, it was time that Carew didn't want to have to wait

"Shit!" Carew murmured.

Two minutes to midnight. Carew lay on his bed peering at the boring white ceiling. The hanging light seemed to burn in his head. He felt stiffness in his arm setting in. He flexed it slowly. His head hurt. The pain killers were wearing off. He cursed as he realised he'd left his phone charger at Pete

Silver's place. His battery was at about 50% he estimated. The phone vibrated. He had turned the ringer off in the hospital. He looked to see that he had received a text message from Frank. Moira was missing.

The news shocked Carew. The anxiety was intense. He felt his heart beating, as if in his throat.

Nervously, Carew rang Moira's number. Then he rang Frank's number. It was awkward doing it left handed. No reply from either, just the annoying: 'Leave your message' announcements. He sent a text to both that simply said, 'Call me'.

Carew felt helpless and sick to the pit of his guts. After what seemed like an eternity, the phone rang. It made Carew jump. The fear of answering it gave him a dry mouth. It was Frank.

"Where are you?" Frank asked.
"Home. Broken hand. Got knocked out cold by some bloody bastard in a balaclava. Moves like one of our old brigade. Anyway. Forget that. What's happening with Moira?"
"Dunno. I haven't seen her in 2 days. I haven't been here the whole time though, obviously. Obviously, she's wasn't at home on her Aussy soap night. So obviously, I rang her. She didn't answer so obviously, I sent her a text." Frank over used the word 'obviously'. There had been a time when Carew had attempted to count how many times he said it in one conversation. He lost count, obviously.
"Perhaps she's out with Simone and Jayne?"
"I rang them, obviously. They haven't seen her. It's not like her to go walk about."
"Any clues?"
"Nothing much, obviously. No yogurt carton in the bin for today."
"So either she's not keeping to her usual habit or obviously, left the house before midday."
"Obviously. I checked for anything, clues and obviously, there was nothing out of the ordinary."
"I'll come over. I'm limping so it's gonna take me at least half an hour to reach ya. I need to see your house. Try a bit of tracking skills."
"Obviously. I can pick you up."
"Rather walk. You know me and cars."
"Obviously."

Carew was even more tired. He felt like he was dragging himself down the street. His hip was hurting and no matter how he positioned his foot as he walked, it didn't help.

As he looked around him. It seemed that every vehicle that drove by was a taxi. Their headlights hurt his eyes.

1960's housing with clipped hedges or rosebushes lined his route. Although effort had been made to beautify the area, it still looked austere and soulless to Carew. This was a legacy left over from World War 2 when people needed housing after being blitzed. Now, the streets needed blitzing again Carew had thought.

He saw the tower blocks over to his left, a few streets over. The sight nauseated him. Graffiti and abandoned hypodermic needles seemed to be the norm in and around these tower blocks. He avoided the area, yet could still hear some depressing and thoroughly bloody awful music drifting from the general area.

The house where Moira and frank lived was on the edge of the estate. There was a playing field behind their house and just beyond that some allotments.

The door was open and the interior had the familiar aroma of apples and coffee.

Chapter 11
Friday

Frank greeted Carew and commented on what a mess he looked.

"You look lovely too, Frank," Carew said as he slumped into a battered armchair. He surveyed the room for any clues to explain Moira's disappearance.
"Tea?" asked Frank.
"Please." Replied Carew, "Usual. Sugar and one lump of milk."
"Eh?"
"Nothing. Unusual."
"Obviously."

After about 2 minutes Carew had a cup and saucer on the table next to him to his left. He couldn't hold the cup. The tea was too sweet but he didn't care. He broke out 2 pain killers from the blister pack. Swiftly he swallowed them with the tea. 20 minutes and they should kick in. His phone was charging from the spare charger Frank had found.

Frank said he'd only noticed Moira was missing that afternoon. It concerned him because she always told Frank where she was going to, and vica versa. She never left without telling of her whereabouts, hence Frank's worry. Carew kept checking his phone to see if there was word from Moira. He rang again only to get the same recorded message. After the tone, he asked her to call.

While drinking the tea, Carew noticed some letters and bills on the table near the window. The letters were all adverts and bore no postage date. There was one brown envelope that looked like a bill. It had a date on the post mark from two days ago.

"When did you get those letters, Frank?"

"I don't know but obviously, Moira must have put them there. They're addressed to her, obviously."

Carew cursed himself for asking such a stupid question.

The letters were all second class so Carew deduced they must have been delivered yesterday. It was a new day now, after midnight. Moira must have been in the house yesterday.

"You call the cops, Frank?"

"Seems a bit early for that, obviously."

"I dunno. Missing person and all that. What has she been like?"

"Quiet. Not really her usual self but obviously, she's not been the same since....you know. She hasn't said a lot lately. She goes out with friends so she says."

"And that's what bloody worries me, Frank."

Carew put Martyn and the Balaclava as a low priority right now. Finding Moira was more important. If Balaclava got to Martyn first then so be it. Somehow, Carew knew that would not be likely to happen.

"I keep trying to ring her, obviously. Left a few messages but nothing comes back."

"No other friends she could have gone to? Relatives? Anyone?"

"Obviously, I keep thinking. But I don't know who else to contact. Can't disturb anyone else at this time in the morning, obviously. It isn't like Moira to clear off like that. I rang the hospital but she's not been checked in there. Her stuff is here. Handbag. Purse. ID. Everything. Even her coat."

"Coat? Mind you it hasn't been freezing out. Anything missing? Anything at all?"

"Not that I know of."

"Was the door shut when you came back? Any sign of a struggle?"

"Well the door has a Yale lock obviously, so it locks itself and it was shut when I came home like normal."

"What about her office?"

"Her boss says she didn't turn up. Didn't ring in sick. No messages. Nothing."

"I hate this waiting game...makes me feel sick."

"Tell me about it."

Carew thought this would be a long period without sleep but he drifted off in the armchair. Frank didn't disturb him. There was little else they could do at the moment.

***

Carew awoke with a start. He was dribbling from the side of his mouth. He must have slept with his mouth open. His throat was dry so he licked his lips and swallowed spit. His hand was aching and so was his hip. The digital clock on the DVD player flashed 9:04am. Frank must have decided to get some rest too. Carew was surprised he'd slept so long. He was disorientated. His phone rang. He answered it in a flash hoping it was Moira. It wasn't her number on the display.

"Mr Carew? How are you? DI Dangerfield here. Can we talk today, sir?"

"Sure. I'm on the Brockwell at the moment. A bit worse for wear and might need your help with something."

"Is it convenient if I come to you then?"

"Sure. When?"

"About half an hour?"

Carew gave Dangerfield the address. Frank wouldn't mind and Dangerfield might be able to help find Moira, after all, he was 'the police'.

Frank appeared at the living room door to see if Carew had news about Moira. He'd just cleaned his teeth and some toothpaste was still on the corner of his mouth.

"Saw you were kipping, obviously," said Frank. "I left you to it. I've heard nothing from anyone. Dunno what else to do."

Carew explained that DI Dangerfield was coming over. Frank agreed it was probably a good idea to get the police involved now, obviously.

"Want some brekkie?"

"Not hungry, Frank, but thanks."

Dangerfield pulled up in his car. He sat for a few minutes looking at some notes. Then he got out of his car. He clicked his pen and clipped it to his shirt front pocket. Carew was already waiting for him. He opened the door when he saw him walking up the path to the house. Dangerfield was wearing his trademark coat.

Dangerfield pinched at the end of his nose to relieve an itch.

"Rather a tangled web, Mr Carew." Dangerfield admitted after having listened to Carew and his concerns about Moira. Carew had stated he was simply gathering 'evidence' that he could present to the police.

"But, that's our job not yours. You could mess it up for all concerned."

"Yeah, well I thought of that but your man Bellamy seems to be blocking things."

"Again, leave that to us, Mr Carew. He's our responsibility now. But I think you're not telling me the one piece of information we need. Just what is it you're trying to pin on Martyn?"

"Rape!"

"Thought as much. Are we talking about Moira here?"

"I'm afraid so. Your man Bellamy prevented her from taking the matter further. I have reason to believe it was Martyn that raped her as you will have guessed by now."

"Well if you want Martyn to see justice you'd better start trusting in me. What about the evidence you mention?"

"I have a mug shot of Martyn with her at a nightclub on the night the rape took place. It was brutal. He shoved a pin up her toenail and tore it about."

"One minute, Mr Carew. A pin up the toenail did you say?"

"Yes. Why?"

"Just getting the facts, Mr Carew. Are you saying that Moira was raped and brutalised especially on her foot by Martyn, and PC Bellamy prevented or withheld any report or reporting of it?"

"Abso-feckin-lutely. Moira was intimidated by Bellamy. She was too afraid to take the matter further. I felt I needed to. Personal reasons."

"Thank you, Mr Carew. Well, whatever your reasons you'll appreciate that this is all very serious, and I mean serious. And you have no idea how severe, I don't think. Can I have the most recent photo you have of Moira?"

Frank, who had been quiet all this time, had a rummage around in the sideboard drawer and finally produced the latest picture he had. Dangerfield was given permission to keep it. Taking his phone Dangerfield took a photograph of the picture.

"Look, er. I'm just going out to my car. I need to make a call about this. It ties in with several factors but I can't say too much. Be right back."

From the window, Carew and Frank could see Dangerfield take the pen from his shirt pocket. He began to write in a small pad whilst balancing his phone on his shoulder and talking.

Carew and Frank both commented that they wondered what was being said.

When he returned Dangerfield had issued a police alert to look out for Moira. He asked Carew who he suspected of being behind the Balaclava and what was the connection to Martyn.

"I'm not sure now." Carew scratched his head. "I thought it was Pete Silver's son, Nigel. I suspected he was home on leave. You know, little things like a light going on upstairs when Pete was downstairs. An extra coffee cup on the kitchen table. Not evidence in itself but I think Pete's son is an old acquaintance of mine."

"But you haven't seen Nigel, you say?"

"Nope. And I know an extra coffee cup may just mean that Pete hadn't washed the cup up from his last drink. A light upstairs could be an electrical fault or a timer switch or something. But I saw the Balaclava and those moves used were fairly identical to what I learned in the old brigade."

"I see. Well, we'll park that for now. Our magnum focus is making sure Moira is safe and I'm bloody concerned in case these mysterious bastards or Martyn might have her."

Frank spoke at last, "Thanks DI. We're obviously worried, obviously."
Dangerfield replied in his own dry way, "Obviously, sir."
"Obviously, what do we do now?"
"Gotta do what you should have done in the first place." Dangerfield stood up and was being brutally honest. "You should leave it to the police, despite Bellamy. We can deal with him and his sort."

He walked back to his car and looked under his coat at his shirt. His pen has leaked in the pocket. There was a splodge of wet blue ink in a wide circle on his chest.

He rolled his eyes and remarked, "Bugger!"

***

Marcia had driven with her friend Carol Reedy, out beyond the viaduct, toward Collingsmote village. There was a quaint tea room there. They decided to visit it as it was a nice day. Carol had her hair in braids that Marcia styled for her. She always used extension hair colour B1. Carol's parents were Jamaican but she hadn't really retained a great deal of the culture. As an example, she preferred Lasagna to Rice and peas. They both decided to take a break near the weir. There were no other cars parked there and no other people in view. It would be a nice spot to take some 'selfies' on their phone cameras.

"There's a lot of flies about, Carol. It's a shame. Otherwise it'd be lovely here."
"Yeah, bloody things are everywhere. Ouch!" Carol winced as a tiny fly got in her eye. She rubbed and manipulated her eyelids to remove the tiny black speck. She looked at it on the end of her finger.
"Rahtid sinting is what my Mum would say." She laughed. Carol laughed too. "My eye's still sore," Carol added. "Feels like the likkle pest is still in there."

There seemed to be a cloud of flies swarming to their left. They decided instinctively, to avoid that area. But out of sheer curiosity they looked in the direction of the thickest congregation of flies. There was something out of context in amongst the bushes. A shape. A dark shadow.

The water roared as it cascaded over the weir. There was a faint rainbow around the base of the torrent. Spray gently flecked their faces as they walked near the crashing water. To their left was a spinney. It was quite thick. There was a shadowy figure suspended in mid air.

Carol gave a scream. Marcia grabbed Carol by the arm in fear. Something large was suspended from a sturdy branch of the tree.

A limp parody of a human was in front of them. It was hanging from a blue tow rope. There were flies buzzing around and landing all over the body. An ASDA shopping bag was caught in brambles at the base of the tree. It flapped and rotated in the cool breeze from the weir.

What a waste. A once beautiful female was hanging lifeless. A discoloured face and tongue hanging out. Scratches on the legs and arms. Hanging from a blue rope. Lank black hair. Pinafore dress stained in vomit. Excrement smeared down the inside right leg. It was clear this person was dead.

Marcia's stomach churned uncontrollably forcing her to throw up violently on the grass. Carol was panting in panic.

"OHMYGODOHMYGODOHMYGOD....(pant...pant).....OHMYGODOH MYGODOHMYGOD....(pant...pant)....."
"Carol. Carol. What do we do?" Marcia didn't expect an answer.
"OHMYGODOHMYGODOHMYGOD....(pant...pant).....OHMYGODOH MYGODOHMYGOD....(pant...pant)....."

It seemed like a life time elapsed until the ambulance and police arrived. By now, Carol was in tears and Marcia was comforting her as best she could. Marcia held back her own tears. They both sat on the grass as the weir crashed its waters relentlessly and without emotion, yet almost mockingly.

Neither Marcia nor Carol really comprehended what was happening. A female police officer with mousy hair in a pony tail, came to speak to them. She spoke in a soft low tone and asked a few questions. Refocusing, Marcia answered as best she could.

Already, the police were searching the area around the body for any clues. It looked like suicide but the police wanted to be sure. Photos were taken. Fingertip searches were conducted. A body bag took the corpse to a cold morgue ready for autopsy and recognition. There was nothing by way of personal belongings or identification on the body apart from the clothes.

Dangerfield was on the scene. He recognised Marcia but not Carol.

"Hello Marcia," he said. "Are you going to be okay ladies?"

They nodded at him. He gave a grim smile and walked over to the body. He looked at the face. Dangerfield looked back at the tree and sighed. "Oh, bugger," he said under his breath.

***

Frank walked over to Carew, who was standing in the rear entrance of the house and looking into the garden.

"Carew. Her phone. She left it here, obviously. I found it under her pillow in her room."

"Any numbers dialled? Calls received?"

"Well obviously, I don't know. She has a pin number to open it and I obviously, don't know what it is."

Carew looked grim. Frank looked grim. They said nothing and yet they both knew that the other one feared the worst for Moira.

There was a knock at the door. It was Dangerfield. Carew and Frank almost missed it but for Carew going into the house for a pee.

Dangerfield looked exhausted. He rubbed his tired watery eyes with a tissue.

The colour drained from Carew's face. He felt the chill wind blowing in his soul again. Frank walked up behind Carew and they both looked at Dangerfield. He asked them to go into the living room and sit down whilst he spoke to them.

"Mr Carew. Mr McNamara." He looked at them in turn and paused as he drew breath. "I don't know if this is bad news concerning Moira but we believe we may have found her. Bad news if it is her, I'm afraid. Would you be prepared to come to the city morgue to identify the body?"

There was silence. Frank said feebly and in a hoarse voice, "Obviously."

Carew was uneasy in the car as usual and tried to fight back the fear. Dangerfield had his coat off and had forgotten about the large ink stain on his shirt. It didn't add any relief to the situation for Frank or Carew. Carew bit his bottom lip and remained silent and grim.

The journey was not long. During the drive, Carew watched pedestrians going about their daily routines. He saw a hopeless world, full of people who would soon die on a tiny planet that would eventually end without a trace.

The doors of the pale concrete building whooshed open. It was cool and ill lit within. Carew and Frank picked up security badges. D014 for Carew and D016 for Frank. Dangerfield just flashed his police badge but the security guard knew who he was anyway.

"Ullo! Er, Andrew," said the man in the apron.

"How are we, Paul?"

The man gave Dangerfield the thumbs up and Dangerfield said, "The Weir Jane Doe, today. These gentlemen are here to ID the body or not as the case may be."

The man in the apron, Paul Hinkins, led them to a cold slab with a body under a blanket. Hinkins was a middle aged man with a paunch. His greasy hair flopped over his forehead. His half moon spectacles balanced on the end of his slender nose.

"Just waiting er, for the results of the dental to, er, come back," explained Paul. "Estimated time of death about 10:30am."

It was agony for Carew and Frank as they watched the blanket being pulled back by the man in the apron. It seemed like slow motion, as if time began to freeze.

They saw the first wisp of matted black hair appear, then the tortured face beneath the cover.

Frank turned away revulsed and ran to the sink to throw up.

Dangerfield asked, "Well? Is that Moira?"

Carew looked Dangerfield squarely in the eyes and gave his answer.

Chapter 12

At the Legister house, Carol sat with Marcia in the living room. Not the traditional 'best room' but the room the family used for TV and meals. A clock, shaped like a map of Jamaica with the Jamaican flag colours on, ticked ominously.

"There's something very weird going on around here lately, Carol."

Carol mentioned that she was aware that a copper had disappeared. She said that a friend of a friend, told her that a local villain had jumped of the Darrow Way bridge, into the path of a train. She'd got that wrong but Marcia wasn't going to correct her because it wasn't important.

Marcia decided that the atmosphere was too sombre after their shock. She decided to change the mood. She put a lovers rock reggae CD on to play Then she offered to get drinks. Taking out her lip balm, she applied it to her mouth like lipstick. 'Pop, pop, pop,' Marcia said, as usual.

Marcia had a creamy coffee. Carol sipped at a 'Grace' strawberry syrup in milk with ice cubes. The syrup was a family favourite. Marcia only ever found it on the market in the city or at an Asian shop.

"For someone who isn't a traditional Jamaican, you sure like Jamaican comforts."

Carol gave a forced grin then asked, "What time are you picking your kids up from school today?"

Marcia looked at the clock and said, "In about a couple of hours."

"The police were nice weren't they," commented Carol.

"They were. I've met DI Dangerfield before. Y'know, that day I found that chap down the track. Garroo or kangaroo his name was. Something like that. They were better than some of the bastards I've met. I mentioned that copper that went missing, Bellamy, he was a real raas pig. Hated black people. Hated all a we. He was the one trying to frame up Ralston and the rahtid Babylon even tried to frame up me likkle pickney dem." Marcia was getting emphatic. She had stood up, put one hand on her hip and was gesturing wildly with the other hand. When Marcia got emphatic she broke into Jamaican patios. Then she realised what she was doing, flopped back into her faux leather armchair and laughed heartily.

Carol blinked and smiled politely. Her solemn mood was lifting. Her eye still felt as if there was something in it. It was sore and reddened in the corner.

Ralston arrived home early having received the text from Marcia about the body hanging near the weir. He walked over and kissed her on the head. She stood up and they hugged.

In his polished voice he asked, "How are you feeling? Been worried about you."

"You needn't have come home, love. We'll be all right. What about the shop?"

"Oh, that's no prob. Left Asif in charge. I'm more worried about you my sweet." He smiled at Carol. "Hi, Cazza. Are you all right?"

"Been better, but Marce is looking after me aren't you, Marce!?"

"Doing my best, peeps."

There was a knock at the door. Marcia's heart jumped and she felt nervous.

"Must be the police," Ralston said. "I'll go."

When he opened the door there was a greying couple standing there with satchels. The man was portly and had an ill fitting navy polyester suit. His tie was knotted all wrong. The rear piece of the tie hung lower than the front and was tucked into his tight waistband. He had dead eyes and a fake smile. The woman with him was the epitome of frumpiness. She had a pious condescending smile and a magazine in her hand. Did that say 'the Washtowel'?

"Hello," said the female frump with an insincere smile. "We're making brief and friendly calls in your area, and talking to all your neighbours. I'm Hazel, and this is my husband Ray. We've been talking about how terrible things are in the world and even in our own area. Do you think things will change for the better?"

Ralston was already bored with the rhetoric from these poor cult members who were so obviously labouring under a hive mentality delusion.

"Sorry. I'll stop you there." Ralston held a hand up to the couple, gave a resolute smile and said, "I'm not interested."

"A lot of people say that, but what is it you're not interested in?"

"God. Cults. Religion. The Bible. Bifurcated viewpoints. Kool-aid. Take your pick." Ralston felt the whole thing was tedious. He remained polite, after all this might be interesting. He decided not to send them away just yet.

"A lot of people would agree with you and I myself once felt the same way as you do now. Let me show you a scripture." She opened her Bible to a convenient bookmark. It was obvious that this was all a rehearsed presentation. The whole thing made Ralston feel embarrassed for the frumps.

"Before you do, can I say that I don't believe the Bible is anything more than a collection of writings put together by the Catholic church to control the masses."

"I see. Well at second Timothy 3:16 it clearly shows that the Bible is the inspired word of God though."

"Yes. But you're using the book to prove the book. That's circular reasoning. I don't believe in the Bible or your God. To me God is just a delusion to make us feel better and a tool of religion to control us. No offence meant."

"None taken," said Ray Frump. "But I know that God has helped me in my life and answered my prayers and he can yours too."

Ralston was relaxing against the door now. He held his tie. This was interesting.

"You know, you could pray to my back door and it would give you the same answers as your God."

"Well...er....I..."

"It's true. If you pray to God for something his answer is either 'yes', 'no' or 'later'. Is that right?"

"Well..er....I.."

"No, it's true though. If you get what you pray for you think it was a 'yes'. If you don't get it you think it's a 'no' and that God knows best...always a get out clause for God........or......if it seems that you're waiting you think God knows best. There is no God. It's all down to our own confirmation bias and the happening of coincidence. My back door will give you the same answers if you pray to it. In fact, why should God give you a new bike and allow a child to get sexually abused repeatedly by one of your own elders and nothing is done?"

The Frumps seemed to be squirming at any accusation being made against their cult. They had been programmed by the powerful thought reform and propaganda techniques of their cult, to reject any negative comments. The sad thing was, they didn't even know it. They had fallen foul of the biggest con trick ever and succumbed to the dangling carrot of living forever.

They remained calm and tried to continue with their rehearsed responses, red herrings and predictable thought stopping clichés.

"You believe in oxygen don't you? God is the same," Ray said nodding his head.

"Oxygen? Belief? I don't have to believe in oxygen because it's a scientific and provable fact. It is demonstrated in a practical way. God on the other hand, which ever god it is, Zeus, Poseidon, Odin, Marduc or whoever, lacks evidence of existence in any provable way."

"I see....er.....what about the creation all around us? Isn't that evidence of God's hand?"

"No because it could be evidence of another process."

"You mean evolution or the big bang?"

"Maybe yes and maybe no. It doesn't matter. What matters is we don't waste our short lives now coz you're a long time dead, friends."

Ralston noticed a car pull up opposite. It was DI Dangerfield complete with ink stained shirt. Ralston didn't know if the driver was a police officer visiting Marcia about the hanged girl at the weir or not. Dangerfield casually watched as Ralston spoke to the frumps. He shook his head and gave a wry smile. He had met them many times before. Nice people but totally deluded. Wasting their time slaving to give money to their New York leaders who don't give a shit about the members. As long as the leaders could live a comfortable lifestyle on the back of their members, that was all that mattered to them. Dangerfield wound down his window to catch any dialogue as it looked like it was fun.

"Well, the Bible tells of a wonderful time where we won't die and our dead loved ones will return."

"Listen. You say the Bible. What about the Koran or the Rig Vedas. How do you know which writings are correct? Let me explain what I mean." Ralston rubbed his face and then pointed outwardly. "The particular God you worship is dependant upon the age you live in and your geographical location. If you were born in ancient Greece you would probably be worshipping Apollo. Odin if you were a Viking. If you were born in Pakistan you'd probably be Muslim. The fact that you are here now in Britain is a high chance you'll have had a Christian upbringing. The way I see it, God is terrible at communicating. If God did exist in the way you say then he'd make his or her existence obvious to all."

"Well....er...this magazine explains how we feel. Please read it and we'll come back next week to see what you thought."

"Thanks but no. Like I said at the start. Not interested. Have a nice day though."

The Frumps gave another artificial smile, said their goodbyes and walked slowly away.

As they walked, the frumps were discussing how sad it was that people hadn't chosen to join their cult. They agreed that God would lovingly murder such ones very soon. Later they would be telling other cult members, at their meetings, that they had a wonderful chat with a man and showed him the light. It was all typical cult mentality or as Ralston called it, 'All a load of old bollocks!'

Dangerfield got out of his car and crossed over the road. He was waving at Ralston. They exchanged greetings. Dangerfield showed his ID but Ralston was too preoccupied looking at the stained shirt.

"Oh, that," Dangerfield said grimacing and touching the stain. "Cheap pens. Cheap pens."

"Use a pencil, hahaha. Sorry. Change subject. I think Marcia is expecting someone from the police to call but you're not female and you don't have a pony tail."

Dangerfield smiled. "Only on a Sunday." He liked this guy's sense of humour already.

In the living room, Dangerfield was invited to sit down.

"Now ladies. Not you, Ralston. May I recommend you speak with our counselling officer?" There was a silence and Carol looked at Marcia. Marcia looked at Carol.

"Well I'll leave that an option for you, ladies. I'll give you this leaflet with the number on." He flopped the leaflet onto the coffee table. "I have news about the body you found. We have a positive ID but until we locate all the relevant next of kin I can't reveal a name. I can tell you however, we are certain it was suicide. I've come to offer our thanks for your assistance in the matter. Oh, and do have a look at that leaflet."

After a brief chit chat, Dangerfield got up to leave. As he did so he caught his shin on the corner of the coffee table. He winced. "Oh, buggeroonie! Scuse my French."

***

Smiffy met Dangerfield at the coffee machine back at the station. He commented on the ink stain with a laugh. Dangerfield knew he would.

"What's that? Is it a map of Cromer, Danger-man?"
Dangerfield rolled his eyes. "No it's a stain on my character."
"Wanna talk about what's been going on in the town."
"You asking or telling?"
"Er…both."
"I'll just get a coffee and my office or yours?"
"Yours. Mine isn't as posh and doesn't have such a lovely view out of the window."
"Sewage works your thing?"
"Yeah. Not to be poopooed at."

They walked to Dangerfield's office. As he opened the door he knocked his coffee cup against the door. Some spilled on his shirt on the opposite side to the ink stain. Smiffy laughed. Dangerfield said, "Oh, buggeration!"

***

John Cruickshank sat at his desk slurping at a strawberry milk shake. He was shuffling some papers and considering the funeral he'd been asked to conduct for Mike Rolph. It had been arranged at the crematorium. John was secretly relieved that it wasn't to be held at the church.

The plaque on the wall told the origin of the name Cruickshank. John Cruickshank was transfixed by it for a few seconds. Then he scratched his head and a grey hair fell into his milkshake. "One less for God to number on my head," Cruickshank said.

"What, dear?" Mona asked as she walked by the office doorway.

"I'm saying that the Lord will have one less hair to count."

"What on earth are you on about?"

"Hair. One fell out. I was just scratching my bonce. Did I mention the funeral?"

"Rolph, perchance?"

"Yes. Rolph perchance. Being held at the jolly old crem in Collingsmote."

"Do you really have to conduct it for that awful villain? I know I shouldn't speak ill of the dead but I usually do."

"Tell you a secret, dear. I'm glad they didn't want the service at the church." He tapped the side of his nose with his finger emphatically and winked.

Mona gave a knowing smile and went about her business in the house.

After about ten minutes she popped her head around the door and asked, "John, dear. I'm going to do some washing. We won't be wearing our motorcycling balaclavas in this weather, so is it okay if I wash them?"

"Certainly. As long as I have a spare one." He paused thoughtfully. "Er, just in case. Cold nights still, even for this time of year."

"Well you are a little ray of sunshine aren't you?!" She laughed. "We will always have spare balaclavas. I love a good face covering. Makes me forget that I look like an old hag these days."

"Oh, behave. You're as lovely as ever. It's me that looks like a mouldy jacket potato with hair falling out. You are as lovely as the day we met."

She rolled her eyes and said, "Is there someone else in here you're talking to? Coz it sure ain't me, honey bee."

Mona went to the kitchen and put the washing in the machine. She added the washing gel and fabric softener. Mona span the dial. The washing sploshed away in the machine. There was a clunking every now and again as buttons glanced the glass of the machine. It was a nice drying day and Mona would hang the washing on the line outside. She loved the aroma of freshly dried clothes from the line. Each time she hung the washing out she still felt uneasy because she wondered if Mrs Bellamy might try to steal it. There was still no news on Phil Bellamy but Mona knew he was dead. Her eyes narrowed as she thought of him in Hell. She had a sarcastic grin.

Chapter 13

Dangerfield's office was warm even with the window open. The hypnotic sounds of cars whizzing by mingled with the sound of the fan doing its usual paper lifting sweep of the desk. Smiffy sat in the mesh chair resting his hands on his belly.

"So what have we got?" asked Dangerfield as he stood next to the flip chart paper on the easel. He had a green felt tip in his hand. The cap had been chewed. There was a map of the Barnowby area to the top left of the flip paper. He knocked the easel with his middle finger knuckle. The easel wobbled uneasily on the flimsy tripod. Something rattled on it. The fan blew the edge of the paper making it curl slightly at the bottom and flap about.

Smiffy began to give his observations and Dangerfield wrote them down.

"Phil Bellamy disappeared. The last time we know of his whereabouts was at Martyn's gaff. We're not sure if he went home or to stop off at Burnsy's for what we suspect is his usual sheep shearing event." Smiffy paused and looked quizzical. "Anyone seen Farmer Burns? He seems to have vacated the village," he said.
"I went to see Burns. He wasn't there. But then he does go to visit his sister in Hull around this time of year. Goes for a week normally." Dangerfield drew 2 big arrows from the houses on the map and wrote. 'PCB last seen here or here.'
"Rolph was splattered on the tracks at the bridge. Any evidence of murder? Nothing apart from a pink flare fired. It could have been to distract the driver from the body? Dunno. Can't rule it out."

Dangerfield circled the bridge. Another arrow with comments.

"Kitter seems to have vanished but his car turned up on Martyn's lawn burnt out. Martyn hasn't been seen since, according to what the neighbours told Richie, er, Detective Sergeant Parr."

Another arrow to Martyn's house with comments.

"Some bloke in a balaclava runs off after flooring a bloke behind Martyn's house. What did you say his name was? Magoo?"
"Carew," Dangerfield said slowly as he drew another arrow from the area behind the Martyn house.
"Someone…ahem…found a shit load of videos of Bellamy buying class A's from Martyn."

Dangerfield drew and wrote another comment.

"The weir. Don't forget the weir. Suspected suicide. Did you find out who she was?"

"I did," Drawled Dangerfield as he drew more arrows. "She was one of those previous unsolved rape victims. You know, the pin mutilation ones."

Dangerfield underlined the word 'rape', gave a bold full stop after it. As he turned to Smiffy the easel fell over with a clatter.

With a droopy face Dangerfield looked back at it and commented, "Bugger, bugger and thrice bugger!"

Smiffy threw his head back and guffawed.

The two men decided to have a cup of water each from the dispenser.

"Martyn. It all surrounds Martyn," Smiffy said thinking aloud.

"Think I should pay another visit there. Perhaps take Parr with me. I haven't even done anything about the car on Martyn's lawn yet. Mind you I do think it's Martyn's problem not ours."

"What about your man Magoo?"

"Shrewd one that. A bit complicated though. You can tell by his body language. You know I thought he was gonna crap himself in my car. He's a terrible passenger. Probably got knocked over as a child or something. His mate Frank is a bloody wuss arse. Considering they were both soldiers together. And he has this nasty habit of saying 'obviously' when he talks. All the bloody time 'obviously' this and 'obviously' that. Bugger."

Then Dangerfield looked at Smiffy with a profound look. "We forgot the son of that Silver bloke. Carew says he thinks he's home on leave, and it's around the same time as all the weird stuff starts happening. And he's a soldier too."

"What are you saying?"

"Let's pay this Silver bloke a call. Can you check if Burnsy is about, and then are you coming to Silver's?"

"I'll be your moral support. But hold on a sec. Why don't you stick a broom up my arse and I'll sweep the bloody floor while I'm at it. Contact Burnsy indeed."

"Sorry. Yeah. That did sound a bit bossy didn't it?! I'll do it." He pursed his lips and continued, "We're missing something here. We're missing something!"

Dangerfield screwed his plastic cup up to throw it away forgetting there was water still in it. The water squirted over his hand and trousers forming a damp patch on his crotch.

"Oh, no! Looks like I've bloody peed myself," he remarked rolling his eyes in frustration.

Smiffy threw his head back and howled with laughter. Then he held his belly. He laughed so much that he had to double up and lean against the wall one handed, knees buckled. Tears ran down his cheeks. As he laughed he farted, which made him laugh all the more. Dangerfield couldn't help but join in. The laughter was infectious. Then, as usual, Dangerfield made a remark containing the word: 'Bugger.'

***

Martyn was huddled on his king sized bed in gloom.

He looked around the room. He stared at the 'Anti-Vietnam war' poster on which a shard of light fell. It was his favourite poster. It was in a tarnished silver frame. The poster was drab and crude looking relic from 1966 that he'd acquired it in New Zealand. It depicted half a skull on the left and a half blank face on the right making a full head. The head wore a top hat with the stars and stripes on. On the blank face were the words 'Mobilise against the war'. He liked it because the blank face gave the impression of a dual personality.

He had his wooden slatted blinds closed.

Martyn clutched his gun. Someone was after him but he didn't know who it could be. It wasn't as if he'd actually seen anyone but all the evidence was there. He was hungry and thirsty. There were no sounds in the house. Martyn slowly opened his bedroom door as he clutched his .38 revolver ready to fire it. The hallway was empty. The carcass of the cat had attracted flies. He moved out into the hallway. No one was there. He crept downstairs. No one was there. Gradually, Martyn relaxed as he searched the house with his gun ready. He found no one there.

He looked at his phone. The screen was cracked where he'd thrown it on the ground earlier. Cautiously, he looked from behind the curtain of the living room and saw Kitter's burned out car. He peered from the kitchen, over at the green house. There was no sign of life anywhere. He went into in the downstairs bathroom.

Heaped on the floor lay a pair of black military trousers and a black military sweater. On the work surface, containing the wash basin, he saw a pair of leather gloves that he vaguely recognised. He looked at the toothbrush holder and saw a black balaclava, that again, looked strangely familiar. He backed out of the toilet confused. When he looked up, he saw a Bowie knife embedded as an angle in the ceiling. Was this a warning? Where did these items come from? Something was screaming in his head that there was no danger here. He didn't listen to it.

He sprinted from the house to the greenhouse. He ran into his office. He glanced at his laptop. Something was missing. The red memory stick was not in the port. He hunted around in a panic but couldn't find it.

"Shit," he said in panic.

***

Pete Silver answered the door. Dangerfield showed his ID. Smiffy did the same. Inside they sat and exchanged pleasantries with Silver. They accepted his offer of coffee which he served in white cups on saucers.

Then Dangerfield got to the point. "Mr Silver. We have reason to believe there is a killer, possibly with military training, and active in this area. We have little to go on but we understand you know a Mr Carew."

Pete nodded and commented that he hadn't seen Carew since the previous day.

Dangerfield tilted his head and continued, "We believe Mr Carew may be in danger from this killer which may also mean you are too, by association."
"Is this about the fight he had with Martyn?"
"What fight?"

Pete explained the brief events from that Sunday outside the Inn.

Dangerfield looked across to Smiffy. Both men frowned. They now realised there was yet another piece of the jigsaw here.

"Mr Carew says you're looking forward to your son coming home."

Pete looked perplexed. Dangerfield observed his coy body language.

"Yes. I'm looking forward to him coming home."
"He isn't here yet then?"
"Not yet. Couple of days." Pete seemed uncertain.
"Anyone else here with you?"

Pete shook his head.

"Just watch your back, Mr Silver." Dangerfield was serious and Pete understood the ambiguity of the words.

Dangerfield picked up his cup. It slipped, spilling on his lap. He jumped up and exclaimed, "Ooooh, me goolies!"

Pete was horrified. Smiffy tried to pretend to be concerned but ended up laughing.

***

Martyn locked his office door and slumped in his leather chair. It creaked. His mind ablaze with fear and puzzlement. He thought back to the last time he saw his father. It was the day he had punched his stepmother in the face. His father had a shouting match with him. It was nearly midnight when he came to blows with his father. He remembered his father's nose streaming with blood. Blood that splatted into a shape onto his silk shirt. The blood stain seemed to be forming a mocking face.

His father ran to the phone to call for an ambulance in an attempt to get Martyn sectioned under the mental health act. Martyn grabbed the base of the phone and smashed it against the wall.

"Let's go," his father shouted to the new Mrs Martyn. The two ran from the house to their car.

Martyn couldn't recall what happened next. Another blackout? He just remembered walking from the downstairs bathroom to find his father's car still on the drive with the door open. The ignition had been ripped from the steering column. Something told him not to worry. It was that voice in his head again.

The next day Mike Kitter had helped him to push the car into the garage, where it remained since.

***

Frank went out. Carew decided to return to Pete's. Frank would call him if there was any news about Moira. He did have his kit bag in Pete's shed anyway.

It was nice to be wearing some fresh clothes. Ruby red 'Staprest' trousers, a 'Lion of Judah' tee and a red Harrington jacket with tartan lining. Instead of the army shoes, Carew had some Adidas Rasta trainers. He felt smart.

Clouds scudded a beautiful blue sky. The walk from his home to Barnowby was uneventful, even boring. His hip was feeling better although his hand was throbbing. He disliked the outskirts of the city. There was something soulless about it. It was devoid of life and ugly. He noticed the hogweed along the banks of the dyke as he approached Barnowby. He remembered the darts he'd made and decided to carry them with him in future.

The whole Martyn/Balaclava thing had taken a back seat in his priorities. Moira was still missing but Dangerfield was handling that and there was no more that Carew could do. It had already become messy with Dangerfield involved. Carew knew he needed to be bloody careful what he did or said now.

The hanged girl was someone called Ruth Rutherford. She was a rape victim in the unsolved file that Dangerfield had revealed to Carew in utmost confidence. It was a confidence that Carew would not dishonour. Loose lips sink ships and Carew knew this to be one of those truthful clichés. Carew recognized the M.O. with the pin used on the victim as the same used on Moira. It was Martyn's work. It seemed that Ruth was a Krok user. It was bloody obvious that Martyn was a seller of that shit, but there had been no evidence. If Martyn had been ring fenced, protected by someone, then it was by Bellamy.

Pete stood in the doorway and seemed hesitant to greet Carew as he strode through the green rickety back gate. He heard a familiar voice from inside the house.

Carew looked horrified. There she stood, half hidden behind Pete.

"Moira?" he stuttered. "What are you doing here? We thought you were dead. We thought all sorts. All your stuff was left at home. What the fuck, Moira?"
"Come inside," she said. "I'll explain. Oh, and don't worry, I already told Frank just a minute ago when I saw you coming. He won't ring you. I told him not to."

Carew was ecstatic that Moira was safe and yet there was a rage within him for the same reason.

They sat in Pete's room. Carew's eyes were wide and his expression intense.

"So. What am I missing here, you lot? Was your disappearance a hoax, girl?" Carew was mystified.

Moira looked down and sighed. She looked as if she was about to cry.

"I'd like you to meet someone," she said.

The door behind opened and a man about the same age as Carew walked in. He was tall, handsome and had short cropped hair. He was clearly of Eurasian mix. There was a small scar just above his left eyebrow.

"This is Nigel," Moira announced. "He's my boyfriend. Nigel Akino-Silver."
Carew looked puzzled. "So you've got a boyfriend. Why the secrecy?"
"It's a long story but basically…." She stumbled, "..basically…."
Nigel spoke in a deep voice, "I was working for Martyn, on the side, selling Kroc to the Brockwell. Yeah, I know, pretty crap right? Then he wanted to kill my Dad for some reason, so I split."
"I don't get it. So what?" Carew was agitated.
"Hold on, mate, haven't finished." He held a hand up to Carew. "So I fucked off and managed to join the forces. In the mean time Moira and I started seeing each other."
"I still don't get it."

"No, well you won't. It was whilst I was working for Martyn on the Brockwell, that I met Moira. She has, er, a certain powdery need, mate." He looked at Moira. "Sorry, babe."

"Moira? You never said? What the fuck?" Carew's mind was racing. "We could have got you help. You never said. We couldn't tell. What was all that with leaving your stuff back at the house....worried us to death........we were going didlow! Even got the coppers looking for you."

It seemed like time was standing still until Moira gave her reply, slowly, deliberately and on the verge of tears.

"I left my stuff at home by accident. Simply an accident, that's all. I picked up the wrong bag when Nigel came to get me. That's all. Just the wrong bag. Left my phone behind too. I thought it was in my bag. The right bag that is," said Moira inadvertently using repetition for emphasis.

Carew thought it was an odd explanation, yet in a strange way, it was so weird it sounded totally plausible. His mind was still racing.

"Did Frank know any of this?"
"Nope."
"Why the fuck didn't you just say you'd got a boyfriend?"
"I was a mess, Carew. Nothing made sense....and I wasn't sure you and Frank would approve of Nigel. The whole thing's a mess."

All the time Pete sat with his head in his hands.

"I sent Pete to get you, Carew. I wanted someone to keep an eye on you. Nigel was coming home so uncle Pete was waiting for you to arrive. I hear you met Martyn already."
"Uncle Pete?"
"Yes, my uncle Pete."
"Small world and getting smaller. So you're the Balaclava then, Nigel, ay?"
Nigel gave an ironic half smile. "Sorry, mate, I'm not. Glad I sodding ain't."

Carew was even more puzzled and wound up. "Woah! Hold on there. What Martyn did to you Moira? What Martyn did to you!"

It was some time before Moira, choking back the tears, explained. "I arranged to meet Martyn that night, at the club. To get my own 'Kroc' coz Nige wasn't supplying anymore. Martyn just came on too strong. Didn't want paying in money. He wanted...." She choked back tears.
"It's all right sweetheart, no need to explain. I get the picture. Isn't it about time to call the coppers?"
"No! No cops!" Moira was firm. "He did the same to me as he does to all those that don't want to pay him. Pay him in the way he wants. He ruh.....ruh...ruh...ruh...." She couldn't say it.

"Martyn's been after me. That's why I've remained hidden," Nigel admitted.

Carew wasn't amused. "I don't know what to make of you, mate, Moira is your bloody cousin and you're dating?"

"Not exactly."

"Whaddaya mean, 'not exactly'?"

"Dating. Yes. Not cousins. When my Mum got married to Pete she was already pregnant by another man."

"Oh, don't tell me. Bloody Martyn's Dad!"

"No. You watch too much TV. But Pete looked after me like a real Dad would though."

"You're right, Moira. This is a bloody mess!"

"Gawd, this is too bloody much! So many bloody questions! Dunno whether to laugh or cry."

They all sat in silence.

Chapter 14

Dangerfield received the call from Carew saying that Moira was safe. Typically, Dangerfield's curiosity was on high alert now. He knew something wasn't quite right, he could sense it in Carew's use of words.

"Time to knock off, Danger Boy. Sunday tomorrow. We do need some time off," Smiffy reminded him.

"Yep. Recon it is. But you know how it is. My gut is telling me something is about to kick off."

"Martyn?"

"The same. I think we should be looking for him. Er, for his own sake. Don't want anymore drama around here." Dangerfield was gazing at his monitor screen that contained the unsolved rape notes with another window showing notes about Martyn.

"Don't you think that's a bit hasty? Not long ago you said to take it easy trusting your gut but now you've changed your tune."

"I have. I have. But maybe you're right. Dunno what to do for the best." He turned in his chair and looked at Smiffy. Then he turned back and banged his fists on the desk. "Shit. What a fuck up."

Smiffy was waiting for something to fall off the desk. Nothing did. The men became sombre.

"Let's go home," Dangerfield said. "Gotta make plans for Cromer tomorrow anyway. Got next week off. I'll bring you a stick of rock back."

They left.

***

Carew wanted to get out of the house for some air and go for a drink somewhere. Moira and Nigel wanted to remain at the house to stay out of sight. Pete was too down to care but agreed to drive to the 7/11 off licence to buy beers and wine. Carew stood outside and casually leaned on the wall watching Pete drive toward town. A helicopter whirred overhead. Carew looked up. It was a Westland Puma transport vehicle flying from Collingsmote.

Pete drove down Venables Street to the 'offy'. As he drove his mind wandered back to his dealings with the Martyn family. When old man Martyn's wife died in the fire, it didn't seem long until he'd met Sue. Something writhed and twisted in his stomach. It formed a lump in his throat.

His wife was in hospital the day Dave Martyn found him in bed with his step mother. It wasn't meant to be like that but the need for intimacy was strong. When she'd offered him coffee as he mended the hinges on the greenhouse door, he'd seen a wicked glint in her eye. She wasn't particularly attractive but her legs were irresistible. He recalls their alabaster like sheen in the greenhouse light. Her words. Alluring. Sexy. Suggestive. Provocative. How had they ended up sharing their bodies? She wasn't very interesting in bed but she filled a need. Her bodily aroma was gorgeous. He remembered how he would touch his penis and smell his fingers just to get that aroma. It was only the once and he never returned to continue employment, for obvious reasons. He never saw Sue again. But then he wouldn't go around that area any more. Now, he kept himself strictly in the city or Collingsmote area to avoid the Martyn gang.

It all seemed like a dream to him now, as if it never really happened. Perhaps he didn't really love his wife or the love had died. When she came into the country to marry him, she had loved another man whilst they were courting. Pete forgave her and she gave birth to twins. Nigel and.........ah best to forget.

In the shop, Pete clunked around the bottles and cans of alcohol. He was still lost in his memories. Suddenly he was jolted back to reality by a voice.

"Having a party, Peter?" Mr Nazir asked.
"I wouldn't call it that, Mr Nazir. More like a bloody wake." Pete gave a half smile.
"Oh, dear. Well maybe you need some crisps or nuts to lighten things, eh?" He pointed to a wire basket with a crude sign on the torn off lid of a cardboard box. "Bumper pack of cheese and onion crisps only 0.99p."

Pete pulled the face he always pulled when considering something unimportant.

"Yeah. Good price."

He picked up two packs. Paid. Then he struggled out to the car with the bags swinging precariously as he carried them. One pack of crisps fell from his hand as he struggled to get the car keys from his pocket. The keys fell on the floor.

"Doing well here," he muttered as a car pulled up.

The occupant jumped out of the soft topped car. "Hi. Uncle Pete," said the camp voice.

Pete looked around and smiled as he recognised his nephew Jimmy.

"Jimmy. I didn't know you were home."
"I'm not. Just passing through. Thought I'd visit the parents back home."

Pete said that normally he'd invite him over, but there were things kicking off that were better left alone, at least for tonight. Jimmy had heard that Bellamy had been missing for days and one of the Martyn gang had died.

"Trust me," Jimmy patted his chest. "Martyn is behind it all!"

Pete didn't see how Jimmy had made that conclusion but figured him for a clever lad.

Jimmy went into the 'offy'. Pete drove home.

Pete entered the home to what sounded like an argument. He threw the crisps onto the kitchen table. He took the tins of lager and the bottle of wine into the room. From the cabinet, he picked out a wine glass. The wine bottle was a screw top so there was no need to use a corkscrew. After cracking open the twist cap, he glugged the wine into the glass and handed it to a trembling Moira.

Carew accepted a tin of strong lager which hissed as he pulled open the tab. A little foam escaped and dripped over Carew's fingers which he then licked. He didn't usually drink alcohol but on this occasion it seemed like a good idea.

"Look." Carew was almost shouting as he looked intently at Moira, "The way you were dealt with by that pervert. You weren't the first and you probably won't be the last. This is madness. If you don't tell the coppers who the rapist is……." He stopped, calmed himself down. Then he spoke slowly and deliberately to Moira with his eyes fixed on hers. "Do you want the pain of other girls on your conscience if you don't speak up?"
Moira looked down. "I just can't."

"I think you better had." He spoke kindly. "Let me call DI Dangerfield. Please. Pretty please?"

"I don't know. I just don't know."

"If we get Martyn arrested and off the street, to keep other poor girls safe, Moira," Carew implored. "I can wait. I will get him. I'm not allowing that Balaclava chap to get to him first."

As the evening wore on Carew relaxed. Maybe it was the drink. Maybe it was knowing Moira was safe. Maybe it was a combination of factors. It was Sunday tomorrow and a week ago since he came to this village. Events were moving fast for Carew and it had knocked the stuffing out of him. He realised he needed to get rest and get back into fighting form, as far as the fractured hand would allow. He figured that if he practiced using his elbow instead of using his hand, he could still fight.

The hogweed darts would be carried at all times from now on. Carew was an expert with a blow pipe. This was all well and good to Carew but he needed to find Martyn first. He looked at the Voodoo mask on the wall and thought about the woodcarving Moira had given to him. Then he looked at Moira sitting with Nigel and he remembered Amy Bell. That chilling gale blew viciously through Carew's heart and soul. His eyes narrowed as he recalled the scene.

"Darling?" Amy had called to Carew who was busy painting the hallway in their new home.
"What is it?" he replied almost sounding absent minded.
"Need a word."
"Coming. Hold the line."

Carew remembered climbing down from a ladder and putting the paint roller in the tray. Gloopy pale green paint slopped over his hand which he wiped with a towel.

"I want you to meet someone."
"Do what? Meet who?"
"Schmoo the gnu." Amy held up a knitted toy she'd made for the baby.

Carew felt tearful remembering. It was only weeks before the accident. He'd kept the toy in wooden a box in his wardrobe. He never opened the box.

He looked at his hands. The paint was long gone and so was his reason for living.

A familiar freezing wind blew through his soul.

Chapter 15
Debbie Burns

Debbie remembered how Gavin Dando, 'the Goth', used to look at her as they sat together on the battered and stained red sofa in their living room. He had long dyed black hair and a thick gold eyebrow ring. She joked that it was a good thing all his tattoos were spelled right.

To all outward appearances, he was an intelligent and studious person doing well in his studies. He was charming. Debbie had fallen for this seeming quality. It was a deception that cost her dearly, emotionally and in future relationships.

These were days of microwave meals and dealing a little weed, or so she had first thought. Dando was now Debbie's scrounging, live in boyfriend. They met at Uni. It wasn't long before they struck up a relationship. It looked like this was the relationship that would be the only one ever. Dando with his love of Metal music and crafty wit amused her. It wasn't until they moved in together that Debbie began to see the darker side of this man.

He kept a sub machine gun in a cupboard with some packets of powder. All were in a large locked metal box. She'd not let on, but Debbie suspected some involvement in a drugs cartel. As for the mysterious powder, if he wasn't selling it he was snorting it. She would usually look away as he carried on playing a game on his X box and think, 'What a tosser!' She hoped he'd change. She was frightened to end the relationship because of the emotional ties that had developed. She didn't know how she would cope ending it when she was still in love with him.

"Where do you get this shit?" She'd ask only to be confronted by his anger and evasiveness.

There were nights she slept on the sofa and would think back to the farm in Barnowby where she grew up. She felt trapped in a relationship that was now soured by Dando's addiction, financial demands and mood swings. He'd had some run ins with the law but always managed to wheedle his way out of trouble. She suspected there was a bent copper that was protecting some drug pushing villains.

It was one Saturday morning. The door was smashed down. Two suited men burst in. Debbie screamed and fell back onto the kitchen worktop knocking over a bottle of ketchup that smashed on the floor.

It was Dave Martyn and Mike Kitter demanding Dando.

"He's not here. What do you want?" She was panicking.
"He owes us money. Where is the cunt?" Martyn shouted.

Just outside the door they heard someone running. As they turned around they saw Dando running down the grubby concrete steps in the musty hallway. Both men gave chase as Debbie watched in horror. She ran to the lounge window to see that Dando had jumped the fence and sped off to the dockland area. Martyn and Kitter split up and tried to head him off at the railway line. He was gone. They stopped running and flung their arms up in frustration.

They ran back to the apartment.

"Pull yourself together, Debs," she was muttering under her breath. She knew the men were coming back and probably to take her hostage.

Quickly, she grabbed the sub machine gun from it's box and waited just inside the door as Martyn and Kitter came back.

They stood there stunned when they were confronted by Debbie holding the weapon at them. Kitter held a knife. Martyn just smiled and calmly told her to put the gun down and there would be no trouble. She fired off a round of ammo. Kitter's knife span out of his hand as a bullet caught it. A bullet grazed Martyn's cheek as he recoiled. Wood and plaster flew everywhere as the salvo tore through the door lintel and wall.

Martyn and Kitter fled. She heard the Transit van screech away. Debbie stood in the kitchen trembling but still gripping the gun tightly.

A neighbour had called the police but by the time they arrived Debbie had gone, taking the gun and a box of ammunition with her.

The police found Dando's body in the river a day later. There was never any evidence or witnesses to him being murdered. The news paper told of a drugged man. They said he had fallen into the water and drowned. Debbie knew it was the work of the Transit men. She didn't need evidence. So she ran scared. First she went back to the farm where she grew up, then to a friends house. Marcia Legister didn't require any explanation but let her stay in the box room. Debbie had no idea that Martyn lived nearby.

The police couldn't find Debbie. When she found out that Dando was dead she went to the local police station. Questions were asked about the machine gun fire. She told them it was one of the men from the Transit van that had fired the shots. She was unable to provide the registration number of the van but gave descriptions of the men to PC Bellamy. All she really remembered Bellamy saying to her was, "I thought that was blood on the floor until I saw the sauce bottle." She thought, 'That sweaty bastard pig doesn't give a fuck!'

Bellamy had used the powder, found in the apartment, to fit Debbie up on a charge of possession with intent to supply. She suspected Bellamy knew who the men were. The machine gun was safely hidden away on the farm. It was stored in a disused building. The gun was wrapped in cloth and hidden on a roof rafter.

That was history but her fear of being visited again by the Transit men remained and as a result. She kept the gun.

Today though, Debbie Burns sat at home in the farm house watching TV. She brushed her brown hair and gritted her teeth when the brush snagged. Her father was away in Hull. She was bored and thought she'd ring a friend. Maybe she could, at least, get out and break the boredom. The first number she rang went on to answer phone. She stuck her tongue out at the phone. She knew Jimmy was in town so decided to ring him. Even if it was just a conversation about his boyfriend, it would alleviate the boredom.

Jimmy was delighted to speak to her and suggested that he picked her up and they could go out somewhere.

He arrived quite soon with a mischievous glint in his eyes.

"Uncle Pete doesn't want any visitors. Intrigue or what? I can't resist a challenge. Let's just drop by. Now let's see what excuse shall I make?"
"Your mother wants to borrow a cup of sugar?" She giggled.
"Oh you are creative...not!" He smiled camply.

The pair went outside to Jimmy's car. The night seemed still. A 'flower moon' as Debbie's mother called it hung in the sky. It was a May moon and 'flower and corn growing time' her mother would say. Debbie would comment that her mother's obsession with all things Native American was fine, but when it came to ordering hand made moccasins online then that was another story.

The farm house living room contained beautiful Native American paintings on the walls. The most expensive was an original by Spencer Asah which was a gouache on paper work. Her mother never revealed how she had obtained it, but it really was the centre piece of the 'Indian wall'. Debbie's mother had no Native American connections but truly admired the culture. Why she hadn't married an Apache, Debbie never knew. It was a standing joke. They sometimes called her father Chief Sitting Burns. He was less related to the Comanche Nation and more to the Cheeky Cockneys.

"I like your hair, Jimmy," Debbie said as she looked at the way Jimmy's hair was cut and dyed.
"Thank you, love. Graham did it for me. The dizzy old queen has his own salon in Chelsea."
"That your other half? I forget."
"Yeah. He's a delicious older man. Remember? I'm a kept toy boy lover." He laughed then put the car in gear and they drove down the bumpy farm track to the road. Then he remarked, "We're off to see the wizard!"

They drove along Collingsmote Lane. Suddenly, Jimmy slammed on the brakes. The car came to a slithering halt and stalled.
"O.M fucking G!" gasped Jimmy. "Did you see that?"
"No. What?" Debbie was shaken.
"Bloody shadow ran in front of the car."

Debbie froze. She couldn't see anything except the road, trees and bushes in the dark.

"What was it? A fox? A deer?"
"God knows. I'm all a lapdab. Looked like a man. Running across the road."
"A man? Did you see what he looked like?"
"No. Just a black figure, head to toe."

"Shit, you're scaring me now. There is a legend of a black Shuck around here. Mind you, that's a giant ghostly dog not a man." She thought a moment, "I didn't see anything."

"Ran, shoop! Right in front of the car. Couldn't miss it, lovie."

Jimmy started the car again. He then went 'pedal to the metal' as he would say, to Pete's house.

When Pete answered the door he looked a little uncomfortable to see the pair.

Jimmy broke the ice, "We come in peace, Earthman." He held his hand up forming a 'V' with his middle and ring fingers.

Nigel saw them from the house and called out, "Cousin Jimbo." He smiled and greeted his cousin with a 'man hug'.

"Last time a man did that to me I lost my wallet," Jimmy quipped.

Reluctantly, Pete let them in. There was a lot of 'surprised' and 'lovely to see you' chatter. Carew recognised Jimmy from school. A few introductions and then Carew's eyes met Debbie's. He was immediately attracted to her quirky and cheeky ways. She had bright eyes that were full of life. Moira had commented that Debbie and Carew were single people as if trying to match make. Carew had no thoughts of any emotional entanglement right now because he felt that he was not over Amy.

Debbie sat near Carew after Moira introduced them. They began to talk about music, art and literature. The conversation was vaguely reminiscent of one Carew had with Amy when they first met. He learned that the Reggae DJ he admired 'back in the day', was actually Marcia's husband.

Debbie had an annoying way of mentioning her ex boyfriends in every conversation. Carew didn't know why this annoyed him because he had no intention of getting into a relationship and Debbie. She probably wouldn't be interested in a wreck of man like him.

Jimmy related the incident with the shadow in the road. Carew paid rapt attention. Debbie said she had seen nothing and that Jimmy was hallucinating.

"Nonetheless," Carew said, "I think we'd better be careful. If it's that Balaclava character he may want us. Not trying to put the shits up you, but that's truth."

There was silence. A loud knock came at the door. Everyone jumped in surprise.

"It won't be the Balaclava," Carew laughed. "He wouldn't knock. Anyhoo, I'll get it."

Carew opened the door to see Frank standing there in his black bomber jacket.

"Obviously, I came as soon as I could," Frank said.

"Did you nearly get knocked over in the road back there?" Carew pointed in the general direction of the road.

"Yes. How did you know?"

"A friend of a friend told me."

Carew told Pete who Frank was but he already knew. Carew felt foolish and Debbie giggled. The room was quite crowded now.

"Where's your car, Frank?"

"Well, obviously I ran out of petrol on the way, so pushed it into a lay-by."

"Sort it out in the morning," said Pete.

"Obviously, I'll need to."

It was getting late but no one was really bothered anymore. The alcohol had lightened the mood and Carew was enthralled with Debbie and secretly she was feeling the same about Carew.

"Debbie," he said clumsily.

"Carew," she replied cheekily.

"Er, nothing." He chickened out.

She looked at him and said, "If you want to ask me out on a date just say, buster."

Carew was surprised and was visibly shaken. He blushed.

"Yeah, well, er.....sorry. I guess..."

"Oh, shut up man. Where are we going then? Cinema, pub, restaurant? Where? Oh, and tomorrow is fine. You know where I live. I'll drive."

Carew was stunned into silence. He sat there eyes wide open. Then he admitted.

"I don't do cars. Erm. That is, I have a sort of phobia about being in them. Had a crash. There was a death. Ever since....y'know."

Debbie looked at Carew with sympathy. Then, she changed to optimistic and chirped, "We'll walk then. How's about a walk in the park? And then we can go and see if Marcia and her bunch are home. If she is, I assure you you'll get fed, mate."

Carew agreed. He had placed the killing of Martyn and the apprehension of Balaclava on hold. Maybe permanently. Debbie was far more interesting, and Moira was going to get Martyn arrested by talking to the coppers, either tomorrow or Monday.

For once, things seemed less chilly in Carew's soul. He wondered how long it would last.

It was late and Jimmy offered to take Debbie and Carew back to the farm, or wherever they wanted to go. Debbie accepted the ride to the farm although Carew was fighting back the fear of travelling again. He felt he had better overcome it, if he could, to impress Debbie who was a bright spark of life to him now. However, this time Carew decided to stay at Pete's place.

Frank would get petrol in the morning and return home. It would be a bit of a walk, so both Pete and Nigel offered to give Frank a lift to the petrol station. As Pete was feeling like a cold or flu was creeping up on him, Nigel took Frank the next day. They didn't say much at first but then began to chat about military life. They spoke of tales they'd heard and mentioned names of people they may know. The name George Ashby came up a few times. Frank said that he'd not met Ashby much, but he reminded him of Carew in so many ways. It was the look. That intense gaze that gave an air of confidence or danger. He was never sure which.

"Did Carew ever meet Ashby?" Nigel enquired.
"I don't know. Obviously, we didn't serve together all that much, obviously, as such but Ashby would obviously have driven to the different bases from time to time. It's just something about the pair. Obviously, I can't put my finger on it. I guess obviously, everyone has a double."
"I think you're right. Maybe they're probably long lost twins or something."
"Well, obviously they're about the same age but I think Ashby is a bit older."
"Unless the horrible truth is that they're one and the same. There. Solved."

Both men laughed.

Both men drove home.

Both men forgot the conversation.

Chapter 16
Jimmy Banyard thinks

Jimmy Banyard lay in his old bed at his parent's place. He couldn't sleep. He stared at the walls and held his iPad to play a game of Swapping Candy.

Jimmy knew he was gay when he was a teenager. It wasn't something he had to learn. He just felt that way. There was a period of confusion for him as he came to the realisation that he was different from others. It was uncomfortable because he dare not 'come out' at that time. There was a strange feeling of being alone. That was until he spoke to Mr Ollard.

Mr Ollard was a round faced, clean shaven and flamboyant interior designer. He lived in a cottage on the corner of Venables Street. His hair was a mop of grey, sometimes dyed blonde or purple. He favoured wearing a brightly coloured artist's smock. Sometimes he wore a cravat. Jimmy didn't know if he only had one pair of trousers or not, but he always saw Ollard wearing navy blue felt trousers.

William (or Quentin as his friends called him), Ollard was never married and had a male friend that dealt in antiquarian books. Ollard believed in mystical things and flirted with Rosicrucianism for some years. He'd been part of the spiritualist group that Mrs Bellamy was associated with. It was a group that used to meet in a room above the now empty and boarded up Cona Café. The boards were now used by local bands to paste their gig posters on. Jimmy's favourite local band name was 'the Grumpy Waiters'. Although it sounded more like a cuisine juggling act, they were actually a great folk duo with witty self penned songs.

Small town. Small dreams. The Bellamy bunch were a wart on the arse of mankind. Despite his connection to the Bellamy bastards, Jimmy was drawn to Ollard but not in a sexual way. He felt there was some kind of affinity but didn't realise that it was because they were both gay. Jimmy thought the word that described his relationship with Ollard was 'avuncular'.

"I don't like you talking to that man," his mother would say.
"Oh, mother. Don't be an old fuddy duddy!" Jimmy would reply waving his hands in the air.

He thought that because his mother was a Christian, she held some archaic views from illiterate iron age goat herders. He was grateful that she hadn't shunned him when he came out as gay. He knew his parents didn't like it, but they were at least reasonable about it. They remained open an honest. So many of his friends had parents that had either thrown them out of the home, stopped communication, or carried on oblivious. Jimmy was lucky.

Ollard died of pneumonia a year ago and Jimmy had attended the funeral. He cried like a baby as they lowered the coffin and Ollard's man friend put his arm around Jimmy to comfort him. The town gossip was the usual homophobic AIDS related slander. Jimmy didn't care if it was AIDS or not because all he felt the passing of a great soul that had been a guide to him. Ollard was no hero in the sense of rescuing a child from a burning building, but he was a hero to Jimmy in his own right. It was the news of the recent deaths in the town that had reminded him.

He recalled Ollard's favourite saying, "Oh well, you live and learn and then in the end you die and forget it all."

That first conversation with Ollard was very awkward and was held over Ollard's garden gate.

"Are you friends of Dorothy?" Ollard asked Jimmy at one stage.

"No. Who is she?" Jimmy asked.

Ollard laughed and then asked, "I mean, are you 'so'? Homosexual?"

"I don't know," said Jimmy. "I find it hard to talk about."

"Well, you'll find out soon enough. Just remember that being gay is nothing to be ashamed of. It's all part of our evolution. Another thing. Just because a man is gay doesn't mean he fancies every other man he sees. That's a common misconception amongst straights."

"I still don't know." Jimmy was confused. "I find girls yukky."

Ollard had laughed in a good natured way and agreed that it was very difficult to know who to trust with such feelings.

"What do I do?" Jimmy asked.

"Just be yourself. Get a job. Get a hobby and get friends. You'll soon find the right people will naturally gravitate to you."

Jimmy took that advice, as nebulous as it seemed, and secured a job as a mental health nurse. The most problematical inmate he ever dealt with was Dave Martyn and his alter ego. He wondered where Martyn was now. When he had driven through Barnowby there was police tape over the door of the Martyn house and around the greenhouse. Martyn's home had become a crime scene. From his past experience of Martyn, he knew that anything involving drugs, death or depravity would also involve Martyn somehow.

He recalled one winter's day. It had been grey outside and sleet was falling. The whole place seemed murky and austere. It was the day he saw Martyn in his room, with pictures of people from newspapers and magazines. Martyn had torn them out. He was arranging them on the floor then tearing off half of their face, from the top down and then putting the half faces in one corner of his room. He placed them upside down and face down. For some reason, Martyn would refuse to eat anything containing cucumber on a Thursday after 12:35pm. There was some strange thing about eating black pudding too, that went beyond personal taste and was almost religious.

Then there was the thing where he would cover his head with a bag, or anything big enough, and call himself Tom Eccleston. If he was asked to remove the mask he would become agitated and refer to it as his 'real face'. Sometimes he had drawn the emblem of the British Royal Marines between the eye holes. The protective Eccleston persona gave evidence of a chaotic thought process that strangely filtered into logic.

It became apparent that Tom Eccleston was his alter ego. Because of this 'safety behaviour' he wasn't challenged when 'under the bag' but treated as a separate individual. There seemed to be some connection between the emergence of his alter ego and his mother. The notes by Professor Paul Kerner-Jackson had been consulted as they matched the Martyn/Eccleston behaviour perfectly. After hypnotherapy and medication he was deemed fit to go back into society. To all intents and purposes he seemed normal.

News spreads fast in Barnowby and it wasn't long until Jimmy heard that Bellamy was dead. Murdered. His first thought was, 'Eccleston did it.' For once Jimmy thought that Martyn or Eccleston had been a force for good. The news that Rolph had been found by the railway tracks, sounded suspicious too.

Jimmy decided not to think about Martyn anymore and his mind wondered to Carew. He remembered Carew from school. Always that intense look. Carew spoke with his eyes. He vaguely recalled Carew was in the last year of school when Jimmy started. Carew was a Jehovah's witness and seemed very inward. The new Carew, who was out of the JW faith, seemed a much better person. However, there was a hint of aggression in his face but not something too obvious. It was like an after taste.

Jimmy had assessed Carew using his observations of body language and speech. Here was a man who seemed to have no hope and yet was on a mission of some sort. Was it to pay for some past sin? He seemed to exude confidence in what he was doing though, as strange as it seemed, he didn't appear to have self confidence. It was a puzzle that, perhaps, illustrated how complex we are as humans. Carew was also a man that appeared to be on the run from something. There was an air of aloofness there too. This man was hiding many things and looked to be bursting at the seams with them. However, now he'd met Debbie, it seemed that Carew's inward freeze was thawing.

Jimmy gave thought to Frank too. He thought about how Frank had the annoying habit of inserting 'obviously' into everything he said. Jimmy just wanted to respond with, 'No. It's not fucking well obvious, Mr Frankie goes to Hollywood!' It was an annoying sentence filler to add merit and undue validity to the shit he was talking. Jimmy had known a dumpy little girl once that over used the word 'basically'. Then there was that tall skinny bloke from the chemist that looked like a vampire only deader, that used 'actually' every damn sentence. Jimmy laughed as he thought of the chemist. He stood bolt upright, had a long face and kept his chin down whilst looking straight ahead. He kept his arms flat to his sides. He looked like he was laying in a coffin but standing up.

Frank wasn't all he seemed to be in Jimmy's eyes. Although he gave the impression he was a bit of a bumbler, he'd been in the forces and even been a mercenary soldier. He had killed people and had a sadistic look when he spoke of it sometimes. Franks did not give the impression he was really interested in helping with anything. Did Frank have a life partner? Was he gay, straight, a-sexual or what? Was he even a bloke? Was Frank a woman dressed up?

Jimmy looked at a framed meme on his wall that he could just about see in the gloom. He knew what it said:

"The freest anyone ever is occurs when they care enough about their integrity to search for the truth. The most enslaved anyone ever is occurs when they are constrained enough to announce they've found the truth and, to protect their pride, stop the search." -unknown

"Too bloody true," he said and began to play his game on the iPad. Every now and again he received messages from his partner as they held a virtual conversation.

He decided it was time for a wank so looked for some porn on his iPad.

After his customary wank, he wiped his belly with a tissue to remove the semen. He screwed the tissue up and popped it under his mattress where it would get flattened. He could dispose of it in the morning. Jimmy snuggled down beneath his light quilt for the night. Before he drifted off to sleep, he heard a passenger plane droning as it passed overhead. Somehow the sound gave him comfort and sent a pleasant shiver through him.

His dreams were in colour.

Chapter 17
Another Monday.

Monday morning. Carew showered. He hadn't slept very well, partly due to his aching hand, but mainly because he had been thinking of Debbie. He couldn't quite remember her face. He wasn't sure if he was doing the right thing by agreeing to walk with her the next day. Surely it was only a walk. No harm would be done. Carew felt bewildered about the way he thought of Debbie.

Debbie met Carew at the bandstand in the park. She brought a carrier bag with some old bread in it to feed the ducks and swans that congregated on the large pond in 'Central Park'. Carew mused over the name of the park as it was nothing like its name sake in New York.

Today the sun was faintly warming despite the breeze. Carew could feel the sun on his forehead. He wasn't sure if he should take his Harrington off or leave it on. It was one of those days. He'd actually decided to dab on some Dunhill aftershave. The park was devoid of many people as it was a working day for most. The trees waved majestically and the breeze made the grass appear like moving waves on the sea.

Carew felt nervous. He mused that he could feel confident facing a killer but not a female. He wanted to smack her arse because he thought it was the best arse he'd seen on a woman. He resisted.

Debbie had invented a pet name for Carew already, 'Colonel'. She said it was because his facial hair seemed to be modelled after Colonel Saunders of KFC fame.

Debbie looked at Carew's shoulder and laughed as she pointed.

"That's good luck, Colonel," she said.

Carew looked. A bird had shit on his shoulder. He took a piece of tissue and tried to rub the mess off. "Not lucky for me. This is my best Harrington."

"Fancy an ice cream, Debs?"

"No but I'll have a rocket lolly if they've got one. Then after we'll see if Marcia is about."

Carew went over to the cream and blue ice cream van to buy their choices. He handed Debbie a rocket lolly. Carew had a 99 cornet. He ate the chocolate flake first. It was a ritual of his.

"I bloody hope Moira rings the fuzz about Martyn," Carew said.

"Yeah, you said. I'm sorry. An ex of mine, Dando, he had a girlfriend who was raped before they met. He had a terrible time in the relationship."

"You mention Dando a lot." Carew made a slight dig with this observation. "Are you sure you're over him?"

"Well, yes but I only speak of him for context, Colonel. I'm well over him. I just felt sorry for him that's all. He had a weird childhood."

"If he treated you like shit it's because he treated you like shit as a man. You're being too soft I think. It will mess up your mind. Anyhoo, change subject. Will Marcia mind me coming over?"

"She was fine about it when I rang her. She's looking forward to meeting you. Oh, and for the record, are you a little jealous of my ex's?" Debbie smiled but was disguising her seriousness.

"Why should I be jealous? I don't even like you." Carew winked. They laughed but in the back of her mind Debbie was wondering if she did seem obsessive over her ex boyfriends. Then she justified it to herself in her usual way.

Marcia answered the door. She looked surprised to see Carew standing there with her friend Debbie.

"This is the Colonel. Colonel Carew, this is Marcia," Debbie announced.

Marcia composed herself and smirked.

"We've met," she said. "Last time I saw Mr Carew he was face down in the mud."

Debbie looked baffled and said, "Please tell me more."

They went inside. There was a song playing:

'Lick shot. Boomshot. Boom boom shot
Police brutality, in dis ya society
Boomshot boomshot
A wah me seh
Mash Babylon to rasclaat.'

"I love this song," said Carew. "The dub version is one of the best ever."

"You like reggae music, eh?"

"Yeah. Debbie tells me your husband was one of my favourite DJs back in the day. I'm a big Reggae fan. Massive."

"I love this song too. The words are a bit rude. I'm careful when I play it usually."

"Oh. The 'R' word you mean," said Carew.

Marcia commented that Carew should have been a black man. He replied that he nearly was, due to his blood connection to Barbados.

They sat in the living room and Carew looked around at the familiar things in there. He felt at home. Marcia served bun and cheese and drinks. Carew and Debbie had black grape cola.

"Not at work today, Debs?" Marcia asked tilting her head.

"Got the week off. Dad's away in Hull and someone's gotta take care of the farm."

"You do it all on your own or are the men still there?"

"Just Ben and Bill now."

Marcia laughed, "Don't you mean Bill and Ben, the Flowerpot men?"

"I know," sniggered Debbie. "That's why I say their names the other way around." Then she asked how Marcia's family all were.

Marcia admitted she had been worried about her son as he came home from school tired and seemed unable to concentrate. He was on report for not handing his homework in and not concentrating in lessons. The father of Devonn's best friend had called Ralston on the phone. He said that he was worried that the boys were taking or smoking something they shouldn't. Ralston said he'd 'keep an eye on it'. So far he'd seen, heard or found nothing.

Carew had seen this behaviour before when kids had started taking substances to get them high. But he decided to say, "Perhaps a teenage thing."

"I'm going to see the head teacher tomorrow anyway. Kids. A real pain at times." Marcia was perplexed.

She looked at Carew and said, "I hope you don't mind me asking, but a masked man attacking you?"

Carew gritted his teeth and Debbie looked intrigued. She knew his fracture was a result of some sort of assault. Carew wasn't specific and she hadn't pushed him.

"A few odd things going on around here but I can't say too much other than things are afoot at the Martyn ranch."

"Are you a copper too?" Marcia wasn't sure. After all, Dangerfield didn't know Carew. Who knows how they work?

"No. I was a soldier. I have, let's say, an interest in Martyn and an old debt to repay."

"So who's this man in a mask then?"

Carew smiled at the irony of the question and replied,

"I do not know. Er, he wears a mask?"

"So why did he attack you?"

"I saw him at Martyn's place. I think he wanted to erase me as a witness. That's my guess at least."

"Sounds like an idiot to let anyone see him in broad daylight anyway."

Interlude: Devonn Legister and Aaron Kitter

Old enough to want girls but too young to vote. His school in Barnowby was an old dingy looking collection of 20th century buildings. Like most of the architecture in Barnowby, nothing matched, not even the name: 'Barnow Academy'.

Devonn, unlike his sister, disliked school. The only redeeming features were his friends and being one of the few black kids in the area. Due to this he was a bit of a celebrity, in a good way. His friends thought he was a cool rap star in their midst. Although Devonn's father had been a reggae DJ of note back in the day, the kids at the school had not heard of him or even particularly liked the genre of music he had played.

Devonn wrote rap lyrics and got together with his friends to record tracks. They had uploaded some to music sites, with little success. They recorded their musical offerings on Aaron Kitter's PC using a microphone Devonn's dad had given him. Some of the music was original, albeit made with a downloaded suite of sound bites. The lyrics were typical street talk dirges about what they had heard or imagined were the problems in tower blocks and estates in London.

They had dreams of making it big in the rap scene. To this end, they had sullen photos taken of them with the Brockwell tower blocks as their background. The boys had plans for an album called 'Butter$ Bitche$' using the US dollar sign in homage to their favourite rap artists. Of the songs they had recorded they had one that they seriously thought would make them rich and famous. It was the track that had inspired the planned album title. Some of their favourite lyrics were:

'Butters bitches bubble butts,
Boomshot bloodclaat batter up.'

Although young they still entertained misogynistic and homophobic lyrics.

Little did Devonn know that Aaron secretly preferred boys to girls as a sexual preference. However, Aaron did not fancy Devonn. Aaron liked older boys with blonde hair like his own.

When Devonn stayed at Aaron's for the evening, they had started rolling spliffs and smoking them in the garage. Their parents suspected something was happening with the boys but had no proof. Although Devonn's father had been a reggae DJ and did smoke weed on occasions, he didn't want that for his son. Too many friends of his had started with weed and ended up addicted to substances much stronger. He'd been to too many funerals to want his son to start on a slippery slope.

It had been raining. The boys had been scribbling rap lyrics down for about an hour. Aaron had a silver packet with a picture of fruit on the front.

"What's that, blud?" Devonn asked trying to sound cool.
"Legal high, blud," Aaron replied.

The boys laughed as they prepared the powder in a crack pipe. Within minutes they were stoned yet unaware of the depression that would result at the come down stage.

When Marcia picked Devonn up, she knew he had been smoking but not what exactly. Devonn's eyes were glazed and he seemed very lethargic yet strangely aggressive. Marcia decided she would refrain from interrogating him but bring up her concerns later. Devonn had a black, full faced, balaclava hanging from his jacket pocket. Marcia was confused as to why he wanted one. She presumed it was because of his interest in guns and the moronic 'gangsta' mentality.

Many times she had told Devonn that black people are rarely 'oppressed' in this country anymore. She observed that the USA black youth mindset is not compatible with UK culture. The whole background was very different, both historically and currently. She stated that the influence from American media had seeped into British culture. It was contaminating it with the racism that pre existed in the US. The race problems in the US were not the UK struggles. Devonn didn't like this line of reasoning and preferred the role of underdog.

"Your friend Aaron is white," Marcia told Devonn. "Why do you associate with him?"
"You wouldn't understand." Devonn really had no sensible reply and the post stoned depression was kicking in. He was becoming increasingly

angry. He smashed his father's CD rack one day for no reason. Devonn claimed it had fallen over. He thought he'd fooled his parents but they suspected there was a problem with him.

"I understand, Devonn. You've got a lot to learn. Life isn't like you see it on the bloody TV. You've got a lot of growing up to do."

Devonn perpetuated the trend of boys with their shirts untucked at the school. It was a small rebellion but it sent a message of non conformity. Despite his parents being clean and polite, Devonn was scruffy, as if he had no pride in appearance.

It was the day of the media studies lesson. The two boys had hidden behind the poplar trees in the playing field. It was a blind spot to the windows of the school. As they sat there Aaron took a pouch of powder from his back pack.

The boys rubbed the powder on their gums and began to feel the rush. Devonn began to perspire and put it down to the weather. They both began to laugh at the most trivial things. Suddenly Devonn stood up, lurched forward and vomited. He fell onto the vomit as he blacked out. Aaron was laughing at Devonn falling and began to perspire. He felt pins and needles in his leg and face.

Both boys awoke and fell back to sleep as the ambulance took them to hospital accompanied by frantic parents.

"It's ketamine mixed with something else," said Doctor Khan.

The noises in the hospital were getting more irritating to Marcia. The lights began to give her headache. As she sat at the bedside she felt despair for the first time in her life. She knew she would never be free of it because this 'sword of Damocles' was her son.

Over the days that followed Devonn's mood became dark. One morning he didn't get up for school. When Marcia went into his room she gasped, "Dear God!"

She saw that Devonn had been cutting himself. They were not deep cuts but typical surface marks of self harm. He was delirious.

He was never the same again and even the medication from the doctor would never stop his deep depression. Marcia always attributed his suicidal tendencies to the concoction of drugs he'd ingested. His mind was damaged beyond repair.

Aaron Kitter committed suicide one morning at 2:25am. He jumped from the multi story car park adjacent to the tower blocks on the Brockwell estate. He had only a folded piece of paper in his pocket that read;

'Butters bitches bubble butts,

Boomshot bloodclaat batter up.'

The coroner pronounced a verdict of suicide. Aaron had not taken any belongings with him. His pockets were empty.

His medical records had shown anxiety, panic attacks and paranoia. There had been his unprovoked attacks on random passers by and an arrest pending trial.

Devonn didn't attend the funeral of Aaron Kitter. He had been detained by the police for stealing a box of CD jewel cases from the Blears department store. His mother had taken him into town to get a black tie for the funeral.

"I only let him out of my sight for two minutes and this is what happens," Marcia told the police.
"You're giving black people a bad name." Devonn was told by his family.
"Allow it," was his rude and dismissive response.

Chapter 18
The Dangerfields Do Cromer

Dangerfield and family, with their entire luggage, crammed into the Citroen Picasso and began the journey to the north Norfolk Coast. No one really knows where the name 'Cromer' originated from but it was held that it meant 'Crows Mere' or Lake.

There had been the most beautiful red sky the night previously. They were convinced it would be a nice day for a seaside vacation. When Dangerfield saw the sky from his window he went outside and took a picture of it with his tablet. The trees in the background were silhouetted against a scarlet, orange, pink and blue sky. Later that night, he uploaded it onto his blog 'Thermidore Cro-Magnon'. The blog title was a fanciful confection that had presented itself to him in a dream. It was also a nod to his wife being French. The photo entitled 'Before Cromer', received positive comments. Dangerfield changed the PC wallpaper from Cromer Parish Church to his new picture. He knew he'd change it the day he got back.

Esme, Miriam and Vanda had all decided where they wanted to go shopping. Dangerfield just wanted to stroll along the beach but the 'belles' wanted to drag him around the shops. Although the holiday was officially 'Cromer', they rented a caravan in Beeston Regis which was only an 8 minutes drive away.

The drive to Beeston Regis seemed endless with Esme and Dangerfield taking it in turns to drive. There was the long wait at a garage to fill up with petrol outside Norwich.

Miriam and Vanda sat on the back seat both wearing earplugs and listening to music on their mobile phones. They were texting their friends. The days of 'are we there yet?' were over. Dangerfield was not sure if that was a good thing or not. With people like Martyn selling filth on the streets, the world was sinking to the rule of the lowest common denominator. The decay was setting in.

He commented to Esme, "You know, all the great empires fell."

"What do you mean?" Esme was surprised by such a random comment.

"Look at the Greeks. Fantastic empire. Then the decadence set in and whoosh, they're gone. Same with the Romans."

"Yes, dear," she replied with an antipathetic tone.

Dangerfield decided to keep quiet and continue driving along the twisting roads. Then he turned right, under the railway bridge, an on to the caravan.

When they arrived at the caravan, Dangerfield made sure the gas was connected for cooking. Varied items were shoved in the fridge. Bags were dumped on beds.

Dangerfield knew he'd be sleeping on his own, on the bench sofa at the end of the caravan, because Esme couldn't bear to hear him snore. He felt outcast but was used to it more these days than when she first bullied him to sleep on his own. He wondered if there was any love there anymore. In any event, keeping his family together was the most important thing.

Esme made a pot of tea then declared, "We haven't got any sugar."

"Any sweeteners?" Dangerfield asked.

"I think so. Remind me to get sugar when we go to the supermarket, dear."

The girls were in their small rooms, more interested in texting their friends than sorting their bed linen out.

"I'm turning my phone off. I do not want to get bothered by all the nutty stuff from Barnowby," Dangerfield said.

The next morning, the Dangerfield tribe decided to go for a walk after tea and cereal.

They clambered down the vertiginous, rickety wooden steps at the cliff face. The sea was raging and roaring. It smashed against the wooden sea defence barriers. A cormorant sat on a post further out to sea. A dull looking man was walking his Labrador, otherwise the beach was forsaken. Dangerfield noticed that his daughters were not particularly impressed with the majesty of the sea. They were more annoyed that their phones struggled for a signal. He picked up a small flat stone and skimmed it over the waves. It hopped 6 times before disappearing from sight into the water.

They ambled in the direction of the concrete slope. Dangerfield picked up a large stone and threw it at the orangey cliff. It hit in a cloud of dust and he watched as a cascade of sand fell down. It reminded him of his childhood. The roar of the ocean and the memories made him feel melancholy. But time moves on and his friend Ronnie once reminded him of a cliché; "All good things come to an end!" He recalled Ronnie, the Vincentian, had said that with a smile on his face. It had seemed like the wrong expression for that kind of cliché.

Esme was walking behind Dangerfield as if disinterested in him now. 'Lugubrious' was the word for it. Is that what the years of marriage did to a couple? He looked at the girls and pondered what their future might be. The melancholy was getting worse.

He recalled almost having a brief fling with a WPC, Jo Marshall. He was supervising her in a sting on street robberies. They had spent time together on police business in Leamington Spa. They were in the same hotel. Nothing happened but it very nearly did. Dangerfield was relieved when she was posted away. It made him think that if Esme was his one and only then no one would come anywhere near in-between them. Perhaps he was wrong. The wind blew Dangerfield's hair askew. He was feeling old remembering when he had a full head of black hair.

The next day would be a visit to Cromer itself and the promise of perfect fish and chips. This was what Dangerfield held on to. It was cold comfort but at least it was some comfort.

That very next day they parked in the pay car park along the front. Dangerfield could see the pier and beach. The girls dragged him around the shops. He was bored and announced that he was going to a second hand bookshop for a 'nosey'.

In the shop he looked at the varied genres. Finally he found a book by a Professor Paul Kerner-Jackson. The book was about the 'Fragmented Mind'. He thumbed briefly through it. It didn't read like a boring textbook. It was actually interesting. Alternate or fragmented personalities that were once termed schizophrenia, suddenly made Dangerfield think about the Martyn enigma he was working on. He resisted the urge to buy the book but still did. It was a read that would make him see the whole Martyn thing afresh. It reminded him that Martyn had spent time with mental heath issues.

He was wondering if Jimmy Banyard may be able to assist with enquiries. Jimmy had worked at Ranstead as a nurse when Martyn was admitted there.

"DaaaAAAaaad." Vanda broke his thoughts. She was beckoning him.

Dangerfield turned around and his family awaited him with varied coloured carrier bags in hand.

He paid the money to the shop owner who was a tall greying man with a tweed jacket and spectacles on a chain.

Then he left the shop and joined his family. There were no slapstick events that would normally make Smiffy laugh or cause Dangerfield to swear. He felt like a clown and that was nadir enough.

Esme was now quite chirpy and feeling good about life. She recalled her childhood in France with the greatest of joy. The vineyards to the west of her village. Her exchange as a student to the UK. She's stopped in Peterborough and although it wasn't a wonderful place, it was made better by the friends she met at the Baptist church. Pastor Tim was a very kind man and his wife was charming. Tall and deep voiced sermons on a Sunday were a treat to Esme. It was because of her love of the church that she insisted that one child at least have a biblical name. They'd planned for three but had two. Miriam was the biblically named child. They chose the names together. Miriam Rebeccah Dangerfield. Then there was the semi biblical one Vanda Tabitha Dangerfield. The name was loosely chosen because Esme was originally a Catholic. Dangerfield hadn't liked the name Vanda at first, but as his daughter grew, she began to look like a Vanda to him.

Finally Dangerfield could go to look at the beach after putting the shopping into the Picasso. Somehow the beach looked drab. The pier looked drab. He watched as a boat sped out across the waters. It looked tiny and insignificant. Dangerfield sighed. Anyway, he was looking forward to a fish and chip meal. He felt the book in his pocket and although he wanted to get away from work, the Martyn thing was haunting him. He felt there was a clue in the book.

They decided to get the fish and chips from the usual place. The man serving recognized them. That was customer service, Dangerfield thought.

His daughters actually preferred kebabs, so that's what they got.

The food raised Dangerfield's spirits. He thought back to when Vanda and Miriam were children and he knew he had beautiful memories with more to follow.

He recalled the day a little Vanda asked him what she had dreamed of the previous night. He replied he didn't know. She replied angrily, "Well you should know. You were in it!"

Tomorrow they planned simple microwave meals, more boring shopping and then the cinema.

They ambled to the car park and loaded the boot with their purchases.

As the Picasso drove from the car park, a silver BMW M3 sedan with blacked out windows followed. It kept several cars back on the road back to

Beeston Regis but it was there, unnoticed by Esme who was driving. The girls were tapping away on their phones as usual and were oblivious of the world around them. Dangerfield looked at his girls and reflected on how perfect they were to him. He couldn't have wished for better daughters. Times like these were precious and he was savouring them. Esme turned right to go under the railway bridge at Beeston Regis. The saloon followed at a distance.

The Picasso drove over the rough ground and parked next to the caravan. The saloon remained in the car park near the railway tracks 300 yards away.

Dangerfield and family entered the caravan which rocked slightly under their weight. Crockery clanked, doors flapped and things bumped. The girls returned to the Picasso, opened the boot hatch and took their shopping out. Dangerfield stood on the steps of the caravan and looked across to the 'Beeston Bump'. I was a very large hill overlooking the sea that somehow seemed out of place. He'd walked over it several times with his family to visit Sherringham. He had been told that the hexagonal concrete surface on the top of the bump, was a leftover from the Second World War. Something to do with signalling he was told. A 'Y-station'. Dangerfield thought, 'and why not station.'

In the caravan they all sat watching TV while Dangerfield became engrossed in his book. He heard the girls laughing at the show and yet it seemed distant and inconsequential, as if it wasn't real. The observations about the fragmented personality became clear to him. Something was coming together in his mind but all the dots hadn't connected yet. There was something here. He read on until the girls announced they were off to bed. He bid them all goodnight with a kiss and continued reading until he dozed off to sleep. His dreams were uneasy. Images flashing. Voices. He awoke with a start and sat up. It was clear what was happening with the Martyn case. Still many questions. Should he curtail his holiday?

At 3:00am when the family were all sleeping, no one noticed a figure in a balaclava sneak to the caravan door. With a swift movement the lock was picked and the balaclava entered quietly. The Bowie knife was thrust hard and decisively into Dangerfield's gut and up toward his heart. There were no shouts from a sleeping Dangerfield as bubbling blood splattered the ceiling and dripped onto the carpet. Balaclava entered each bedroom and administered to same manoeuvre to Esme, Vanda and finally Miriam.

Balaclava closed the door which slowly swung open again later. Balaclava returned to the BMW and drove away cautiously.

It was Mrs Pitts, a local resident, that called the ambulance and police. Each morning she went for a coffee with Esme when the family were on holiday. They'd known each other from Esme's college days.

Body bags took Esme and the girls away.

Somehow there was a spark of life in Dangerfield. They rushed him to intensive care. The trauma team worked hard to keep him alive. The blade had missed his heart and instead punctured his left lung. There seemed to be tubes everywhere. The surgeons worked to restore the lung tissue by entering tubes down the throat that led to the airways. Another tube was inserted to remove unwanted air. They removed surplus fluids in the pleural space.

At 7:32pm the heart monitor flat lined. At 7:35pm after being hit with a defibrillator his heart started again.

He survived with one lung. When he woke up later, he realised his world was shattered. He wished he hadn't survived.

***

Carew rang Dangerfield. No reply. Not even the answering service. A dead tone. It was about time this charade ended and Martyn got justice. Not being able to contact Dangerfield was a big spoke in the wheel.

As Carew picked up the newspaper the colour drained from his face as he read how a family had been brutally slaughtered. Instinctively he knew it was the Dangerfields.

One: he knew Dangerfield was on holiday, even though he rang his number. Two: it was rumoured in the article, that it seemed to be a revenge attack because of police action. Three: Dangerfield's number was totally dead. Why it was totally dead was a mystery but there it was. Carew was uneasy. He really didn't trust just any copper. Dangerfield was a good man and not power tripping or apathetic like many coppers Carew had met.

Moira was an adult and as such should be responsible for her own actions. Carew still felt like she needed brotherly help.

Moira's rape needed exposure. Martyn needed reeling in. All this blood lust was getting out of hand. Now there was Debbie on the scene and this made thing totally different. Meeting Debbie had softened Carew. Now, he didn't wasn't to kill Martyn so much as make him face justice. Carew didn't want to go to prison for murder either. He'd made up his mind that if he did go to jail that he'd go after paedophiles and rapists in there and kill them if he could. Unlike before, when he didn't care, Debbie had changed the game.

After Amy and before Debbie, Carew hadn't bothered whether he lived or died. In fact death had seemed almost like a friend he'd longed would visit. He had considered suicide but realised it wasn't really death he wanted but the end of the pain. Suicide was a terrible thing and what if it went wrong?

Carew knew a guy that had tried to electrocute himself but survived with no arms as a result. There was another friend who'd had enough of the killing he'd seen in Africa and took pills and alcohol. He'd woken up the next day in a pool of vomit and never recovered from the internal organ damage.

There was Lydia who jumped from a multi storey car park. She lay in a quivering heap before she died. Drowning? No thanks. There was that frightening body shock as the cold water hits, followed by the panic as the lungs fill with filthy water. Never hanging. Slowly choking as excruciating pain wracks the body.

Now here was Debbie. Carew felt strange because he didn't know if he was willing to move on from Amy yet. A few years had past since the car accident but he was still haunted by it all. He knew it was early days. He still wondered how his feelings for Amy would clash with anything that may or may not develop with Debbie. They were only friends but Carew felt there was something very different with this one. Could it be a rebound thing? Surely not after so long.

Carew rang Moira. "Hey, I think DI Dangerfield has been killed. Moira. You need to tell the coppers about Martyn like I said."

Moira was reluctant but agreed that she would call the police and report Martyn soon. Carew was anxious. Would Moira do it or would he have to do it for her. He hadn't told her he'd attempted to call Dangerfield to report the rape.

Sid Banyard had seen his brother in law Pete, at the GPO and they spoke for a long time. Although Pete had not had much contact with Dangerfield, he was sickened when he found out about the slaughter. The official word was that they were all dead. Even at the hospital, Dangerfield was under covert police protection. For now, they believed the whole family were to be buried at St Matthew's church after the inquest was over.

Mona Cruickshank had revealed that there was to be a funeral for the Dangerfield family who were ex residents in the parish.

Pete told Carew what Sid had told him in confidence. Carew and Pete sat in the living room at Pete's. The Voodoo mask seemed to look on with a mocking expression. Debbie was to arrive in half an hour with Jimmy again. Carew sighed deeply. His fears had been confirmed. A sticky cup ring on the coffee table took Carew's attention. He thought to himself that things were now coming full circle.

***

Dangerfield attended the funeral of Esme, Vanda and Miriam. He was slumped in a wheelchair. He could barely breathe despite the oxygen mask he wore. The Reverent John Cruickshank conducted the funeral at St Matthew's Church. A great number of people attended. Dangerfield noticed Carew was observing from a distance. There he stood in the dappled shade of a tall tree. Carew wore his red Harrington jacket and his hair was wild. He looked leonine and had a resolute look on his face as if he was planning something. Debbie Burns was with Carew.

Carew was surprised to see Dangerfield alive. Relieved even and yet he felt a deep sorrow for his loss. Carew thought it best to stay at a distance. After all, he didn't really know Dangerfield well enough to make contact.

Smiffy had informed Dangerfield, on a daily basis, of the progress the police made. Someone Dangerfield hadn't met but knew by reputation was leading the murder investigation. Detective Inspector Mason LeBeau. LeBeau was a very confident man with sharp features and spiky black hair. He had a constant, clenched teeth, stern look on his face. Dangerfield liked him, he was a hard bastard and not one to be tricked easily.

Due to the circumstances, his injuries both physical and mental, Dangerfield accepted retirement from the police force.

Sitting at home Dangerfield looked at his phone and hovered a shaky finger over Carew's number.

Chapter 19

LeBeau sat in his modest office. The light came in through the slatted blinds. He could hear the busy traffic outside. Occasionally there would be the sound of an angry driver sounding his horn. He ran his fingers under his collar as the shirt and tie combo made him uncomfortable. There was a hair in his mouth which he picked out and yet it seemed as if it was still in there. About 2 minutes later, after moving his tongue around, he picked out another hair.

He rang Smiffy and told him he wanted all he had on Martyn. "Listen," he said to Smiffy. "I know you're related to Martyn but as far as I'm concerned you're a police officer now. When you're at work, family means nothing in these circumstances."
"Yes, sir. Thank you, sir."
"I want the memory stick as evidence. Where did you get it?"

LeBeau was playing with Smiffy. He knew exactly where it had come from and who had taken it.

Smiffy hesitated then replied, "Er. Anonymous informant, sir."
LeBeau smiled to himself and said, "Better stick to that story!"

Then he hung up.

Both men knew the other knew the score. It was a mutual respect thing.

He looked at the photos taken from inside the Dangerfield caravan. He'd been there, at the crime scene investigation, and sickened by what he saw. He splayed them on the top of his desk.

He peered at the forensic results. There were clues here. Method of murder: Bladed instrument thrust under the ribcage to pierce the heart. Approximate blade length: 8 inched not serrated. Viscous bastard.

When they'd employed the tracker dog it had taken them to the car park. It lost the track there. LeBeau knew from this that the murderer was in a vehicle. He requested information that may be on any CCTV cameras in the area. They'd found a bloody footprint on the caravan carpet and three long dark hairs that didn't match any of the Dangerfield family or Mrs Pitt. DNA tests had revealed nothing. The footprint revealed a UK army 'defender' boot size 42, heavily worn down at the heel. The same tread was found in the car park next to tyre tread marks. Judging by the width and placement of the tread marks in the dusty ground, they were Mitchelins on a BMW M3, possibly. The tyre dimensions at the front were measured at 255/40 ZR18 95Y and at the rear 275/40 ZR18 99Y. This is what forensics had said.

LeBeau directly linked the Dangerfield incident with the report from Smiffy.

"Let's get Martyn," he barked. "This has been sat on for too long. Martyn's going down for life for supplying class 'A' filth and murder, I do believe."

With military precision he led the men to Martyn's house. He had a search warrant.

There was no reply and after a search of the greenhouse area. They battered the door down. The alarm screamed. The house was searched. No one was there. They found the remains of the dead cat upstairs.

"Right," commanded LeBeau. "Let's do a thorough search. Bags and tweezers at the ready men."

His radio squawked. No one had been found in the green house.

He ran over to the greenhouse where the men had entered by force. Glass lay inside the doorway. It crunched under his boots as he strode in.

He stopped and looked around at the plants. Then he noticed a small camera hidden in the cycads. The wire led to the office at the back. No surprise there he thought.

"Nothing here, sir," said PC Barstow.
"What's in there?" LeBeau pointed to the large metal door in the far wall of the office.
"It won't open, sir."
"Right. Let's get someone to open it. Oh, Barstow, get some men to search the back to see if there's an exit."

The radio squawked again and he ran back to the house. Meaden had found something. It sounded significant.

LeBeau looked at the box that had been found in Martyn's bedroom. It was full of ripped thongs and briefs from different females. There was a name sewn into one pair but the ink was badly smudged. There were lipstick tubes in the box. In one corner, he saw a handful of pins that had congealed together with something gelatinous.

"This looks significant. Better get forensics to look over this lot. Oh, and that name. Let me know the moment the lab guys figure it out," LeBeau ordered. Then, into his radio, "Where's that bloke to open that metal door in the green house?"

"He'll be about ten minutes, sir," replied the voice.

LeBeau looked around the Martyn house but found nothing significant apart from a deep knife groove in the ceiling above the downstairs toilet. He requested that someone check it out fully and see if it matched any markings found on the inside ribcage of any of the victims. He had a hunch about this and he wasn't telling yet.

The radio squawked at LeBeau, "Iqbal's here to open the door, sir."

He went to the doorway and looked at the stocky, mixed race Cockney, Paul Meaden. "Meaden, with me please." He gestured with his radio toward the greenhouse.

At the greenhouse a young Iqbal, who had dark rings under his eyes, was in the process of heaving open the heavy door. He released the seven locks with his lock picks and bolt cutters.

LeBeau said, "Good work Iqbal. Now stand well back."

LeBeau and Meaden shone their lights into the gloom whilst sheltering behind the doorway. As one of the few coppers in the area allowed a firearm, LeBeau unsheathed his Walther P99 pistol. He side stepped into the darkness. Pistol and torch ready, he moved cautiously forward. He saw a flight of steps leading down. There was a foul stench rising from below. As he looked around, he found a light switch and pressed it. A bulb came on above his head and he could see clearly. He switched off his torch.

"Coast is clear. Meaden. With me please," he called.

Meaden followed down the dank steps to another heavy door. It was painted in red gloss and was damp. There was rust on the edges.

Iqbal was required to open the door with his usual precision. As the door squealed open the foul stench hit their nostrils. They all recoiled. LeBeau placed a handkerchief over his nose and mouth. He switched on the light and viewed the inside of the narrow room.

"Good God," LeBeau gasped. "What do you make of this?"

There was a stunned silence for a brief moment.

Chapter 20

The phone rang. Carew answered. It was Dangerfield.

"Thank you for coming to the funeral, Carew."
"No problem. I am so, so sorry. Look. If there's anything I can do. Y'know."
"Actually there is. Can we talk? I can't drive. I'll pay for a taxi for you. Or a bus."

Carew said he didn't like traveling in cars but the bus was fine. He asked to bring Debbie.

The bus ride was uneventful. Carew observed the people getting on and off at the stops along the way. There was the ignorant looking man chewing gum with his mouth open. The large shouty mother with the runny nosed toddler. A man that had a face like a boxer dog. Several teenagers and some dispossessed looking men in hi viz jackets. The bus drove through a grotty looking estate. It turned onto a pleasant residential area festooned with bushes and trees, instead of hypodermic needles and burnt out cars.

Carew and Debbie got off. The stuffiness of the bus was forgotten as they walked out into the refreshing air. They followed the directions Dangerfield had provided.

Debbie tugged on Carew's arm.

"There it is. Number 27. Looks like a nice place."
"Yes. Full of memories too. Poor old Dangerfield. Shit. I don't know what to say."
"Take it as it comes."

For the first time Carew grabbed Debbie's hand. She gave a twee smile.

"Does this mean we're officially dating then?" Debbie asked.
Carew trying to be cool replied, "Sure. If you want."
"I want," She replied. "Now," Debbie winked, "Let me hold your other hand."
Carew gave a one sided smile and said, "And on the other hand!"

Debbie threw her head back and laughed aloud.

The door opened. There stood Dangerfield hobbling and holding his side. Carew noticed how ancient Dangerfield was looking now. Unshaven. Unwashed hair. Harrowed and stressed. Lacking sleep. A rag doll of his former self. He looked skeletal almost. 'Understandable considering the trauma he's just experienced,' thought Carew.

Inside the pale green living room, Dangerfield slowly lowered himself into his armchair. He gritted his teeth as the pain lanced through him. Around him were pictures of his family. There were portraits on the wall and one family photo on an occasional table. The table had an aromatic tea candle burning in front of the picture.

Just beyond the patio doors there was an unkempt lawn with an apple tree. It made sense to Carew that the garden had been neglected since the murder of his family. If no one could help him then he was incapable of mowing the lawn in the state he was in. When a man has nothing to live for then nothing is worth bothering with. On the larch lap fence sat a tabby cat that looked around slowly with, what appeared like, disdain.

"Get yourself a drink if you want," Dangerfield said. "I find it a bit hard to move about at the moment."

"Can we get you anything?" Debbie enquired opening her eyes wide.

"No thanks. Well, maybe a coffee? White with a sweetener. While you're there, you can help yourself. Tea. Coffee. Squash."

Debbie went into the large kitchen. The clear kettle boiled. Drinks were served in bone china mugs. While she waited for the kettle, she put dishes in the dishwasher and activated it. Dangerfield said it was kind of her. He looked like he was about to cry.

"So," Dangerfield asked, "Are you a couple?"

At the same time Carew answered, "Yes," Debbie answered, "No."

"I perhaps, shouldn't have said a word. You don't seem to know." Dangerfield raised an eyebrow.

Debbie and Carew looked at each other. Then at the same time Carew answered, "No." Debbie answered, "Yes." Then they looked at each other and turned to Dangerfield.

"Well," Debbie said, "We only just met a few days ago. We seem to be getting on well though. Nothing official."

Carew added, "We're good friends. It's going well though."

"Look after each other whilst you can." Dangerfield's eyes had that far away look and his face looked even more pained.

"Who's looking after you?" Debbie broke the trance.

"Oh, I'm Okay. Er, miss?"

"Debbie. Burns the farmer's daughter."

For the first time Carew saw a flicker of a smile on Dangerfield's face.

Debbie persisted, "Mr Dangerfield. I know we don't know you very well but still. We're all just trying to get along in life even so. Who is looking after you? Really I mean."

"I look after myself. Smiffy comes over to visit. LeBeau contacts me. Oh, they're coppers by the way. You probably never met them, sorry. I'm talking like you know me from years back."

They discussed trivia and generalities. Then Dangerfield looked at Carew and came to the point.

"Look at this."

He handed a book to Carew.

"Professor Paul Kerner-Jackson. Yes. Read some of his stuff before. I like his style. Easy to follow."

Carew flicked the pages. Looked at the index at the back then scanned the introduction. All this time Dangerfield was looking at him with a burning intensity.

Carew asked Dangerfield why he was sharing this book with him.

"Because, Mr Carew, you and I are now on the same page about Martyn, for different reasons."

"Was it Martyn who did this thing to you?"

"Yes it was but at the same time it wasn't."

"You said I spoke in riddles," smiled Carew thoughtfully. "Are you implying that Martyn and the Balaclava are one and the same person?"

"Yes! Sort of. The same body but not the same person." Dangerfield was deadly serious, "That's my theory. It sounds crazy but there it is. Martyn and Balaclava inhabit the same body but are different people essentially. I at first thought that Martyn was just playing a dual role but I've seen how he is afraid of the Balaclava so he doesn't even know it's himself."

"That's quite a theory. Have you fed this back to your friends on the force?"

"Not yet. I don't think my views count anymore. LeBeau, the new kid in charge, is leading an investigation with no thought of anything apart from catching the man."

"What did you want to see me for then?"

"You're driven. I know you came here to kill Martyn and don't deny it, please."

Debbie looked horrified and simply asked, "Colonel?"

"I came here to see that Martyn faced justice one way or another.' He was bending the truth because he had actually planned to kill Martyn, combatant style. However, since he met Debbie his plans had changed, "Yes, I'm an old soldier but I'm not a murderer like Martyn and his 'shadow'."

Dangerfield looked at Debbie and knew why Carew had said that.

Debbie responded, "Sorry you had to hear this Debbie. I guess I'm just being careless now that......."

"It's no problem, Mr Dangerfield. We all have our missions in life."

"Thank you. Anyway, I want Martyn to face justice too. I'm in no position to do it. I know LeBeau is quite capable of catching Martyn but I think he'll be given the slip. If I'm right, and I usually am, Martyn will keep giving him the slip."

"I don't know what I can do though, to be honest. If he gives the police the slip he could give me the slip and I don't exactly have transport if he buggers off somewhere."

"Oh, he already has buggered off. I think I know where to and LeBeau should too."

Debbie needed to go to the bathroom. When she was out of earshot Dangerfield whispered to Carew.

"I want Martyn dead. LeBeau won't do this for me but you can. I know that's why you went to Barnowby, Mr Carew."

"True. Guilty as charged but the game's changed." He indicated to the direction of the bathroom.

"I can see that, Mr Carew." Dangerfield looked at the rug, "My game has changed too. Martyn must die and I can't do it. I'll offer you payment by way of this house and certain funds I have."

"This house? Where will you live?"

"Cromer. Anyway. I know you were a mercenary soldier so I figure you'll consider my offer. Think about it and let me know. I know you can outsmart LeBeau and avoid capture. That's my offer."

Carew was quiet and thought for a few moments then admitted he'd think about it. However, the problem he foresaw, was his own lack of transport along with a broken hand. If Martyn was on the run then how could he catch him?

"I'm very tempted, Mr Dangerfield, but I wouldn't have you messing your life up like that."

"Mr Carew. How much more messed up could my life be? And of course, you only get anything if you do kill Martyn and I get proof. For the record I'm selling the house anyway, even if you don't kill him. Too many memories. Don't want them. Not my way."

"Here's the thing." Carew paused, "If I accept or not I'll be over in the week to mow your lawn. We can talk then."

"You'll do it. Kill Martyn I mean, not mow the lawn, although I'm sure you'll do that. I can see the lust for his blood in you. You have your reasons and I won't pry. You may risk losing the girl but having said that, you've only just met, it'll only be a small beheading."

"You've got it all figured out, haven't you?!"

"I try, Mr Carew. I try."

The toilet flushed and the men went back to idle chit chat. Debbie returned and offered more help for Dangerfield.

Debbie asked Dangerfield if he had any painkillers to ease his pain. He replied that he had but his prescription was almost run out, so he was using them sparingly. Carew and Debbie asked him if he had the repeat prescription. He had the slip that needed handing in to his GP at the local surgery. Carew and Debbie decided to take a walk and hand it in. It was only a few streets away.

They walked along Lombard Avenue where some men were working on the pipes beneath the pavement. One of the men looked at Debbie then at Carew then away again. Carew was ready for a fight if the workman got cheeky with Debbie. The workman knew this and also knew that even though Carew had his hand in a splint he'd be no push over.

"Colonel." Debbie looked at Carew, "Were you really going to kill Martyn?"

Carew drew a deep breath and replied.

"It's a long story and I don't expect you'd approve but the game keeps changing."

Debbie said nothing. They walked in silence not holding hands.

After a few minutes Debbie grabbed Carew's hand and said, "So tell me, Colonel. What's this game."

Carew smiled. He was relieved. Maybe he could confide in Debbie after all.

"I wanted to kill someone once," she admitted, "I was ready with my father's shotgun. I bottled out though."
"Don't suppose it was that bloke you keep rattling on about, er, what's his name? Er, Dandy by any chance?"
"You're not letting that go are you? No. Worse."

Carew winked. Debbie continued, "It was a copper called Bellamy. Local bully boy. Absolute scum. He was using my previous trouble with drugs and threatening to plant false evidence to ruin my life. There's more but it's not savoury."
"Yeah. Bellamy was a sheep shagger. Used your Dad to get his loving in."
"How'd you know that, Colonel?"
"Dando told me."
"Oh, piss off."

Carew gave a triumphant grin and Debbie mocked a look of hatred. She hadn't mentioned Dando that was dead.

They waited at the GP's surgery and finally obtained the repeat prescription with a letter of authority that Dangerfield had provided. Then they headed off to the chemist and waited while it was dispensed. The chemist had that typical clean aroma that was slightly pungent. Carew sat on plastic chairs and looked idly around in their boredom. Carew decided to buy a whistling lollipop for them. It had a stick within the main stick that moved in and out that made it sound like a swanee whistle when blown.

***

"It's the remains of a drugs factory," offered Meaden as the peered around the room.

"There are some funny patches and drag marks on the floor here. Looks like blood. Better get the lab guys to analyse them." LeBeau was unconvinced the stench was from the drug lab alone. "Over in the corner there, what's that?"

Meaden walked to the far corner. He took a photograph of a man's gold ring, then picked it up with his gloved hands. The ring was chunky and engraved with a lion's head. The eyes were small red stones that looked very expensive. With one eye partly closed, he dropped it into an evidence container. It fell in with a plop.

The room was a total mess, as if someone had attempted to trash it before the police arrived. Meaden had always imagined a drug factory would be full of test tubes and beakers on Bunsen burners, until he joined the force.

There was white powder next to crushed tablets scattered away from an overturned table.

Meaden picked out another container and scooped the powder into it. He'd always been amazed, if not horrified, how the TV portrayed coppers tasting the powder to analyse it. This was not how real police worked.

***

"Got some lab results, sir," said Smiffy handing LeBeau a folder. Meaden stood with his hands leaning on the back of a chair.

LeBeau took the file with a look of ruthless efficiency. He nodded and pointed to the chair at the side of his desk. Smiffy sat down. LeBeau's desk was arranged in a defensive manner as if he was cocooning himself behind it and keeping everyone else at bay. Smiffy sat in the creaking blue fabric office chair. He swivelled toward LeBeau. 'Does this man ever smile?' thought Smiffy.

"Bingo!" LeBeau said slapping his desk with the papers, "Blah, blah, Krok powder. Blah de blah. Ah, here we are, listen. The DNA on the underwear found in Martyn's bedroom. Positive matches to rape victims. The pin had blood on which also matches one rape victim at least. The name on the label in the female's briefs reads Faye L Jaracz."

LeBeau looked at Smiffy and without smiling said, "Martyn's our man alright. That was his sicko trophy box we found."

LeBeau continued reading. He made grunting noises as he read. Smiffy felt uneasy.

"The blade mark in the ceiling in Martyn's bathroom matches the cut marks on Esme Dangerfields ribs. Martyn is the killer."
"What about this Balaclava figure, sir?"
"No evidence that the Balaclava even exists, let alone done any wrong apart from an alleged assault on Mr Camus."
"Carew, sir."
"Same difference. And Mr Carew hasn't reported the incident so there's nothing more to add at this moment. I'm ruling out any connection with this vigilante type because we only know of one sighting. it's hardly proof of anything. I am well aware that DI Dangerfield thought there was some link and that Martyn was suspect."

Smiffy watched as LeBeau muttered to himself. Then he flicked the papers with the back of his hand, looked at Smiffy and told him, "The stains on the floor. DNA matches Bellamy. Bellamy's dead by the looks of it. Keep it from the press for now and better get his rellies informed."

Smiffy looked shocked and yet at the same time it was what he'd come to believe about Bellamy.

"The ring you picked up, Meaden. Not sure about that. Did Bellamy wear a ring?"

Meaden shrugged. Smiffy didn't know but said he believed that Mike Kitter had a ring like the one in the photograph.

"What happened to Martyn's laptop?" LeBeau asked Meaden who was unwrapping some gum to chew. He was leaning on the chair back with one hand and popping the gum into his mouth with the other.
"Boffins got it back sir," he continued. His tongue moved the gum to the side of his mouth. "I've got the report." Meaden shuffled through some files and handed them to LeBeau. LeBeau placed them on the desk and simply asked, "What's the nub of the findings?"

Meaden explained that there had been evidence of money laundering on a small scale via on line markets. Martyn set up multiple IDs. He then used an ID to sell a product, like a Rolex watch for instance, to some unsuspecting victim. It looked genuine because there would be a few positive comments and feedback on the account, all from the other of IDs of Martyn. On line Payment would be collected and transferred to another of Martyn's IDs. The selling account would mark the item as dispatched and then be closed. The payment would be used to buy another fake item from yet another ID. This time, the item would be marked as received by the 'buyer' and the money banked by the 'seller'.

"How did he do that all from his place?" LeBeau thought he knew but wanted confirmation.

"Well sir, he used a sneaky bit of software that gave fake IP addresses for each account. It would have been a swine to track him down. He made a grand in one hour according to the report."

LeBeau simply said, "Thought so."

Outside they heard shouting and a scuffle.

"Is that Mr Merchant having a fracas with god again?" LeBeau was getting used to the sounds that occurred once or twice a month now. Mr Merchant was a poor soul on medication for his mental illness, but every now and again he would bring a tin of sliced carrots to the area to banish the demons. Due to his mental state, he was never arrested but would be taken back to the hospital. The scuffling would be Merchant resisting the ride back. He had never been violent or thrown a punch but he did try to run away. LeBeau felt sympathy for the overstretched NHS staff and knew that they couldn't cope any more than the police could. The country was in decline in his view and there was only so thinly things could be spread.

LeBeau stood up. "Right. Let's get the men and go to Cromer. Mr Martyn senior has a bungalow nearby apparently." LeBeau pointed to a post-it note then ripped it from the top of his laptop monitor screen, briskly screwed it up and flicked it at the wall. It bounced off the wall and into his waste paper bin. He still didn't smile. "Let's see if Martyn is holed up by the sea."

Chapter 21
LeBeau and Dangerfield

Lebeau walked up to Dangerfield's house in the suburbs. He didn't know what to expect and knocked on the door with trepidation. He wasn't sure if the door bell was working. He didn't hear it.

A cobweb caught his attention in the top corner of the arched entrance way. There was something austere about it. It looked as if the spider was long gone but the trap remained. It reminded him of the case of 'Tommo the bomber'. He'd worked on the case back in 2010. Tommo, Melvyn Thompson, had already been arrested, tried and imprisoned but he'd left a trap behind. An explosive device. It detonated killing the occupant of a bungalow Tommo had worked in as a plumber. They should have seen the signs. Tommo was infatuated with the man that lived in the bungalow. It was unrequited love.

Dangerfield opened the door and was quite obviously struggling. This was not the Dangerfield he'd seen pictures of. This was the husk of a man.

Dangerfield recognised LeBeau instantly and gave him a weak smile.

Wheezing, Dangerfield gestured for LeBeau to enter the house.

"Sit yourself down, Andrew. Can I get you anything?" LeBeau asked quietly.
"Coffee please. Milk. One sugar. Help yourself."

LeBeau looked around the kitchen and located the coffee making items. LeBeau made instant coffee.

He knew Dangerfield had lost the will to live and so brought some snacks from the local Spar shop. Dangerfield was grateful but his appetite had totally left him. However, LeBeau had an air of command about him. Dangerfield could see his humane side despite the facade. LeBeau had brought chocolate digestive biscuits with him and put them on a plate. Dangerfield couldn't resist dunking them in his coffee despite his inner darkness. It was the first thing he'd eaten since the previous day when he'd simply had a pot noodle.

After the usual introductory chat, LeBeau came to talk of the point of his visit.

"I know you're not on the force anymore so I'm not at liberty to discuss too much of the case with you, but I will tell you this, David Martyn is the perpetrator of the crime. No idea who this man in the balaclava is or if he even figures in any of this."
"It's Martyn."
"What is?"
"Under the balaclava. It's Martyn, but he doesn't know it. He has an alter ego that he doesn't even know about himself. It's his protector."
"This all very theoretical, Andrew. I'm not sure how you arrive at that but the cold hard facts show that Martyn is our man and Martyn we shall get."
"Yes. I am sure you're right. I know Martyn has a protective persona. It manifested when he was in Ranstead hospital. Jimmy Banyard was a nurse there at the time. Another patient was involved in an altercation with Martyn. That night, Martyn with a pillow case over his head went to assault the other chap."
"Well. Schizophrenia or not. David Martyn will be arrested and we'll make sure the charges stick."
"I know it sounds fantastic but you'll notice that Martyn is still alive. Those around him are either dead, missing or in danger."
"Why would that be? I'm not saying I believe you, but, just for argument sake, what are you saying?"
"The Balaclava alter ego, as I say, is the protector. The alter is probably so protective that he wants to destroy all friends and family Martyn has so he can be alone with him forever."
"If the killings and disappearances are, as you say, an alter ego of Martyn it begs the question: Why now?"

"Who said it had only just begun? Remember Martyn assaulted a guy in Ranstead. Ask yourself the question: Where are Martyn's parents? His real mother died in a fire and he was there at the time."

"A line of enquiry I've considered, but they haven't been reported missing so it's on a back burner. All I know is David Martyn will be arrested and the rest will fall together. I'll keep you posted anyway, Andrew."

They spoke of their lives as police officers. Despite LeBeau's outward appearance of efficiency and mercilessness, this was all a front.

He told Dangerfield of his life. He went to an old style infants, juniors and comprehensive school before going on to further education. His father was an engineer in a factory and his mother was a housewife. In those days it was not the thing to do to have the wife out to work. He had one step sister Glenda, who was older and from his father's first marriage.

LeBeau's mother was a bitch to his step sister because she reminded her of her husband's first marriage. Their first car was a Ford Popular Deluxe. He remembers looking form the kitchen window of their council house as his father drove up in it. Before that his father had a Vespa scooter. LeBeau recalled liking the smell of the exhaust fumes from the Vespa.

There was a lot of shouting in the house and it was usually his parents, having disagreements over Glenda. LeBeau was a quiet child and just observed the world around him. At school he was good at creative writing and art. Maths was not a strong point but then who cares now that, we have calculators. He remembered large and really expensive calculators. Now of course, you can get one the size of a credit card for free.

Glenda had left for Scotland in the seventies and married an air force man. She met him at 'the Collingsmote' when she worked as a receptionist there.

LeBeau had been to see the Special AKA at the free trade hall. The show was brilliant. After the gig he went to 'the Duke' public house. A fight broke out between rival neo Nazi groups. LeBeau couldn't stomach racists. He'd sneakily kicked a skinhead in the nose and smashed it. Another Nazi caught LeBeau's knee in his bollocks. He knew the police had been called by the barman. When he saw the barman on the phone, LeBeau had hurled a beer glass at him.

As he was exiting the premises, a burly police officer named Jarvis arrived and grasped him by the arm. He grabbed Jarvis by the little finger and twisted it until he was almost on his knees with his arm behind his back. LeBeau gave a heavy kick to Jarvis and propelled him over the tables in the pub. Jarvis glided across the long table on his belly. Glasses seemed to be flying everywhere. Another copper named Frain, got out of the pale blue and white panda car and came over to the pub to get LeBeau. But LeBeau had climbed the fire escape and made a getaway across the flat roof.

The copper was too unfit to give chase but muttered something into his radio.

LeBeau joined the police force and rose through the ranks. He later met the two coppers, Jarvis and Frain, when he was posted to that area. One of them had looked at him and said, "Where do I know you from?" LeBeau had simply answered, "That's, where do I know you from, 'sir', to you." He admitted this was when he realised he was not on the force to make friends. It was a time for brutal efficiency.

LeBeau's father died of cancer. It was only days before his father's birthday. The funeral was held at the crematorium one autumn. He thought about death and decided that it was time to protect the living.

It was the feeling that he could make a difference that attracted LeBeau to the force. He was jaded now and felt that justice was just a process and not a morally successful force for good. In fact it was shit. Nevertheless, LeBeau was determined to do the best he could before the apathetic justice treadmill took over.

Dangerfield agreed that the old saying: 'The law is an ass' was correct.

Dangerfield related his own life to LeBeau. It consisted mainly of caring for his disabled brother until he died. His mother was bed ridden and his father was working at the local railway station as a station master. His grandfather looked after horses at the Co-op dairy. This was before electric milk floats. He recalled his grandfather taking him for a ride on a horse and cart along the Lincoln Road, before they removed the level crossing. Dangerfield was not a naughty or rambunctious child, just a little mischievous.

At school and just before a maths lesson, he put his special piece of chalk on the ledge of the blackboard. The chalk had been 'borrowed' the day before and taken to the woodwork lesson where he'd drilled a hole down the middle to form a chalk tube. A non safety match head had been snapped off and placed at one end and covered in chalk dust. The hollow was filled with gunpowder from a firework and another match head to stop the other end. More chalk dust made the chalk look whole and not tampered with.

Miss Lawson marched to the blackboard, picked up the only piece of chalk available and announced, "Right. Pythagoras' theorem."

As she drew a triangle the chalk fizzed and sparks flew out of one end. She picked up the board rubber and threw it across the class room. "Dangerfield," she shouted.

How did she know?

That was a defining moment for him. He decided that detection and insight into people would somehow form his career. Then the police force was suggested by his career adviser. 'The rest was history,' he thought.

133

He started to speak about Esme and the children but began to get choked up. LeBeau stood up, walked over to him and put his hand on his shoulder. LeBeau seemed callous but he had a heart.

"I'm going to make you some lunch," he said, "Then, I'd better get back to the station."

LeBeau heated up tinned Chili con carne and microwave rice. They ate together in silence. LeBeau left with the feeling he hadn't accomplished anything. Dangerfield felt as if LeBeau had accomplished a great deal.

***

Back in Cromer, LeBeau and his team entered the Martyn bungalow. There was little evidence that anyone had been there recently. They found little of any use to the investigation in the garage, apart from oil patches on the floor. A team was assigned to check for tyre tread marks to see if anything matched a BMW M3.

"Where's Martyn senior? Anyone been able to make contact?" LeBeau asked with the team assembled.

Meaden had researched the whereabouts of Mr and Mrs Martyn senior to no avail. They had only found their car with the ignition ripped out, in the garage at the house in Barnowby. The company in Greece he worked for hadn't seen him in months. LeBeau had wondered how it was possible for Dave Martyn's parents to disappear without a trace. He considered that they had been murdered by Martyn himself in some bizarre lust for power. Those that might know had either gone missing or been killed. Only Martyn himself was the key.

"Dangerfield said there's been a fire here some years ago and Dave Martyn's mother burned to death. Insurance covered the rebuild but we are not sure of the details there considering the circumstances. We think Mr Martyn senior had connections with the insurance company," Meaden said.

***

On the top of a concrete water tower, Balaclava was observing the police search the bungalow. He peered through his field glasses at the scene. The BMW M3 was parked in a barn nearby and hidden from view. Although it was hot, he wouldn't remove the balaclava. It was his face, his true identity, and what was beneath it was not considered reality.

Through the round mouth hole in the balaclava he fed himself a piece of beef jerky, chewed on it, then continued to observe the bungalow until the police had gone. The farmer who owned the field where the water tower was, had told balaclava not to trespass on his land. Balaclava felt he had no other option but to stab the farmer in the throat with his Bowie knife, carry him up the water tower and drop him inside the brick structure that housed the tank. Blood dripped onto the floor from the neck of the farmer. His contorted face amused balaclava. Balaclava licked some blood from the blade of his knife as he laughed.

A bird flew overhead and squawked as if laughing too.

Chapter 22

Carew and Debbie returned to Dangerfield's house to find him asleep, mouth wide open, in his chair.

"Is he breathing?" Debbie asked in a whisper.

Carew nodded. Debbie quietly placed the tablets on the coffee table. They turned to leave but Dangerfield was waking. He asked them to stay in a feeble voice.

"Got something for you," he said. He pointed to a box on the coffee table. "Go on, open it."

Carew opened the hinged lid of the dark wooden box. Inside were the keys for a Citroen C2 VTS 1.6 and the registration documents.

"It belonged to the wife, Mr Carew," Dangerfield wheezed. "It's yours. Please take it."

"Thank you, Mr Dangerfield, but I can't drive, I mean it's just......." Carew tailed off. He squinted and screwed up his face in mock pain.
"I know you have a licence, Mr Carew. I know you can drive and even drove tanks in the army..."
Carew interrupted, "How'd you know this?"
"Doesn't matter. This is my gift to you. Get the car insured and drive it. Hodophobia, Mr Carew. Get over it. Face your fear."

Dangerfield explained in front of Debbie, that he had no close family left to give the car to. He didn't mention the deal he'd put to Carew who would respond the next day. Secretly, Carew had already decided that killing Martyn would be his greatest challenge. Even so he would do it. Despite his right hand being in a splint and despite his Hodophobia, Martyn must die. If Martyn was also the Balaclava, as Dangerfield suggested, then it would be double the satisfaction.

Carew was thinking of the weapons he could use apart from his martial arts. He remembered the Hogweed darts and mused that they were just for sadistic fun.

Debbie was smiling at the conversation. She personally agreed with overcoming fear by facing it, in many instances. Of course, if you're afraid of being murdered, it was best not to find a murderer and ask to be murdered.

Carew's mind was in overdrive. On the one hand he had the fear of travelling but on the other hand he had the allurement of payment for killing Martyn. But how would Debbie react?

If it wasn't for Debbie's encouragement, Carew would never have accepted the car. After several calls, he finally obtained an emailed certificate of insurance then taxed the car online. It was hell for Carew to give details of his past driving experience and the accident that happened within the last 5 years. Debbie watched with deep sympathy as Carew's demeanour changed during the verbal ordeal.

But where could Carew find Martyn and what would he tell Debbie?

They sat in the car as Carew familiarised himself with the dashboard.

Debbie looked directly at Carew and said, "I know you're going to try to kill Martyn before the coppers get to him, and I'm coming with you. I want to go back to Dad's place and pick up a gun. I'm coming with you. I believe Martyn has raped one of my friends."

"You're not going to be carrying a bloody great shotgun around are you?"

"No, Colonel. A German Heckler and Koch MP7A1. I kid you not, and don't ask where I got it from, or whether I've got a license."

Carew raised his eyebrows. He was impressed. This was some girl he was with.

Debbie asked, "When are you going to start this thing?"

Carew looked awkward, "Yes. Well. This feels all wrong. I don't feel good."

"Just turn the key, let the engine idle and go from there."

Carew turned the engine on. He adjusted the interior mirror. Sunlight glanced off the wing mirrors as he adjusted them. They sat together as he fondled the metal gear knob. Then he gritted his teeth, thought of killing Martyn, slammed the car into gear and screeched from the driveway and onto the street. The back end slewed out with over steer. Debbie whooped as Carew gained control of the Citroen and drove. He was now in control and had that look on his face of determination.

Dangerfield looked sadly from his window as the couple drove away. He changed the sadness to a wicked grin knowing that Carew was now on board with the deal to kill Martyn.

"Proper little Bonnie and Clyde aren't we?" Debbie said as the car cruised the streets. She could see that Carew was getting more relaxed driving again. Casually, Carew turned the radio on. After a few bars of a song, he changed channels until he was convinced there was nothing worth listening to. Then he turned it off and said, "Wish I had a CD."

They went back to Dangerfield's place and thanked him profusely. Carew was yet to let Debbie in on the deal.

They stopped off for Gammon and eggs at a motorway café. Inside the café Carew was looking out of the window with a distant look on his face. It was as if he was saying a farewell to Amy Bell after all this time. The old nostalgia wasn't hurting him now. He looked at Debbie and knew the world around him was changing. By the time the moon was rising they returned to Barnowby and to the Burns farm.

"You can come in the house, Colonel, but no sex."
Carew was surprised. "I don't do sex until I'm fully committed in a relationship, Debbie. I do snogs though."

Debbie smiled. They kissed affectionately just inside the doorway. Carew stroked her body. As his hand smoothed its way down to her bottom she grabbed it and stopped him. She whispered sweetly to him that she was on her period and he'd best stay away from that area because she felt unclean. He understood totally.

"You can sleep on the sofa, Colonel, if you're not going back home or to Pete's."
"Yeah. Sofa, if that's good with you. Driving totally took it out of me especially struggling with a splint on my hand and the bloody phobia."

They talked about how the phobia had evaporated once Carew got back driving and how strange it was that it had returned, now he was not in the car. They decided to leave it that people are complicated.

Carew looked from behind the curtains at the clouds moving slowly across a moonlit sky. For once he felt secure despite the knowledge of events he knew he would face very soon.

He received a text from Moira to say she was ready to tell the police about her rapist, Martyn. This was good news and about time too! The police were on Martyn's tail but had found nothing in Cromer, Dangerfield had told him.

What was Martyn thinking and where would he go? Carew would watch the news, check for reports of murdered or missing people and await tip offs from Dangerfield. He knew this wasn't like a fictional story where coincidence just happened to move things along. This was the real world and you had to make things happen.

He sat down with Debbie as she watched the TV. Carew began to read selected chapters from the Professor Kerner-Jackson book. Things were beginning to make more sense.

***

Carew waited for Debbie to wake up before making a drink. She emerged, via the living room door, yawning. She walked over to Carew and bid him a good morning. Debbie requested that he didn't get too close to her as she hadn't cleaned her teeth. She referred to her morning breath as 'minging.'

Carew gave a wry smile, grabbed her roughly and snogged her passionately. Carew put his hand down the top of her tee shirt and found her nipple. He gently squeezed it and rubbed it. Then pulled the breast out from under the tee shirt and sucked on it. Debbie groaned and held his head. Her fingers ran through his hair as he sucked each breast in turn. They fell onto the sofa in raptures of lust that would be partially unfulfilled due to her period. Carew had an erection that was visible beneath his trousers. Debbie unzipped his trousers, grabbed his throbbing penis and rubbed the foreskin back and forth until he shot sperm over the floor. Debbie went down onto Carew's penis and sucked and swallowed the residual sperm from it. They both enjoyed the intimacy of the moment.

They rested for a while holding on to each other in a loving embrace.

Carew made coffee. They sat down on the sofa and Debbie asked, "Colonel. How can you stand kissing me when I haven't cleaned my teeth yet?"

"I know. It's bloody awful but thank imaginary sky daddy that I'm a masochist. Seriously, you worry too much," Carew said with a grin and then kissed her on the ear. She smiled inwardly but didn't want Carew to know how it made her feel.

Carew looked out of the window upon the new day. A green Chinook helicopter flew overhead toward Collingsmote.

"When is your Dad back?" Carew asked.

"Next week, I think. Depends. If things tick along well here. He might take another week to stay in Hull."

"Ever been to Hull?"

"Yeah. Loads. That's where aunty lives. Why is that?"

"No reason. I can't remember if I've been there or not."

"Age catching up with you, Colonel."

"It did that a long time ago."

Carew watched the Chinook disappear into the distance and behind the swaying trees.

"I hated parachuting," he said.

"Why do you say that?" Debbie looked puzzled.

"I just saw a Chinook go over. Reminded me of being dropped into combat zones."

"Oh, I see. Afraid of heights?"

"Yes and no. I was more afraid of being shot at as I floated down. Sitting duck really."

"Looks like you survived. Ever get shot at like that?"

"Oddly enough, I didn't."

"What's it like killing a man?"

"At first it makes you feel sick. I had nightmares. Post traumatic stress they said. Then I just got disengaged from it. It began to feel like justice. I'm not proud of it but I felt the need to do it."

"Sounds deep, Colonel."

"You are not wrong. It's taken away my fear of anyone. I really am not afraid of violent confrontation now."

"You sound like a vigilante, Colonel."

Carew looked back at Debbie. He paused. Then he replied, "I think I am."

He looked back out of the window and let the subject hang. Debbie went to the bathroom to shower and freshen up. Carew just continued pondering his past and the people he'd killed in war and peace alike. Some would say he was a murderer and others would call him a saviour. Whatever he was he knew he was just a man with a hole in his soul. Somehow the hole seemed smaller now Debbie was around.

Carew felt inside his jacket pocket and the small Voodoo wood carving inside it. The feeling of well being did not return to him. So much for happiness in small things, eh?

Then Carew remembered someone saying that happiness isn't found by avoiding unhappiness. His take on it was that if you are trying to avoid unhappiness then you know where and what unhappiness is. If it's in your mind then you cannot avoid it. Better to live in the moment. He thought about the battles he'd been in. He remembered the friends and colleagues he'd lost. Captain Powers violent death was a real sickening loss. Not to mention a sickening experience that Carew still had a scar from.

Dan Payne was a death that needed to happen to balance justice. But had it? Was justice actually served or was it Carew's desire for power? He wondered. Payne being brutally murdered hadn't brought back the parents of Moira and Frank. Yet it felt good. Perhaps Carew had tasted the kind of blood lust that was now insatiable. However, he felt that Debbie had tempered him now. Some of the cold and hatred was diminishing within him.

Carew pondered how the events of a few brief moments could change a person within. A chance meeting. A few words spoken. Perhaps life was just a state of mind after all and all one needed was a tweak of attitude.

After Debbie emerged from her shower, Carew went for his morning clean up. He felt his stubble and asked Debbie if there was a razor he could borrow. Debbie found a new disposable BIC for him. She told him that no one shared razors, any more that they would share condoms.

Carew frowned at the irony but got the point.

As he showered he sang.

It was a song he'd heard by the Grumpy Waiters:

"He pads and he pads don't wag his tail,
That bloomin' cat gobbed in my ale.
He wants to sit upon your knee,
And get his claws in you and me.
Oh, no, the dribbling cat
The pussy is on the mat.
I like pussy can't ya see?
Oh, no, the dribbling cat,
A night of pussy for you and me!"

Debbie listened outside the door giggling.

Carew was unaware of her laughter.

She recorded it on her phone.

Chapter 23
Frank and Carew

Frank sat on the sofa thinking about recent events but his mind kept wondering off to a young Frank just leaving school. He'd been in the army cadets and loved the security of the discipline and friendships he'd found. Cameron was his best friend who had quite an insane sense of humour. Neither of them wore school uniform.

One Thursday they were walking home from school and Cameron decided to open a man hole cover that was outside some flats for senior citizens. He decided to clamber down inside the small drop. A blue rinsed lady peered from her flat window and asked, "What are you boys doing?"

Frank had taken out a plastic wallet with his Joe90 fan club membership card in, flashed it at the woman and replied, "Obviously, we're hedgehog inspectors following a lead."
"How fascinating." Her tone changed from accusing to approving.
"He's gone. Dammit!" Cameron was vehement. Then he looked at the lady and said, "Ring us if you spot anything, Ma'am." They gave a salute and walked away.

Cameron had joined the merchant navy as an engineer. He died of alcoholic poisoning a year ago. After he died, Frank received a Joe90 comic in the post from his estate. Frank had saved it in a metal strong box, in the original envelope the solicitor had sent it in. He hadn't been able to attend the funeral as Frank was in the Congo at the time being shot at.

Frank and Carew had military experience. There was a time that they both wanted more excitement. Frank had seen little action. Both men were recruited by a man named Hans Garrison who had an agency based in Liverpool. Garrison looked like a thug in his sun glasses, leather jacket and combats. He had multiple facial scars. In the mercenary soldier outfit, Carew had become Frank's bestie.

Carew was fairly quiet as a person. He was ruthless in battle and no quitter. Frank had seen Carew incapacitate an enemy by blowing home made darts in their eyes when his sub machine gun had jammed. When Captain Powers had been blown up Carew had seemed to show no emotion.

Frank was convinced Carew was Asexual. He never spoke of love or sex. Some things seemed forbidden to talk about to Carew. He'd once told a joke about a vicar and a butcher but Carew has not laughed. Rather he looked pained and changed the subject. There was a strange aloofness about Carew.

Frank remembered the day his own parents had died. A young police officer and WPC came to the door. Frank and Moira's parents had only gone out for dinner at a restaurant. A container lorry had started to overtake another lorry on the motorway. It was a stupid move as the lorries were lumbering and slow moving. The driver hadn't paid attention to the Red Ford Mondeo already overtaking. The idiot had swung out and crushed the car against the wall of the Uxford Tunnel. Frank had used his connections to find out details of the lorry driver, Daniel Payne. Payne was a wiry man with a bald top but had a scruffy pony tail. He had ill fitting false teeth and the top plate fell down when he spoke. He was an arrogant bully when he'd had a drink.

Having located the man and discovered he regularly drank in 'the Texas Bar' on a Friday, Frank and Carew decided to become regulars and get to know 'Dan the man'. After some months of getting to know him and sharing drinks with the bastard, they decided to make their move. Payne had been boasting about how Frank's parents had been killed and how he'd got away with it. He didn't know Frank was their son. Frank and Carew had agreed they would only rough Payne up a bit and he wouldn't know who they were in their full face balaclavas, but now the game had changed. Dan the man had crossed the boundary with his pride in the death he had caused. Both men were intent on justice mercenary style. The day after Payne's haughty boast they were ready.

Frank and Carew had been working on a building site as labourers whilst there was no action in the world of combat. After a usual Friday drink,

Carew offered to take Payne home as he sometimes did. Carew drove Frank and Payne, in his Vauxhall Vectra, from the 'Texas' and out along the canal. Carew was playing 'Boomshot' on the CD player. Payne said that he didn't want to listen to 'shit by blackies'. He wanted to listen to Country and Western. Carew smiled at Frank and turned the volume up on the reggae dub.

'Lick shot. Boomshot. Boom boom shot.
Police brutality, in dis ya society.
Boomshot, boomshot
A wah me seh.
Mash Babylon to rasclaat.'

There was a railway bridge that they could park beneath. It was dark. There was deserted wasteland nearby. A train rattled over the bridge.

"You get out here, Danny boy," Carew ordered. Payne looked surprised.

"Fuck off and take me home," Payne spat in a conceited tone.

Carew grabbed Payne roughly and dragged him from the car. He pinned him against the black brick wall of the bridge. Carew wedged his right shin and knee against Payne's right shin.

"Right you fucker." Carew growled spitting the words in Payne's face, "I want you to meet my friend Frankie boy."

Payne looked puzzled and said he already knew who he was. Carew then said, "You killed his parents you cunt. Ford Mondeo? You showing off? You walked free?" Carew head butted and smashed Payne's nose.

Frank looked at Payne and spat mucus at his face. Payne's top plate of teeth had fallen down and were covered in blood from his broken nose. Frank was too wound up to speak. Payne was muttering something but neither man could understand a word.

"He's all yours, Frank." Carew gritted his teeth.

Payne was struggling and Carew let him go. As he ran away Carew smiled and bowed theatrically toward Frank. He held his hands toward him as if to say 'your turn'.

Frank smiled at Carew and took a small crossbow from his jacket and fired a dart at the fleeing Payne. The dart caught his right Achilles tendon. Payne smacked to the wet ground splashing his hands in a puddle.

The neon light danced on the water as Frank rolled him on his back. Carew pulled out a rusty Stanley knife and slashed at Payne's eyelids then cut his ears to shreds. Carew took a pencil and shoved it up Payne's blood caked nostril. Frank forced a scrim, that he'd just wiped in dog shit, into Payne's mouth to stifle his screams. Within minutes, Payne was tied hand and foot with nylon cable ties and bundled into the boot of the Vectra. Payne had tried to spit the rag out but just about managed to move it to allow him to breath. A wood screw was sticking out of his penis where Carew had jammed it through his trousers. Blood slowly soaked around his crotch. He was in agony but hadn't blacked out.

They drove to the building site on the edge of the city. There were no security guards. Frank and Carew quickly pulled the large wooden boards from a deep hole cut into the foundation concrete of a house they were going to build. After throwing Payne's writhing body into the hole they threw in broken bricks to cover him. After mixing it, Carew poured concrete over Payne as he tried to wriggle free from the hole and brick covering. It had taken some time but both men felt the effort was worth it. There were no witnesses and now that bastard had been served justice.

'He had become a foundation of society,' thought Carew.

To prevent suspicion after Dan the man, Danny boy Payne had gone missing, Frank and Carew still went to drink at the 'Texas' for the next few months. No one mentioned Payne apart from a woman who asked, "You seen that bleedin' twat Danny boy lately?"

Carew just shrugged.

Frank said, "We haven't seen him in ages, obviously."

That night they had kebabs from the take away to celebrate. If justice wouldn't work in this country then Carew and Frank were determined to make it work.

"Nice chili sauce," Carew said to Frank.
"Obviously," Frank said.
"Do you think we should have let Payne live?"
"Not on your nelly. He would have obviously cost more in rounds of drinks."

They drove away. Carew turned the volume up on the CD player. They sang along,

'Lick shot. Boomshot. Boom boom shot.
Police brutality, in dis ya society.
Boomshot, boomshot.
A wah me seh. A see me deh.
Mash Babylon to rasclaat.'

Chapter 24

John Cruickshank readied himself for the funeral of Michael Rolph. He didn't know who would be in attendance but feared there would be no one there. He'd only just conducted the funeral of the Dangerfield family, which had come as a shock. He'd thought it would have been held after Rolph's but for some reason, the date had been altered.

He drove to the crematorium and parked in the tree lined parking area. With his heavy pilot case he strode over to the venue. He was early and no guests had arrived. He spoke to Mr Spottiswood who was in charge. All arrangements were in place. He spread his sermon on the lectern facing empty chairs. The coffin was in place near the burner. To his right were the windows over looking the garden of remembrance. To his left a wall with windows high above. From the window to the rear he saw a BMW arrive but paid no attention to it as it circled the car park and drove over to the woods beyond.

Eventually, a handful of mourners arrived and waited outside in a queue. Black clad people. He recognised Kay but not many others. The attendant ushered them in and handed out hymn sheets specially printed for the funeral. Solemn music played as they took their seats. Kay looked well and didn't appear to be grieving at all.

As Cruickshank began his sermon a couple arrived late and sat at the back. It was Debbie Burns and a man in sunshades. He had his hand in a splint whoever he was. Both Debbie and the man were suitably dressed in dark colours. The man was in a very smart dinner jacket with trousers that didn't quite match. He paused as the hymn began and the mourners arose. Cruickshank couldn't place where he'd seen this man before but it was of no consequence at the moment.

As the mourners sang Cruickshank noticed a figure, in a balaclava, running through the garden area to the rear entrance of the hallway. There was a crashing sound. Gasps of fear escaped some of the mourners while others looked apathetically around.

Carew was on the move.

"Get down everyone," he shouted, "Get down."

Balaclava burst into the room and threw his Bowie knife at Kay. It narrowly missed her face and buried itself into the bottom panel of Rolph's coffin.

Balaclava ran toward the coffin. Carew swept his leg around and caught Balaclava's feet making him spin around and somersault onto his shoulder. As he sprang up, he threw a shuriken star at Carew. With an almost relaxed motion Carew caught the star in his left hand and propelled it back to Balaclava's face. Balaclava dodged but the star stuck into his left deltoid. His arm was useless in seconds. It swung paralysed. Carew moved into Balaclava's space and smashed his right elbow into his nose. There was a nauseating crack and blood sprayed from the mouth hole.

144

Debbie ran out to the car and was raising the boot to retrieve her gun.

Inside one of the mourners was on his phone to the police. Cruickshank had run behind the curtain and was calling the police too.

Balaclava swung his right arm over around Carew's neck as he pushed his knee behind Carew's. In an effortless motion he threw Carew onto the floor and stamped on his splint. Carew briefly felt pain as a kick to the jaw knocked him out.

Carew heard music as he blacked out,

'Lick shot. Boomshot. Boom boom shot.
Police brutality, in dis ya society.
Boomshot, boomshot.
A wah me seh.
Mash Babylon to rasclaat.'

As Balaclava went to stamp on Carew's throat, two of the mourners, rugby players, attempted to tackle him down. He kneed the first one in the groin and, as he buckled over in pain, he pushed the other over him with a shoulder butt. Balaclava span around to pull his knife from the coffin but it had gone. Never mind, he had more. He growled and ran from the crematorium the way he'd arrived and back to the woods. He'd kill Carew next time he vowed. For now his plan to kill Kay had failed but with his arm out of action he needed to plan again.

Debbie ran in through the entrance holding her machine gun but Balaclava was not to be seen. She went to Carew to help. He was already waking up.

"It's only a toy," she shouted pointing to the gun. "Just wanted to frighten that masked loony."

They both went to their car. As the police arrived, they had parked out of sight. They saw one police officer in plain clothes with gun ready but didn't know who he was.

"I bet that's LeBeau," Debbie said. When he went inside they drove toward the woods. There was no sign of Balaclava, but they saw fresh tyre tracks from the water of an overflowing drain. Judging by the spray left, the vehicle was heading north down Mayholme Lane.

Driving slowly to avoid attention, they travelled north along the lane. Debbie drove as Carew nursed his hand. He was in agony.

They knew it was a long shot but at least Balaclava was near.

***

LeBeau delegated information gathering to Paul Meaden, Rachel Bogle and Kayleigh Rolph (who was no relation to the other Rolphs). He decided to follow the path of the attacker.

'So the Balaclava figure is real,' he thought, 'And apparently bleeds like a man too.'

He followed the spots of blood on the ground that had dripped from Balaclava's smashed nose. They led out to the garden of remembrance and toward the Mayholme woods opposite. He decided not to go alone and requested Meaden to go with him.

They both followed the line of bloody dots to a grassy verge. From there it was harder to follow, but the grass was slightly flattened where someone had crossed. The trail of blood seemed to stop. They both stood at the roadside facing the woods. The sun shone above the treetops in a blinding array. Meaden shielded his eyes with one hand. LeBeau just squinted.

"There." LeBeau pointed to an opening big enough for a car to drive into.

They jogged over to the spot. There were small spots of blood just near an overflowing drain. Tyre marks made by a car driving through the water, were evaporating in the sun. There was still a drying muddy imprint left.

"Think it's our man, Guv?" Meaden asked.

LeBeau just nodded but was wondering to himself if it was worth taking a drive down Mayholme Lane in pursuit. There would be no convenient police cars in that direction. He decided to follow with Meaden as his sidekick,

Bogle and Rolph continued to gather information from the mourners after being informed by radio, that LeBeau and Meaden were going in pursuit.

Cruickshank had decided that the funeral would conclude as soon as possible so asked the police officers to wait until after. There was just the dispatch of the coffin and the conclusion. LeBeau was angry. He wanted the knife cut in the coffin to be analysed and now it was too late. At least there was the throwing star and a photograph that Meaden had taken of the coffin prior to this chase.

"A toy gun. Do you believe that, Meaden?" LeBeau was thinking out loud.
"What, Debbie Burns? Probably an umbrella knowing her. She's harmless. If it wasn't one of her dad's shotguns of course. I don't think we need armed response. Probably be ages before we got any out here anyway."
"Well, we'd better send someone to see her. No one wanted to complain, but better to tie up loose ends. If she says it was a toy then we'll take no further action but we have one other witness that has gone walkabout.

The man in the sun glasses who got knocked out by the assailant in the head covering. I think that's Dangerfield's mate Cashew."

"Carew, sir."

"Same difference."

Chapter 25

Moira's hands were trembling as she dialled the police. She thought her fear had become a mountain that she could never climb. Nigel sat on the arm of the sofa next to her slumped form. She was gripping the cushion and her knuckles were white. This was the third attempt she'd made. The first two times she hung up before she spoke to any one. She knew that she'd spoken to Bellamy about this all those months ago but hadn't given the whole story and anyway, Bellamy didn't care.

Finally she had just enough nerve to speak to someone. They arranged for a WPC to meet with her to go over the trauma which Moira knew would break her. She couldn't let on there were any drug related issues in the whole thing or her story would lose all credibility. She didn't really want to go to trial with this but Martyn needed stopping, once and for all.

LeBeau would be informed in due course but as it was, he was busy with his enquiries and out at a crime scene. 'This could wait.' thought WPC Bright.

Nigel had left the room as requested. He really didn't need to hear the gory details. He went outside for some air. He saw a teenager from the traveller site ambling over a field. It was Callum Jones. Nigel knew the Jones family. He knew Corry Jones through connections. Chorry worked security at the Club Paradigm and had given Carew the photo that identified Martyn as Moira's rapist. Nigel was recalling an occasion when he and Chorry had attended a funeral together. It was Chorry's very old uncle Joe Hinkins who had died of a heart attack in town at the age of 98. One moment he was walking as best he could with his walking stick, down the street, and the next he just fell backwards and was dead on the pavement.

After the funeral a few of the travelers and locals mingled at the Warrow Hall for the gathering after. Some Romany traditions remained and some did not. The old days of the stereotypical travelers were gone. Some of Joe's possessions had been burnt. These days though, his caravan wasn't incinerated. When the funeral procession left Fengate, all the travelers lined up along the road in respect.

Chorry told Nigel about how Joe Hinkins enjoyed his drink on a Saturday night. He would go to the public house on a horse and cart and get blotto. His friends would carry him out and throw him onto the cart, release the brake and the horse would return home. More than once he woke up Sunday morning still on the cart. Joe had sired 23 children but only 13 survived.

Chorry also related how Joe had gone away on a holiday and left his nephews to keep an eye on things, including his Donkey, Penelope. When Joe returned home, he found the police were trying to move the donkey from obstructing the road. Joe's nephews had decided to give Penelope whiskey to drink. If Joe hadn't seen it with his own eyes, he wouldn't have believed it.

Joe would always be missed and not all of his family remained as travelers. One of his daughters married a gadje soldier by the name of Banham Allen. They were a good couple and had a good hearted family. Times were changing and with people all over the globe and so were traditions too.

***

Mrs Banyard received a phone call from her close friend Madge about the debacle they'd just had at the funeral. Madge was a mourner but didn't like the 'deceased'. She was there out of duty. Madge rang from the doorway just after Balaclava had fled and Carew was waking up. Debbie Burns had barged past her with a toy gun. Or so Debbie had said. She thought that it was more like something from a thriller novel or Hollywood blockbuster.

"Some marauding killer in a balaclava tried to kill the mourners," she told Sid who sat reading a gutter press news paper.
"Sounds a bit exaggerated to me," he said as he read something even more fantastic that was passed off as fact by the journalist

As she looked out of the window she saw a Citroen C2 drive by and Callum Jones walking across a field. Just a few minutes ago she's seen a Ford KA pootle along the road. A BMW had only just driven by at breakneck speed already and would catch up with the Ford KA in no time. As she turned away her peripheral vision caught another car driving in the same direction. It was LeBeau and Meaden.

"It's getting like the Wacky Races out there," she said to Sid.

Sid just laughed politely to pretend he agreed with her. In truth he didn't hear a word she said. Instead he put his paper down and said,

"Ay, here. Listen to this. Why is it that when we leave dry food out it goes damp overnight but when we leave damp things out they go dry?" He laughed and looked at his wife. She was looking back at him puzzled.
"I really think this town had gone mad, Sid."

At that moment Jimmy walked in and said, "Oh, mother. Don't be so melodramatic. Nothing ever happens around here that isn't to do with Dave Martyn and his queens."

Then she laughed. There was something bitterly ironic in the words Jimmy had spoken. Whatever it was she found it amusing.

"What have you been up to, Jimmy?" Sid asked, "Anything good?"

"Just been over to see uncle Pete who's getting a cold or something. He looks like death on legs. Er, seen Debs Burns. Her pater is in Hull visiting her aunt, er, nothing enthralling."

"Burnsy always goes to Hull. I didn't know Debbie was back. Is she still as mad as a hatter?"

"Deliciously so. I wrote a poem about Hull you know."

Sid laughed and said, "You'll have a book full of poems soon. Give us a rendition then."

Jimmy put his finger in the air to indicate that they should wait, then exited the room. When he came back he opened what he called his 'art book' and read,

"This is a little recitation entitled, There's Always Hull. By me Jimmy Bee.

I prayed to my god, asked for relief.
I heard nothing, so turned a new leaf.
The world is bland, bored off my skull.
............never mind there's always Hull!

I went to Montrose, I went too far
I left my balls in Leamington Spa
I am a seal awaiting the cull
............never mind there's always Hull!

I wear pink trousers, all the rage
The high heels suit a man of my age
My cup runneth over but it's never full
............never mind there's always Hull!"

The Banyards laughed.

"Got any more Jimmy? You know you should get them published, they're real gems," Sid said as his wife nodded her head.

"Oh, plenty but you don't want to hear me drone on. I want ice cream," Jimmy admitted.

"Where from," asked Sid, "Hull?"

The Banyards laughed for some time. It was nice to have their son back for a visit. He had been missed.

Their laughter would never be shared with the driver of a Ford KA who had stopped to enjoy the view of the country side on this day. There was a sudden smash of her door window and a figure in a bloodied balaclava held a Bowie knife to her face.

"If you wanna live do what yer told," commanded the gruff voice.

149

She started the car engine hoping that the car jacker wouldn't be in the car by the time she drove away. The engine stalled. It was just long enough for the balaclava figure to get into the passenger seat and hold the knife to her throat.

Balaclava lied. When they reached the viaduct he stabbed her throat. As the life ebbed from her Balaclava looked into her eyes. He watched as their vitality died with her. He loved to watch the life drain out of the eyes of the dying. Despite his bloody nose he gave a grin, showing bloodied teeth.

Laughing, he ran toward the river. Once he was wading in the water he knew tracker dogs couldn't track him. It was unlikely that the cops could arrange the helicopter either.

The water was cold as he entered the shallow side of the river.

Chapter 26

The unmarked police car sped along the lane. Far up the lane in front, was Debbie and Carew searching for the Balaclava. Carew was wincing in pain. He got the bottled water and two painkillers. He put some water in his mouth with the tablets and swallowed.

Debbie had told Carew he should go back to the A&E department to get his hand looked at again. He refused vehemently.

"Better to enter one handed into the kingdom." He mused ironically.

Debbie would have been petrified chasing Balaclava normally but the machine gun made her feel invincible.

"Stop," Carew said quickly.

Debbie slammed on the breaks. The Citroen skidded to a halt and the engine cut out. She restarted the engine and pulled onto the grass verge. Carew got out of the car awkwardly and walked back behind the car to where a large five bar field gate was swinging open.

There was broken auto glass scattered on the road. He walked through the gate. There was a cornfield to his right and a heavily wood area to his left. Debbie ran behind him carrying her machine gun concealed in a backpack. The barrel was sticking out of the top of the backpack which she had covered with a Rasta scarf that Marcia had given her.

They walked about 100 yards to find a BMW M3 dumped in the bushes. The driver's side door was open. There was blood from a nosebleed on the seat and steering wheel.

They didn't touch it and Carew said that he believed Balaclava had jacked a car.

"His BMW. It's automatic. No wonder he could drive it with a dead arm."

"Do you think his arm will take long to get back to normal?"

"Depends on what the throwing star was tipped with."

"Shit! He's probably got a bloody hostage. Probably the driver of another car. I think that's what the broken glass is about. Locked driver in a car so he breaks the glass and threatens them."

The Collingsmote viaduct could be seen in the distance. Carew believed that Balaclava was heading there.

"Get back," Carew ordered and pulled Debbie behind the bushes. A car sped past.

"What is it, Colonel?"

"Thought so. Keep down. It's the coppers. You can tell by the car. Extra aerials and not very well hidden lights. I recon that's LeBeau. Mr efficiency himself."

LeBeau and Meaden drove past Carew's Citroen but ignored it, apart from commenting on how it resembled a car Dangerfield had.

When the dark blue saloon was gone, Carew and Debbie returned to the car. Carew knew that now he had a slight advantage.

LeBeau would have no idea that Balaclava had abandoned his BMW. LeBeau had been looking for sightings of a BMW M3 since the Dangerfield murders. LeBeau had been told by Dangerfield, that Balaclava had a BMW M3 which was originally the property of Martyn's father. Dangerfield suspected the vehicle most likely had false number plates on it now and that they would have been copied from a similar BMW somewhere.

Carew and Debbie headed in the direction of the viaduct. They noticed LeBeau's vehicle heading in the same direction.

"Stay as far behind them as possible," Carew advised Debbie.

Debbie made a sudden right turn down a small lane.

"Short cut." She grinned. "No gates this way. Not a lot of people know this route."

It was a very bumpy ride in the Citroen. Carew's hand was throbbing, although the pain killers were helping slightly.

They hit a pothole, heard a scraping noise and a bump beneath the Citroen. Debbie pulled a mock disgruntled face. Carew did the same back. They made jokes about needing a new exhaust soon.

Carew felt in his pocket at the small woodcarving and pulled it out. There was a spent air freshener hanging from the rear view mirror. He unwound the elastic, pulled off the air freshener and replaced it with the woodcarving. He hung the carving from the rear view mirror. It swung around but pleased him.

"Protection from the spirit realm, Colonel?"

"No. Decoration from the souvenir realm. Debbie webbie."

"How's your hand?"

"Bloody awful but I'll live."

Then he replaced the carving into his pocket.

The car bumped along the small lane being scraped and whipped by bushes. They parked at the far end of the viaduct beneath a small arch. They saw a brown Ford KA with the driver side window smashed. It was parked at an angle beneath a large viaduct arch. The shadow of the arch covered the rear half of the KA.

In the distance, the roar of the weir could be heard. LeBeau could be seen on the approach road at the metal gate, which he couldn't open. They remained behind the cover of the arch.

"LeBeau will be here in five. Better move fast," Carew murmured.

They ran crouching as they went, to the KA and looked inside. There was a corpse slumped back and toward the passenger seat. A forty something large woman with bobbed hair. Stab wound to the throat. There was blood splattered over the inside windshield and the steering column. It was already beginning to stink in the sunshine.

Without wasting a moment, Carew surveyed the surrounding area. There was no evidence of any other vehicle tracks or even footprints on the concrete.

LeBeau had opened the metal gate and driven into the area of the arches. Debbie and Carew crouched down and crept back to their car.

"I think Balaclava will be around here somewhere. They'll get the tracker dogs in soon to sniff him out. Now, if I were him where would I go?" Carew was deep in thought. Debbie opened the car door and vomited. The shock of the corpse suddenly hit her.

Through the bushes they could see LeBeau and Meaden examining the KA. LeBeau was barking orders into his radio. The dog van would be here soon and that meant Carew and Debbie would be pursued when the dogs got their scent.

They decided to reverse the car out behind the arch and turn right over the track toward the motorway. They really didn't want to go that way but it was the only direction they could go to avoid LeBeau seeing them.

Along the track they found a left turn to a small power station. They parked at the side. They could hear the humming of electricity. It felt unsettling and dangerous. There were seven padlocks on the metal gate leading into the power station. This seemed a little over the top to Carew.

From the power station, a path led to another overgrown path. It would lead back to the weir.

"Once they get the dogs on the track it'll be all over for Balaclava. So, he's gonna head to the water to obscure his scent. He'll head with the flow of the water too, but where he's heading is still a mystery."

A flock of birds flew overhead. Carew looked at Debbie and pointed to the direction the birds came from.

"He's in that direction. He's frightened the birds. I see you've got your back pack. Planning a camping trip?"

Debbie laughed and replied, "No. Just a little insurance."

"Do you seriously intend to use that thing?"
"Yes. If you seriously intend to kill Martyn, the Balaclava." Debbie squinted at Carew with a grin and continued, "I know about Dangerfield's proposal to you. You better mow his lawn today."

Carew was dumbfounded. How did she know? She was a shrewd one.

"Left my phone on my chair. Voice recorder on. Listened to it last night in the bathroom. Wanted to know what was really going on, the house and the money. Dangerfield is shit at disguising his body language. And you were shit at changing the subject when I came back."

Carew laughed. This was good. He was relieved that he didn't need to hide anything and it felt like all systems go now. He would mow Dangerfield's lawn but maybe not today.

"Are you ready to get your best clothes filthed up, Colonel?" She asked as they made their way to the weir.
"Yeah. Better than messing up my favourite clothes."

Carew had put his sun shades on top of his head and was observing LeBeau and Meaden through the bushes. They'd found the body in the KA. LeBeau was on his radio to get a dog van and a team to clean up loose ends. At least neither of the coppers were coming over to the weir. Debbie took her sub machine gun from the back pack that she had straddled over one shoulder. She'd already changed from her black Paten leather high heels to flat pumps for driving in.

Carew knelt by the bank of the river and watched the water flow. He pointed to the right. He couldn't see any tracks. They slowly made their way along the muddy river bank until it came to a fork. The fork was from a dyke that terminated at the river. Carew saw some sandy coloured cloudiness in the water of the dyke. This was evidence that the bottom of the dyke had been disturbed, and very recently.

'Careless,' he thought.

Debbie skidded down the bank and into the dyke. She landed on her bottom getting the back of her dress caked in mud. Carew slowly waded toward the flow of the dyke with his blow pipe in hand. Debbie followed behind holding the MP7A1 ready to fire it.

"Is this what jungle warfare is like, Colonel?"

Carew held up his hand to silence Debbie. Debbie kept quiet as Carew listened for tell tale sounds from further ahead.

More birds flapped overhead. Carew indicated to move forward. Debbie followed behind. Carew recognized the area as the place he'd collected the hogweed. He was hoping that Balaclava was not heading to Pete's house. If he was he'd better be stopped right now.

He whispered to her, "If you want to go back, now is your chance. To be honest, I think you should. I'm a trained fighter, you're not."

"I've got a gun. Shut up."

Up ahead there was a splash. Carew held his hand up indicating Debbie to stop. They both listened intently as they heard more splashing.

Chapter 27

LeBeau cursed and took his radio from his ear. He slowly, gently and emphatically thumped the bonnet of the car.

"No helicopter available," Lebeau said tersely.

When the dog unit arrived, Bobo the tracker jumped out of the van and heeled at Boothby's feet. Jeanette Boothby was a pale faced ginger young woman with small teeth. 'Rat tooth' was her school nick name. She had excelled in equine studies and regularly volunteered as a groom at her Uncle Vaughan's stable. Snowball was her favourite horse. He would snort when she offered him sugar lumps. She'd been told not to, but Snowball wasn't going to tell. There had been times when she'd walked Snowball around when he had a bad belly.

For now, she was feeling nauseous at the sight of the corpse in the KA, but knew she had a job to do. She took a deep breath and let Bobo get to work. It wasn't long before Bobo was leading them toward the weir area. LeBeau had his gun in hand. Meaden had a tazer, which made him feel like the weakest link.

LeBeau was wondering if there was a connection between the hanged girl that was found here and the Balaclava character they were now chasing.

Bobo came to the water's edge and continued sniffing around but then it became obvious the trail was lost.

"He's been wading in the water and probably with the flow too. That's my guess," LeBeau said.
"We could be here all day. Shall we take a sweep of the area in the motor, Guv?"
"That'll take us the long way around the area, by which time he'll be long gone, but might just be worth it. Get a unit to check out Martyn's place for any sign. Oh, and every plod in the area to be alerted."
"Already done, sir."
"Good man. Yes. We'll leave forensics here and delegate some uniform guys to inform the family of the KA victim. Positive ID was on the driving license." LeBeau looked around then continued, "Thanks, Jeanette and Bobo. Right. We'll circle over to the main road."

They got in the car and drove away. LeBeau watched as the team seemed to fade into the distance in his wobbling rear view mirror.

They drove around to the main route which was just an old country road connecting Collingsmote to Barnowby. It was a bumpy ride and a bird decided to shit on the windscreen. The washer and wipers simply smeared it in a milky arc across the screen.

LeBeau saw it as a minor irritation and continued driving whilst looking for Balaclava. They stopped on a grass verge and got out of the car. They both looked around at the fields, some of which were yellow with rape seed. There was no sign of anyone, not even a farm worker.

"Desolate. Absolutely desolate," Commented LeBeau. Neither of them could see that below the bank, behind the brambles and hogweed, Carew and Debbie were wading along the dyke.

Meaden nodded. Then they drove toward the small hump backed bridge leading to near where Pete Silver lived. Beneath the bridge, as they drove over, sloshed Carew and Debbie. The water was quite shallow. Debbie looked at her legs to see a large slimy brown leech had attached itself to her. She gasped in revulsion and clawed it off.

155

Carew smiled and quietly said, "You're not supposed to do that with a leech."

"Well, what would you do, Colonel?" Debbie whispered back.

"You're supposed to wait until it has fed and it will just fall off."

Debbie gave a look of 'no way!'

They heard the thrum as LeBeau drove over the bridge. Their splashing echoed under the bridge. The air was cooler in the murky shade. Carew and Debbie stood still until they were sure the vehicle was out of sight. It disappeared around one of the many bends in the road.

They both listened but heard no more tell tale sounds.

"What do you think, Colonel?" Debbie asked with her hand on Carew's elbow.

"Time to emerge. I don't know where he's gone but I'm hoping it isn't to Pete's place."

"Oh hell, no."

As they came from under the bridge, Carew looked up from the left of the arch to ensure Balaclava wasn't waiting to jump him. There was no one there. A bird flapped away, startled by Carew.

"I think the car is further away than Pete's house. I think we should stay together. I don't want you going back for the car and getting murdered, young Debs."

They decided to take the road straight to Pete's and get the Citroen later.

Debbie became quiet as she looked up at the sky to see the criss crossing trails from passenger jets. Her mind wondered back to Dando and a conversation they'd had once when they visited Boothby Graffoe.

Dando had been researching conspiracy theories.

"They're spraying again." he said. Debbie had looked at the gardens for sprinklers. "No you silly cow, the sky. Look at the filaments falling."

"What do you mean? What am I looking at?"

Dando pointed to the sky and added, "Fucking H.A.A.R.P. signatures are pushing the chemtrails overhead."

"You mean the contrails?"

"They're full of chemical shit to kill us off. They're fucking chemtrails not contrails."

"But why who would do that and why?"

"They're spraying all kinds of stuff from those aeroplanes. You can see it. It's the Illuminati. They're trying to depopulate the Earth."

"What do they gain though?"

"The Earth as their inheritance."

"Is it worth worrying about a future that is based on possible fantasy? Like those poor blighters in Japan, in the war, when the nukes hit. They couldn't do a thing about it. They were most likely worried about other life problems and never expected the dreadfulness that would come after."

"I know you think I'm paranoid, but you'll see when they start the mind control and when they mess with the weather." Dando was not raving so much as trying to get across his explanation.

"Earth calling Burnsy," Carew made Debbie snap out of her memory. "Penny for your thoughts."

Debbie refrained from mentioning Dando as she knew it seemed like she was rubbing Carew's nose in her past relationships.

They'd talked about it. He admitted it was illogical but he was overpowered by some inexplicable, primal emotion that brought out the fighter in him.

She just asked, "What's your take on chemtrails and the Illuminati?"

"We will probably never know. There probably is no Illuminati, just greedy bankers or some clique of fuckers, with a bit of control. Greedy bankers. That's not Cockney rhyming slang either but fits. It's all just big money that makes the world go around. It makes my world go around more often than not."

"You've heard of the chemtrails and stuff?"

"Yeah. Mind you there might be some crazy stuff going off at H.A.A.R.P. but as I cannot control it or know what it is I'm just getting on with life. What about you?"

"I dunno. I don't think anyone will ever tell me, Colonel."

They both emerged onto the road. They were dripping with water and mud. In the heat of the day they would soon dry. It still felt uncomfortable being dirty. Their feet felt awful slopping around in wet footwear. Debbie had placed the machine gun back into her backpack. She wasn't about to march down the road like she'd just landed on Normandy beach.

As they walked, Carew was watching their surroundings very carefully for signs of Balaclava. He found none. He observed how long their wet footprints and trail remained on the tarmac before being evaporated in the heat of the overhead sun. Ahead, they could see the row of houses where Pete lived. Carew knew that Moira was there and it was little comfort that Nigel was also there. Even though he was a soldier now, he might not be as tough as Balaclava. Nigel seemed to lack the killing edge.

They traipsed toward Pete's house. They were not talking much but feeling hungry and above all thirsty. Carew had left his bottled water in the car and was cursing himself. Schoolboy error.

***

Although being alert, Meaden was thinking back to growing up in the East End of London with his parents. Many a time he'd just listen to his short stocky mother tell her stories to anyone that would listen.

She was telling a neighbour once, "So this geezer was like, in the middle of Clissold Park with this dodgy looking bird and you'll never guess what bleedin' well happened. They looked like they were kissing but he was actually trying to take some dust, or a fly or something, out of her eye with the corner of his hanky. Whilst he was doing that she had her hand in his grotty old grey hoodie sweater pocket. I think she's a tealeaf. Sorry. I mean she was trying to nick some money. You'll have to forgive my way of talking. Cockney and proud, me. I ain't well educated so sometimes I forget that not everyone speaks the old Cockney rhyming slang. See, I like Clissold Park, even though I live here at Wanstead Flats coz it's only about 8 or 9 miles away by frog."

Meaden remembered the Sri Lankan neighbours had been a little confused and hadn't realised that 'frog' was short for 'frog and toad' that rhymed with 'road'. Meaden smiled to himself as he recalled her way of explaining things.

She'd said, "So. Talk about a laugh. This whacking great London fog. Dog that is, comes hurtling like a bat out of hell across the grass being chased by a deer. Both of the creatures bowl the geezer and his bird over with an awful racket. They ended up in a hedge. It looked like a bowling alley for knocking hippies over. There were legs every bleedin' where, I even thought the dog was wearing denim jeans and trainers in the confusion. There was a Park Keeper following, waving his arms like a windmill. His titfer, that's his hat, darlin', fell off and he didn't know whether to go back for it or carry on running. The owner of the dog came running over. Well, I say running. More like walking, a bit quicker than normal, and huffing away like bellows trying to smelt metal. The bleedin' ground was shaking as he ran over. I was afraid he'd fall over. Poor fellah. I felt sorry for him. I tell you what. I don't mean no harm, it's just my way. Now beings as how I'm a public spirited bird, I went to check on the couple that were tangled in the leggy mess. I tell you, if this had been a cartoon you wouldn't have half heard some funny noises. So, I walks over to take a butchers, y'know, see what's going on, and the dog runs off toward the playground followed by old lumber bum. Then I asks if they're okay and they say they are and gets up. Then I noticed this geezer was wearing a shirt with 'I'm with this berk' written on the front with an arrow pointing to his bird. I asks him if he knows what 'berk' means. He says he does and it just means 'idiot'. I just told him he was having a laugh because it's rhyming slang. Berkley Hunt, cunt!"

Meaden remembered her laughing in her bad chested salacious tone.

Suddenly, something hit the windscreen shattering it. LeBeau did a handbrake stop and spun the vehicle around whilst punching the shattered glass. He didn't know what had hit the car. He suspected it was from Balaclava and he knew he needed to make some space between them. He skidded to a stop behind a concrete bus shelter on the right.

Both men got out of the car and looked around.

"Think that was him, guv?" Meaden squinted as he asked.
"It wouldn't surprise me. Let's keep a cavy here for a while. No good calling for back up. We're in the sticks here. Just keep your eyes peeled."

Up ahead was a small wooded area where LeBeau suspected Balaclava might be hiding. What didn't make sense was if he was hiding why break the car windscreen?

From the woods they saw movement. It was a teenage boy running over the field away from them.

"There's the culprit," LeBeau observed.
"Shall we get him, sir?"
"I'm in two minds about that one but I think we've got bigger fish to fry at the moment. Let's see if we can find our killer before anyone else gets topped."

Chapter 28

Callum Jones was a bored teenager. He had jet black slicked back hair and swarthy skin. Callum was born into a travelling family that resented the 'Pikey', or as they said, 'wanna be' travellers, for giving their people a bad reputation.

Callum, the nephew of Chorry Jones, found half a brick embedded in the ground and worked it loose. Beneath it a worm quickly disappeared, back onto it's hole. It was a real bonus when he recognised the police driving in their car. Callum hid in the small wooded area for it to get closer. Without giving thought to the possible consequences, he waited for it to come into range and then he hurled the half brick. It was a result. He ducked down as the screen shattered. He laughed. Then he saw the car skid in the road and retreat to an old dilapidated concrete bus shelter. He noticed LeBeau had a gun and decided that maybe, this prank had gone too far.

There was a noise behind him. He turned around to see a figure in a balaclava enter the wooded area. Callum hadn't been spotted. The figure was massaging his shoulder and flexing his arm as if to get the circulation back or unfreeze it. He was watching the police car but seemed oblivious of Callum, for some strange reason. Callum slowly crawled down the dyke bank for cover and remained squatting for a moment before deciding to make a break for it.

There was something about this figure that frightened Callum. He looked like a Ninja or a member of the S.A.S. Callum had played enough games on his console to recognise a Ninja when he saw one. Why the Ninja hadn't paid any attention to Callum was something not to be questioned at the moment. Escape was the only choice.

On one side, there were the cops and in front knelt the Ninja. Ninja was rubbing his shoulder and making tiny windmill movements with the bad arm. The sunlight lancing through the trees should give him enough cover to creep to his left, along the bank. His hand was spotted with stings from the nettles he'd fallen onto. He didn't believe dock leaves helped either. A bramble had wrapped itself around his ankle. He slowly pulled his leg as it ripped into his jeans.

"Shekka," he cursed under his breath, in Romany 'jib'.

Then his other foot accidentally crushed an empty beer can. He looked to see if the noise made the Ninja look over. It didn't.

There were no options. He couldn't continue along the bank, it was too overgrown. If he crossed the road or went right, the 'shanglos' as the travellers called police, would get him. Through the woods and the Ninja would probably kill him. The only option was to run toward the Traveller camp, diagonally over the field. At least that way he would be out in the open and the Ninja would think again before attacking. The shanglos would have difficulty catching him and if they did, he'd say the Ninja had thrown the brick. If they asked why he was running away then he'd tell them he was afraid of the Ninja.

As he ran, half crouched, up the incline of the field, he kept looking back. Ninja was hiding in the woods looking directly at the coppers. When he got back to camp he'd warn them that there was a Ninja on the loose and to beware. He knew the community would protect each other from the shanglos and the mullomush in the woods.

The camp was serene when Callum returned.

There were a mixture of caravans and an old style Vardo in the corner. Some chickens were running free and a couple of horses were stabled. A dog was yapping in the Hinkins' yard. Just outside the Vardo, sitting on the steps, was uncle John. He was boiling water in kettle over a log fire. Callum wondered why he did this when he could just boil an electric kettle, without having a live fire. But Callum knew that John loved the traditional way of boiling his 'pani', so left it at that.

Yollanda Hinkins was hanging out her washing on the line between her caravan and a thick post near her chicken run. Long gone were the days they would use home made 'faiders', clothes pegs. These ones were plastic ones from Tesco. Callum had been told of the old ways but was a young person and accepted the new.

She saw Callum looking and asked with a smile, "What are you dickin at, chavvie?"

"I ain't lookin' at nothing. Where's Eric?"

"He's in town."

"Oh. I need to see him. Some mullomush over the field threw a brick at a shanglo's drag. The mullomush looks dangerous."

"That's outsider business. None of ours. If the shanglos want to deal with whoever you saw………" She tailed off in meaningful way.

Callum considered her words and decided that the Ninja mullomush and the shanglos would fight amongst themselves.

Then he asked, "Seen Didlow?"

"He's over the tan yard."

"Thanks."

Callum decided he'd go down to the tan yard to see if his friend John 'Didlow' Hinkins was there. First, he went to his wardrobe to get a change of top in case the shanglos were looking for him. He had a perfect excuse but still didn't want hassle. He knew the shanglos disliked travellers. That was obvious from how 'Pig bastard shanglo' Bellamy treated them. Bellamy had kept his distance though because he'd been warned by Chorry, that if he laid one finger on a traveller then he'd be sorry. Chorry hadn't told Bellamy what they'd do but it involved being tied up in the back of a van and taken to a field in a desolate area. Then the shin bones would be broken and the soles of the feet slashed to ribbons.

Callum only knew of one person, Russ Baisden, that faced this and he hadn't returned to the town. He didn't know whether Baisden was dead or not. Frankly he didn't care. Baisden was a filthy druggie who tried selling the Krok powder to a few on the camp. He was warned off but came back repeatedly when he found a customer. Eileen was still at school. She died of an overdose. Justice was required as outsider justice didn't work. Baisden had an accomplice. Dando something or other, but they never found him. Someone said he owed the drug lords money and they killed him. Some say some travellers killed him but kept quiet. Others say it was karma and he died at god's hand. Callum Jones didn't care anyway.

Chapter 29

"No sign of our man and the windscreen's gone." LeBeau sighed as he put his sunshades on.

Driving was awkward. There were windscreen pellets over the seats and crunching underfoot on the mats. Driving with no glass slowed them down. Meaden winced as a fly hit him in the eye as they rounded the bend toward the police station. He dug at the corner of his eye trying to remove the insect. His eye watered and he couldn't keep it open without blinking rapidly.

161

LeBeau's radio squawked. It was Smiffy.

"They've found something at the Martyn house," LeBeau told a distracted Meaden. As they drove into the car park.

Lebeau and a blinking Meaden got a coffee from the vending machine. Then they joined Smiffy in LeBeau's office.

Smiffy spread some photographs in front of LeBeau. LeBeau looked at them with a serious look on his face. He took a deep breath as he considered what he was seeing. The pictures showed the bodies of Bellamy and Kitter. Bellamy was tied to a chair with Kitter draped over him. There were two bodies that were beyond identification. One was rotted and the other was headless with a charred torso.

"Where were these taken?" LeBeau knew it was an obvious question and that Smiffy would tell him anyway, but he still believed it needed asking.

Smiffy answered, "They were found in a room that was adjoined to the one with the drug factory in it, sir."

LeBeau looked puzzled and with a knitted brow, slowly asked, "How did we miss that?"

Smiffy scratched his head and gave an embarrassed grimace, "We found a door hidden behind a large metal shelving unit. Parr spotted that a very faint trail of bodily fluid on the floor led there once we dusted the area with powder. There were no scrape marks where it had arched open across the floor. Parr found a release mechanism situated in one of the struts."

LeBeau rubbed his hand down his face, squeezed his chin and asked, "So have the bodies been given a positive ID?"

"Well, sir," Smiffy continued, "It's Phil Bellamy, Mike Kitter, Mrs Martyn and an unidentified stiff. No dental records for obvious reasons, and the DNA tests are still pending."

"Have we informed the families?"

"Not yet, sir. Awaiting orders."

"Better get to it. There's been some bad press about the force prevaricating in these things. Who's best to go in person today? Can you tell Phil's mother with a WPC?"

"Fair enough, sir. Everyone hates this part of the job but the other best candidates are WPC Reid and Prechodny. I think as far as Mr Kitter is concerned, we'll have a job finding anyone apart from the transvestite he was dating."

"Very well."

As Smiffy walked from the door LeBeau stopped him and said, "Oh, and let me know how Mrs Bellamy reacts. And another thing, take Prechodny with you."

LeBeau looked at Meaden who wasn't blinking now but had a red eye. Meaden shrugged.

"Great," LeBeau said with irony, "We've got a killer on the loose, a cellar full of corpses, a vandalised car, a dead copper and I'm hungry. I want chips. I'm not sure which is worse."

Smiffy looked at LeBeau and realised the real human side of this man was beginning to show albeit for the moment. He guessed that LeBeau would be back to his hard edged and efficient self soon enough.

***

WPC Suzanne 'Sue' Prechodny was a blonde haired blue eyed woman with her hair dyed brown and styled into a bun of braids. She had a round face and always looked dead pan. Someone had commented that her eyes were dead, 'shark mode'. Her father was the son of a Czech architect and an English woman from Cockshot, Northumberland. However, despite her surname, the family had carried no Czech culture over. Suzanne was living with her partner in Collingsmote Village. Her colleagues had no idea if her partner was male of female. She was a very private individual and seemed emotionally distant most of the time. Although she disliked the part of the job that involved informing people of the death of a loved one, she showed no outward emotion, although she seemed very empathetic to the recipient of the bad news. After the initial contact she would calmly say, 'I regret to inform you.....'

Smiffy and Sue drove to the Bellamy residence. They parked a little way up the road and walked slowly to the house. As they walked up the path the odour from within was evident. Even the gentle breeze and he rustling of the trees didn't detract from the smell. The honeysuckle from the neighbour's border wafted softly with it's sweet aroma lessening the stench. The doorbell was broken. Smiffy knocked on the door. There was movement from behind the curtain. The door opened and Mrs Bellamy emerged looking suspiciously at Smiffy and Sue. Then her eyes darted around either side of them. She grasped the door and asked, "What do you fuckin' want?"

For the first time ever Smiffy noticed Sue was taken aback slightly. It was only slight but Smiffy could see her recoil and not just from the stench. It occurred to Smiffy that the stench was like scorched hair as soon as Sue began with her "We regret to inform you......"

Upon hearing the news, Mrs Bellamy looked down at the ground and then made a strange motion with her hand, uttered some words under her breath and looked at Sue and said, "He's fine. He's with his ancestors."

She promptly closed the door and went into the house. Sue knocked and was asking, with her head to the door, "Is there anyone we can contact? Do you need any help with anything?"

They waited for a short while and noticed Mrs Bellamy was in her kitchen moving around doing tasks. They walked back to the car feeling a mutual astonishment without speaking a word. As they sat in the squad car a Silver BMW motorbike came in the opposite direction. It was Mona Cruickshank on her way back to the vicarage after her once a week 'blast' on the bike.

It had been John's idea to keep the bike's 'juices flowing', as he put it. This was because they mainly used the car and didn't want either of the bikes seizing up. Mona was coming from the direction of Collingsmote Village. It was a place she loved to visit due to the duck pond outside the public house. It reminded her of bygone days of innocence and naïveté.

She recalled a previous boyfriend would park his E-Type jaguar just outside the pond. They'd drink in the pub. His name was John, John Emery. John had been in the Civil Service. He was a real gentleman. She'd heard that he died of cancer some years ago in Australia, where he had settled and raised a family. Theirs had been an innocent relationship that lasted just under a year. She recalled that one day, when they were sitting in the garden in the pub, and she looked at him. He had a small piece of wax in his ear. It had revolted her. She realised at that moment that she didn't love him.

As she rode by, she glanced briefly at the Bellamy place and knew the coppers had been there.

She concluded from this that Phil Bellamy had actually been found dead. Although she couldn't explain it she was secretly relishing the thought of his death. She imagined him in pain, in eternal torment of Hellfire, and she smiled. It was at times like these, she hoped that Hell wasn't just a place of being cut off from the Lord until the sinner found themselves back into God's Grace. She knew that thoughts differed from church to church and individual to individual. Her husband John was not convinced that Yah'veh would allow Satan, a fallen angel, to have his own kingdom to rule over. Hell was just a metaphor to him. Sometimes he believed differently. It just depended on what he'd read. Sometimes he sounded like an atheist to Mona, but she knew he was a thinking man and his heart was with the Lord. The world was turning and changing all the time and so was cultural thought.

***

Mrs Bellamy lit thirteen incense sticks around a pentagram inlaid into the table, in her living room. A CD of Wiccan chanting was playing on repeat. This was to be her own confection of the mystic, based on her own way of doing things.

She closed the drapes and lit two black candles either side of a circular scrying mirror at the far end of the table. She walked to the back door, opened it and gave a single knock with her index finger knuckle to the deck of Tarot cards she held. This, she believed, cleared any contaminating essence from the deck. She closed the door and sat at the table. It was time to relax and contact the spirit world. She took a drink of cool water and uttered some Latin words under her breath, "Et odio dolor, ultrices rhoncus, Domini testimonio cupiditatis arma excors," and concluded aloud with, "So mote it be!"

She picked up a jet black 'Athame' dagger and waved the blade through the incense smoke. She drew an imaginary circle of protection around herself.

She held her hands in the air and shouted, in a strange willowy voice, "Batrachophrenoboocosmomachia!"

Then she lit a burner and placed a small challis over it on a stand and said, "With salt I summon thee, O spirits of guidance and light."

She threw a pinch of salt into the challis. She repeated this ritual using her own pubic hair, water from her glass and blood from her hand that she drew with the athame.

Finally, she covered the strange mixture with an ill fitting lid. The room became misty with incense smoke. It resembled a scene from a 1950's 'B' movie horror film.

She sat down and relaxed in the high backed wicker chair that was draped on red cloth emblazoned with stars.

With her right hand, with thumb and forefingers pinched and pointing away from her, she drew an upside down five pointed star in the air. "Left hand path," she hissed.

The Tarot deck was shuffled and cut. Five cards were placed face down on each point of the upside down pentagram on the table.

Each card was then turned face up. Mrs Bellamy gave herself the interpretation based on her question, 'where is my son?'

The cards drawn represented the passage of time to her. The first card representing the past, the last card the future and those in-between being the link period.

The first card drawn was the Ace of Wands. Mrs Bellamy reckoned that this meant that her son was a creative man. One of his kind.

The second. The five of Coins seemed to tell her that her son faced problems.

The third. The Queen of swords, meant a reaching to another person. Perhaps this was Phil wishing to join with his ancestors.

The forth was Death. This was just a transitional thing. Changing one thing for another. A brand new start, for nothing really dies.

The final card was The Magician. This confirmed to Mrs Bellamy, that her son was now in the spirit realm, safe and sound. His journey was complete.

Such was her delusion. The body of Phil Bellamy lay in a cold metal drawer in the mortuary.

She sat back, happy that her son was in such a good place, but she became anxious that her supply of Krok was gone. Even though she could easily buy the stuff, she didn't know where to obtain it now.

This could be resolved by communion with the guardians of light. She stood up and crossed her hands, palms toward her shoulders. Then she unfolded her arms and held her palms toward the mirror.

"Osiris risen. Osiris slain," she whispered.

She continued with her own, made up delusional rituals for an hour or more. She became satisfied that all would be well.

Her son would be buried upright in the wall of a Wiccan house in Eye, Suffolk. This had been arranged many years before.

***

When Mona arrived home she went to tell her husband about her suspicions. John Cruickshank was hoping he wouldn't have to conduct yet another funeral and especially not one for Bellamy.

"I don't want a masked lunatic showing up at that funeral," he said.
"Have the police said anymore about that?"
"No. It's all hush, hush and I'm still shaken to be honest. Got some coppers going to ring me later about a statement or something."
"Any idea who'd pull such a stunt, John?"
"Wish I knew. The whole affair was very nasty. It turned into a rugger scrum. Very nasty. Then Debbie Burns ran in with a toy gun."

John related what had happened, even though Mona had heard it earlier.
"Who do you suppose he came for?" Mona asked.
"I'm sure it was Mr Kitter's fiancé. He threw a knife at her."
"That'd be Kay. Who would want to kill her?"
"Well, all those people waiting to be served in the convenience store I'd imagine," he said. He smiled with obvious insincerity, "She used to buy a stack of scratch cards, scratch them off and hand in the winners. It wouldn't be so bad but she held the queue up while she scratched."
"I remember," she laughed, "you asked her to step aside and she gave you a real unholy mouthful of interesting words, like the devil himself wouldn't dare use."

"Perhaps it was an angry customer in the balaclava that tried to kill her. No. I mustn't be mocking the afflicted."

They both laughed and decided to simply sit in the garden with strawberry milkshakes and mint chocolate biscuits. Finally their tranquillity was broken by John's phone ringing. It was the police requesting to visit him. He agreed and the day would end for the Cruickshank couple with John praying for them as they knelt at their bedside.

Chapter 30

Debbie and Carew made their way to Pete's house. There was no sign of the balaclava. The Citroen would have to be picked up tomorrow. The sun was beginning to go down. They were famished. Carew still had some things left at Pete's house, which he wanted to pick up. Travel arrangements would have to be worked out when they got there. Even if they got a lift back to the Citroen they could work something out.

They arrived at Pete's house. Moira let them in. They sat down together. The pair refreshed themselves with cold drinks and some beans on toast. Debbie washed Carew's splinted hand and cleaned it up.

Carew warned that the Balaclava figure would likely be coming to their house. Nigel was ready for a fight. Debbie had her machine gun and Carew had his wits and hogweed darts. Moira was afraid.

"Where's Pete?" Debbie asked tilting her head, like she's seem Marcia doing.
"He's in bed. Got the flu, I think. Not seen him all day," Nigel volunteered.
"Well," Carew said, with that intense look on his face, "We won't worry him right now coz chances are nothing will....."

The sound of a small amount of smashing glass cut Carew off.

Moira gasped in fear. "Is it him?" she wailed.

Carew put his finger to his lips requesting silence. Nigel picked up an empty wine bottle and Debbie took her machine gun out.

There was the sound of movement coming from the kitchen. Carew switched the light off. He motioned for everyone to take cover, away from the door and get behind him. Slowly, he opened the door, squatted down and looked out. He saw the Balaclava jump to the stairs and stride up them. Balaclava hadn't noticed him.

Carew picked a coin from his pocket and tossed it at the stone tiled floor beside the stairs.

As Balaclava instinctively looked toward the noise, Carew fired the hogweed darts from his makeshift blow pipe. Balaclava saw him at the last minute and ducked. The first dart missed its target and entered the wool nicking the ear. The second dart caught Balaclava in the corner of the eye. It was just enough to blind his right eye. Balaclava gave a grunt and threw out two shuriken stars. Carew batted them both out of the way with his blow pipe. One embedded itself into the wall and the other skittered across the stone tiles.

Debbie jumped from behind the door and sprayed bullets up the stairs. The bullets missed Balaclava as he jumped over the banisters. Plaster showered down. Debbie was going to fire her gun into the ceiling directly above her head, in an attempt to get Balaclava. Carew stopped her. This was, after all, Pete's house. Pete was upstairs and might get hit with stray bullets. Both Carew and Nigel hurtled up the stairs. Carew's hip was beginning to seize up and his hand was agony.

Pete's bedroom door was open and Pete was in bed cowering with the sheets over his head. His window was wide open. Carew ran and looked out of the window. He looked down and around. It was dark and he saw very little. Balaclava was nowhere in sight. All he heard was the breeze and a bottle being knocked over.

"Shit! Bloody gone," he cursed.

Nigel was assuring his Dad that everything was under control. But Pete still crouched in the corner of his bed hiding himself.

Carew and Nigel sped downstairs and out of the back door. They were slowed down having to unlock it. Nigel followed Carew outside. Both men stayed close to the wall and looked around. Carew indicated that they should split up. Debbie waited at the back door, gun ready. Moira was cowering behind the sofa in the living room. She was petrified with fear.

"Could be anywhere, any direction. At least we foiled the bastard," Carew said.

Debbie remained in the doorway as Carew and Nigel searched the perimeter of the houses.

"Does this bloke ever run out of energy?" Nigel asked Carew. The question was rhetorical so Carew refrained from answering.

"Help me sure up this window." Carew pointed at the kitchen window.

"What was the smashing glass?" Nigel asked. "Bloody useless stealth tactics."

"Perhaps he's tired. Making mistakes. You can see where the glass has been cut. Looks like some broke off the main pain and fell onto the floor when our friend was trying to get in quietly. Clumsy twat!"

"I wonder why he went upstairs immediately?" Nigel asked as they got some planking to nail over the hole.

"Did he know your Dad was up there? Did he think we'd be in bed? I am very surprised he didn't notice the living room light on and try to bung his bloody stars at us."

"This Balaclava bloke seems to work on a different wavelength to the rest of us."

"He's fucking dangerous. I still suspect it's Dave Martyn with an alter ego. Jimmy mentioned something about it didn't he."

"Yeah. Forget the details. Martyn's a right fucked up cunt by the sounds. Do you suppose he's gone back home?"

"Nah. Place will be crawling with coppers. I reckon he's probably holed up somewhere. But where? That is the mystery."

There was a revving of a car engine. The car at the end terrace reversed out of the drive with a screech and sped toward the town.

Nigel shouted, "My bloody car!"

"Fuck me," Carew shouted rushing to the road to see the car disappear. "That crafty sod was hot wiring your motor."

Pete came down stairs looking dreadful with flu.

Debbie went inside to see how Moira was. Moira was crying and shaking on the sofa so Debbie sat with her arm around her.

"Take my car," Pete said with a cough as he held himself up on the door lintel, "Just don't get hurt or wreck it."

"I'm coming," shouted Debbie running from the house. She had her back pack with the machine gun sticking out uncovered.

Pete threw the keys at Nigel who fumbled them and dropped them. Carew was in agony with his hand, but was fighting through it. He swallowed a couple of pain killers and gulped them down without water. He pulled a 'lemon sucking' face as he did so. He didn't think another trip to the hospital was appropriate because, he thought, it would just result in another splint. He already had one, as soiled as it was. Carew wondered if anything else was broken now. Meanwhile, Martyn, the Balaclava was getting away.

"If you tell the coppers your car's been nicked it could mean they get to him before we do. What you reckon?" Carew asked as the trio ran around the side of the house to Pete's car.

Moira went into the house and looked through the window. She stood and watched in fear. She bit her lip and breathed heavily through her nose.

Nigel flung himself into the driving seat. Debbie and Carew piled into the back.

"Bloody taxi, am I?" Nigel made the comment wryly.

Carew and Debbie still looked dirty and haggard from their chase earlier, despite having had a bit of a wash and clean up. Carew was limping more than usual and seemed to be struggling with his hand, as far as Moira could tell. Pete went inside and sat on the couch. He slouched down. His head was thumping in pain and he felt wretched. He heard his car drive away. At least Nigel hadn't taken off with a screech. The not knowing would be hell for Pete and Moira.

"I don't know where to go but I can see car lights over there." Nigel pointed toward the town where they could see a car speeding in the distance.

They peered out over the field. Nigel was convinced it was his car in front. This was because the passenger side rear light was dull and blinking slightly. Nigel observed that it seemed strange to be in an escaping car with the lights on. Debbie had said that either he wanted to be followed or he couldn't see the road. That's why Nigel had his lights on too.

"Of course," she continued, "Balaclava might just be a total dickhead."

"Bastard's heading for the city," Carew observed. "He's gonna fuckin' miss the town. He's going too fast to turn down the Venables Street route."

"Where is the bastard going. It makes no sense. What the fuck did he go to the viaduct for?" Debbie wondered.

"He's picking off friends, enemies and the family of Dave Martyn. He tried to kill that bird at the funeral. I'm not sure why. Must be to do with Martyn." Carew explained cradling his hand, "When we turned up he had to fuck off and lose us, so went to the viaduct to find water to cover his tracks."

"You suspect he is Martyn but an alter ego, Colonel?" Debbie wanted to hear the explanation again.

Carew answered her whilst rubbing his hand gently,

"He's a dual ID bloke. He's Dave Martyn and he switches to another persona by another name. I think the Balaclava persona is the protector and maybe, a bit possessive too. I reckon, for what it maybe worth, that the Balaclava alter ego is so possessive that he wants the Dave Martyn version all to himself."

"That's why he's on the killing spree. But why now?"

"I think it started before now but maybe there was a stresser that triggered him to go ballistic."

"That copper, Bellamy, that Dangerfield said was killed?"

"Could be, but that still doesn't make sense. Not that any of this shit has to though. Thinking about it, it just appears to be anyone that posed a threat to Martyn like poor old Dangerfield and his family. Then, it appears to be anyone that was close to him. Bellamy wasn't but could be a potential threat in the future. Did I tell you, I remember Bellamy from school?"

"Get away. Bellamy the copper, you mean?"

"Yeah. The only thing I remember about him was he called me a fucking nobody, so I smacked him in the gob."

"Think he did the same to Martyn and that's why this other ID went for him?"

"There seemed to be a lot of interest in Martyn lately. Dangerfield said he'd been to visit him."

"I think also, Martyn was getting stressed, so maybe it was stressing his alter. The weird loop here seems to be that Martyn was scared that Balaclava was going to kill him, not knowing they were one and the same."

"I wonder if you'd call that a self fulfilling prophecy? You'd make a great pop psychologist, Colonel."

Nigel was swerving the car around the bends in the road and they were almost airborne over the humps and bumps. He wasn't paying attention to Carew and Debbie as his attention was focused on following the Balaclava.

"Bastard," shouted Nigel as a pothole made him swerve and almost drive into the bushes. The glove box fell open and some of the contents, mainly empty sweet wrappers, cascaded onto the floor.

"Ouch," gasped Carew as his hand was jolted.

The car narrowly missed a hedgehog that rolled into a ball in the road. Moths were splattering on the windshield. Nigel applied the wipers which only seemed to have the effect of moving them around the screen.

Overhead a lone jet aircraft flew toward Collingsmote. It appeared and disappeared through the clouds in the sky.

The spire of St Matthew's church was visible as they turned onto the main road. The car they were in wasn't as fast as Nigel's and seemed to choke and judder as the accelerator was forced down.

As they travelled down the main road to the Brockwell outskirts, Nigel said, "We lost the bugger."

Debbie wondered, "'Did he know we were after him?'

Carew considered the question then answered, "It doesn't matter, I guess. We just need to find him. But why here? Why Brockwell?"

The neon lights of the city lit up the area like daytime as the question hung in the air. The pizza parlours and balti houses had people walking in and out, as they drove down the main road. Taxis were crawling in every lane, picking up fares and dropping off. They could hear music blaring from pubs and clubs. They were passed by brightly decorated scooters. It was the local Mods and scooter boys out for a run. Carew admired the scooters with their British roundels. Some scooters had Ska influenced themes.

***

Pete was back in bed feeling like crap.

Moira sat on the sofa crying. As she looked around the room the Voodoo mask on the wall seemed to be mocking her. It reminded her of the birthday gift she had given Carew. Everything to do with Martyn was clattering noisily around her brain. The events of the last few days were too much. Her boyfriend Nigel and Carew her best friend, were both chasing a murderer, and it was her fault. The guilt was overwhelming. Where was Frank? She rang his number but there was no reply. His phone didn't even go onto the answer service immediately, it was ringing and ringing. Should she ring Carew? She daren't.

She stood up and paced the room. She clenched the tissue she used to wipe her tears and snot away. Her breathing was becoming rapid. She was beginning to panic. The room was closing in upon her. The phone in her hand began to feel heavy like a brick.

Moira took a deep breath and steadied herself on the sofa back. She took the phone and began to dial the number WPC Bogle had provided. The cognitive dissonance was too much. She was torn between loyalty to her friends and family, their secrecy and their safety. This was shit, shit and double shit.

For the first few times she didn't continue to dial and abandoned the call. Finally she spoke to a copper. She didn't know or care if it was WPC Bogle or the bogeyman. Carew, Nigel and Debbie's safety was at risk. They may hate her but she could no longer refrain from looking after them.

She told the officer at the other end, as much as she could. The registration plates were only one digit different so she remembered them easily, even in her mind numbing state. After she'd made the call she slumped onto the sofa and thought about all the possible consequences of her actions. After all, this was all her fault and she could no longer live with herself. She got up. She sat down. She looked out of the window. She sat down. She put the TV on. After flicking through the channels, turned it off and threw the remote onto the sofa in frustration. She knew this was going to be a long night. Genuflect against the sofa, Moira prayed in Catholic fashion.

Then she spoke her own words, "Oh, Lord. Please help us all. I know I've done wrong but I do love and worship you with all my heart. Send me a sign. Let me know that Nigel, Carew, Debbie Burns and Frank are okay Father, forgive them, for they know not what they do. If they survive I will be at Mass regularly and refrain from sin. O, Lord my God. Father, if thou wilt, remove this chalice from me: but yet not my will, but thine be done. Glory be to the Father, and to the Son, and to the Holy Spirit. As it was in the beginning, is now, and ever shall be, world without end. Amen."

She crossed herself. This made her feel somewhat better but still, there was an element of fear that god may not be listening.

She recalled a conversation she had with Carew. She'd asked him what he'd say if God appeared to him. His reply had been, "I'd ask him, her or it, which one are you? Zeus, Thor, Elvis, Apollo? You haven't made it obvious."

Moira wept.

Chapter 31

"So did we get a VRN on the cars, Meaden?" LeBeau asked as he clipped on his gun holster.

"Yes, sir," Meaden replied as he attached his earpiece.

"I was at a bloody restaurant and was half way through my seafood risotto when I got the call. They said this MacNamara girl was pretty distraught too. Taking this one seriously. We may need SWAT .but better recce the area first. Can't waste useful resources. We don't know where either car is headed but I bet the one is chasing the other."

"Could be a bloodbath, guv."

"I don't care if those jokers get hurt. I want Martyn in cuffs, in the back of the van with the general public safe and out of this."

"I've told plod not to give chase but to report back. Oh, and not approach or give it the old blues and twos, sir"

"Excellent. Has the car been repaired?"

"Not yet, sir. I have an unmarked replacement though. I've got some heavies on their way already, covertly."

"Who?"

"Jackson and McMullen, guv.

"Good work, Meaden. Let's roll."

The gravel churned under their tyres as they sped out of the car park and onto Collingsmote main road. They headed toward the city at speed. Meaden was tired and put on his glasses for driving.

The radio squawked. Pete's car had been spotted and the unmarked cars were following it in their classic box style. As one car turned into a street from behind Pete's car, another pulled out and followed at a distance.

"Don't pull them in," LeBeau ordered. "Just keep track. They may lead us to Martyn if his car isn't spotted."

Just before he finished he continued, "Oh. And don't let plod pull either of them over unless I give the order."

LeBeau gave Meaden the location of Pete's car.

"Erm, about ten minutes away from them then, sir," Meaden confirmed.

"Better put your foot down then."

"Yes, sir."

Although they were travelling over the speed limit, Meaden sped up. The road they travelled was clear of vehicles. As they came to a blind 'U' bend Meaden slowed down. Directly in front of them was a tractor moving slowly. It would have been dangerous to overtake and there was nowhere for the tractor to pull in. When the road was clear and straight they swerved around the tractor trying to make up time. They were losing valuable minutes and the car they were pursuing was now in denser traffic and a narrow pedestrianised area. LeBeau was confident that their unmarked cars would not lose Pete's car.

"I think our best bet is to go to the Brockwell flats," Carew observed. Suddenly Nigel exclaimed, "There's the fucker!"

He'd spotted his car moving slowly through the revellers in Uldale Street. Uldale Street was a narrow remnant of the days of horses and cobbles. The crowds were mainly dressed in faux Caribbean carnival clothes. From one of the bars, reggae music was pumping. The poster outside advertised 'Jah Vital'. There was a familiar track playing albeit a techno remixed version,

'Da Boomshot Da Da Da Da Da Boom Boom Boom,
Da Police brutality tee tee tee tee tee,
Da society tee tee tee tee tee'

Then the thumping beat started and the song played with a remixed fast beat;

'Lick shot. Boomshot. Boom boom shot
Police brutality, in dis ya society
Boomshot boomshot
A wah me seh
Mash Babylon to rasclaat.'

"Get out of the feckin' way," Nigel muttered under his breath as he drove down Uldale with revellers spilling all over the road.

He followed Balaclava despite the crowd.

"I keep seeing that bloody car," Carew said as he looked out of the rear window. "Reminds me of a bloody ambush we had in Ireland once. They're using the box move. Probably another car onto us too." He looked at the occupants and gave them a knowing smile. He put his finger to his eye and pointed at the driver, McPhee, who saw him. McPhee remained deadpan and simply ignored Carew as if he had seen nothing.
"That car belongs to your friends and yours the Peelers," Carew spat. "Extra lights on the bumper, too many aerials and it's a fucking Mondeo. How come they're onto us I fucking wonder!"

LeBeau received the message from McPhee, "They're on to us, sir."

LeBeau thought for a moment then said, "Fall back and let car Charlie November 3 pick up the chase. Hopefully they won't cotton on."

Suddenly Balaclava sped up and disappeared into the dock area.

"Where's he going?" Debbie asked as she got her machine gun from her backpack. She kept it low and covered in a cloth as she did so.

"Fuck knows. It's just a bloody game to that twat," Carew exclaimed.

From the corner an unmarked police car pulled out and crossed behind them going behind the warehouses in Cromley Road. It was car CN3 with driver Farrow and his partner Pascal. They parked up behind Frij-A-Kool warehouse. Farrow remained in the vehicle and Pascal jumped out and ran to a gap between the tall grim buildings and spied on Carew's car party. Pascal was a man of few words and when Farrow asked him if he could see the car he simply answered, "Aye." in a monotone.

"Drive just behind there," Carew said pointing to a grimy brick building that looked disused. "I think we've got another piggy on our tail."

"Thought I saw something. That car that crossed at the back of us was slowing down as it went behind the warehouse and none of the other cars did. Careless Dixon of Dock Green," Nigel agreed.

"Dixon who?" Debbie asked.

"Before your time."

There was no laughter. The mood was serious now and Carew was psyching himself up for a final battle.

"Have we lost Balaclava boy?" Debbie asked unsure of why they'd stopped in the first place.

"He's hiding and when he's hiding he's bloody dangerous," Nigel offered.

"He might have driven away though," Debbie objected mildly.

"Not around here. All boxed off with walls. This is a dead end," Nigel continued as he shifted into gear and drove behind the building Carew had pointed to.

The area was grim and devoid of any 'soul', as Carew called it. It had dog shit and rubbish scattered across the roads and foot paths. A crisp packet glided across the street slowly in the breeze. There was a tiny swirl of dust in a corner where the wall met the building.

Carew was quiet and nursing his hand. The pain killers had only limited effect. He was gritting his teeth. Debbie looked at him. She knew his hand was no better and he would need a trip back to the hospital, without hesitation.

"I haven't seen any movement," Debbie observed holding her gun tightly.

"I have," Carew said dismissively and looking distant.

From the corner of his eye, Carew had seen a shadow grow tall and diminish against a wall to the left where Balaclava had driven. It wasn't there for long but enough to identify it as a person moving swiftly but unsurely.

Carew guessed that Martyn was now blind in one eye from the hogweed sap, hence the stumbling. How clumsy of him to telegraph his movements because he should know they were on to him by now.

"Sod this," blurted Carew, "I'm getting out."

Carew flung open the door and got out. Crouching down, he moved to the corner of the building, to cover himself. Quickly, he looked around in all directions and up and down. Nothing. He continued to squat and ran along the perimeter of the grotty building that was festooned with bright graffiti and tattered posters. He could see Nigel's car parked at an angle near a metal lattice tower. The driver's side door was open but no lights were on. Carew surveyed the scene. A bent streetlight. The lattice tower with barbed wire around the middle. A flat roof, next to a high fence, with barbed wire along the top. Across the railway lines, in the dip, and directly opposite stood a Brockwell tower block.

Carew knew that Balaclava had chosen this spot deliberately. It provided access to the tower block, away from the public eye and the CCTV that was now active in the street. Carew guessed that there was someone in the tower block that Balaclava was trying to kill. Carew looked for the easiest path over the fence and to the block. It would be across the flat roof and up the lattice tower, part way. Then a jump down to the grass verge that sloped down through nettles to the railway lines. The shadow he saw would have been made from a passing train, shining light against Balaclava.

Carew saw, in his peripheral vision, Pascal watching him through a crack in the buildings, to his far left. Carew knew that he would not be able to climb to the flat roof very well with his bad hand, so he looked for an alternative exit through the fence.

Nigel had joined Carew and ran to his abandoned car. The keys were left in it.

"Careless," He whispered to himself. "I would have thrown the keys away so no one could drive the car."

Debbie was on her own in Pete's saloon, crouching in the back and clasping her gun until her knuckles were white.

"I'll take care of this. You get Debbie the hell out of here. That's an order," Carew commanded through his gritted teeth.

Nigel got into his car, gunned the engine and reversed it at speed over to Debbie. As he approached he swerved the car in a handbrake turn and drove forward. He slammed on the brakes and through the open window shouted, "Get in. We're out of here."
"Fuck off," replied Debbie as she opened the rear door and got out, "I'm taking this car then, and going over to that tower block. I know darn well that's where the Colonel is going."

"Ah, right. Well, er, hurry up then, Burnsy. Follow me then. I know a shortcut."

Debbie scrambled into the front of Pete's car. The engine was still running, she slammed it into gear and the two cars sped off. Nigel waved at Pascal as he drove by. Pascal looked blankly back.

The cars screeched out of the turning. Instead of going left, they turned right and into an alley way between buildings, out of Pascal's sight. Nigel's car was slightly wider than Pete's so, as he drove, both of his wing mirrors scraped along the walls. He hit a sharp bump and sparks flew from somewhere beneath his car. Debbie was not relaxed and breathing quickly with every bump and scrape.

"Shit," cursed Nigel as he saw a fence at the end of the ally. He put his foot down and smashed through it into the where the garages were. A headlight shattered and wire fencing sprang out in front of him and skittered across the tarmac. "Bollocks," he shouted. He yanked his steering wheel and turned sharply right. His tyres screeched and smoke violently spewed from them. Debbie followed in a wider arc almost smashing into a garage door opposite. Her rear bumper slightly glanced the door making a reverberating clang.

"Shitshitshitshit," she said almost singing it. The same rear bumper clipped a wheelie bin flinging it into the road. The contents poured out as it rolled.

"Shitshitshitshit," she sang.

Pascal ran back to the car and tripped over on the way. He rolled with the trip but gave himself a dead leg on the curb stone. He sat there rubbing his knee before getting up and hobbling over to the car. Farrow was laughing despite knowing they'd lost time in pursuing the cars that had driven through the garage compound.

"Bloody Keystone Cop," Pascal cursed as he scowled.

Car CN3 shot off down Cromley Road in radio contact with base. Farrow drove carefully down the alley and saw where the fence had been knocked down. He commented, "Obviously don't make 'em how they used to. In the old days, that would have netted them both."

Pascal in his typical manner, just nodded. He still rubbed his knee.

As CN3 turned into the garages, he stopped at the end of the driveway and looked to for any sign of Nigel and Debbie.

"There," Pascal said pointing to the tower block.

Farrow turned the car and headed over to the tower. He couldn't see the cars but trusted Pascal's judgement.

"You really must learn to talk, Pazzy. I can't deal with your mono syllableistic conversations."

Pascal smiled and said, "Shame."

"Daft bugger."

There were a few pedestrians around the tower block. A jet black BMW R 1150 Enduro motorcycle with a rider in jet black overtook them, cut in front of them making Farrow slam on his brakes. The bike screeched to the back of the block.

"Mad," remarked Pascal.

"I think that was an invite for us to follow. Probably one of our boys but I don't recognise the bike."

"No."

"It looked like a foreign plate and it moved so fast I couldn't get the reg. Pascal, did you get the reg?"

"No."

Farrow frowned at the single word and even single syllable responses from Pascal.

"Can you see those cars anywhere?"

"No."

"BMW main dealer around here so these bikes are all over the place. Looked like a foreign plate on it as I say, though."

Farrow decided to ask Pascal a question that required more than a singular word answer then thought against it. He didn't want to overload Pascal's vocal cords.

Farrow followed in the same direction the BMW had ridden, down an incline and behind the block. Both men expected to find the cars there but the enclosed car park was empty, apart from the BMW. The rider was nowhere to be seen.

They decided to get out as they would be able to cover the ground better on foot. Both men felt a short sharp sting on the neck before they blacked out. From the roof of a garage the rider of the BMW, still wearing the black crash helmet, stood up holding a tranquiliser gun.

The figure jumped down to the grass verge at the back, went over to Farrow and Pascal, then removed the hypodermic darts. The next move was to car CN3 and slash the tyres with a curved blade. The radio inside squawked requesting information from Farrow. The biker simply turned the radio off. The fob key was taken from Farrow's pocket and dropped through the grille of a drain. There was the familiar 'plop!' and the biker returned to the BMW. With a swift move, the biker removed the fake registration plate from the rear, then sped off to the other tower block, over the roundabout and through the tunnel. The bike echoed loudly in the tunnel.

A screech of tyres echoed as the BMW pulled up and veered right, barely missing the front of a bus. The bus driver sounded the horn but the biker was not bothered and continued over to the other tower. This tower block was where the name over the doorway originally read, 'Cundell Tower'. The name had been changed by a graffiti artist to "Cunt all Tower'.

***

Carew found an opening some yards along the fence. Probably where kids had used it to get through. The kids would then throw stones at the trains. The tracks curved into a tunnel on both sides and to cross the lines was perilous. You either needed to know when the trains were due or risk the run. Carew would risk the run across the tracks.

As he descended the bank through the nettles, a passenger train sounded the two tone horn that reverberated inside the tunnel. The train roared from the tunnel to Carew's left. It entered the tunnel to his right. It clattered rhythmically as it whooshed by. Carew felt uneasy crossing the tracks but at least he was confident, that the track the train had just been on, wouldn't have another train following. His hand got stung by a nettle but he wasn't paying attention to it.

Carew knew that it would be difficult to dodge trains that shot between tunnels, even if they sounded their horn because the sound was confusing. He ran across the first track, then listened hard for the sound of the rails thrumming and signalling a train's approach. Carew bounded over the rails and made it to the opposite bank, with no trains passing.

He scrambled up the bank to the high wooden fence that partitioned the tower block from the railway. Directly in front of him, he saw where some planking had been dislodged from the concrete posts. He was able to bend them back and climb through, to the grounds of the tower block. He saw car CN3 with Farrow and Pascal slumped on the tarmac. He ran over and checked their necks for pulses. They were out cold but alive. He suspected it was Martyn. Why would Martyn let them live? Carew stood wondering for a moment unsure of which way to go. He suspected the Balaclava was targeting someone in the tower block.

He rounded the building with his back to the wall. He looked swiftly around the corner to where the entrance was. No one was there. He jogged over and beneath the sign that read, 'Fallon Tower'.

Inside the tall building there was a stair well and a lift. Carew was met with a stench inside that defied description. Someone had dumped a filthy roll of used carpet in front of the stairs. The lift was going up the floors but Carew noticed a boot print, that looked fresh, on the damp carpet. He positioned his head to look directly up the stairwell as far as he could. No sign of movement. He listened for any telltale noises.

There was a thump and a crashing sound from a door being bashed in. Carew ran up the grimy concrete stairs. His foot falls echoed gently as he crept onto the first level and through the fire door. Nothing. Next level. Nothing. Next level, the fire door was wedged open on the uneven floor. There was the broken down door ahead. Carew ran to it and placed his back flat on the wall next to it. He peered cautiously into the flat.

The TV was on showing some inane reality show. The images flickered and send weird shadows darting over the walls in the room ahead. The lights were off and someone sat, head hanging down, in the winged high back chair. It was a woman, and although Carew didn't know it, it was Kitter's male girlfriend, Frederick (Brandine) McClean. There was no blood but the way the head was hanging told Carew the neck had been snapped. Carew suspected it was someone connected to Martyn. A hamster was running in the wheel of its cage. Fish were gliding in the illuminated aquarium.

'Probably how he got in,' Carew thought whispering to himself, 'Martyn requests entry and the doors unlock and don't shut properly. Then I get in. But why is the door smashed?' Carew guessed that the victim had kept the door closed after seeing Martyn in a Balaclava.

There was a movement near the door and Carew saw a silhouetted figure dash out of it. Carew ran in pursuit and saw Balaclava running up the stairs.

"Where do you get your energy from?" Carew shouted as he pursued Balaclava.

He decided that speaking just wastes body moisture, so just chased Balaclava. It was as if Balaclava wanted to be caught. Carew knew that Balaclava was looking for good ground to fight on now and the roof would provide a battleground, out of the sight of anyone, including the police.

Carew was ready as he emerged from the door and out onto the pitch covered roof of Fallon Tower. There were aerials. Pipes were venting steam. The wind was strong making the aerials rattle. As Carew ran to face Balaclava, his hair was being swept back by the wind.

He needed to manoeuvre out of a direct wind as Balaclava would use it to his advantage. Carew knew this was the final battle and stood side ways on to Balaclava. Balaclava had blood around his mouth. His eye was milky white from the hogweed sap and the skin around was blistered purple. Carew could see this through the mouth and eye holes in the woollen mask. Balaclava stood majestically, feel shoulder width apart. He was waiting for Carew to attack.

"Are you ready Martyn?" Carew taunted.

"Not Martyn," came the gruff voice, "Tom Eccleston. Protector."

"You're the protector, are you? So, switched from manky Martyn to twatty Tom have we?"

"Now, I own David," he growled, "All mine. No one else in the way. I eradicate all those close to David because they sully him with their presence."

"You've missed a few haven't you, Tom the twat?"

There was no reply from Balaclava, apart from a fast flicking hand movement. A shuriken star flew toward Carew's face. Carew sidestepped effortlessly, slightly tilted his head backward and the star embedded itself into the door lintel behind him.

Balaclava, sensing Carew was distracted, ran the short distance to Carew and lunged at his ribs with a Bowie knife. Carew dodged spinning sideways. The knife tore Carew's shirt and grazed his side. Blood began to seep onto his shirt. As Balaclava continued his momentum, Carew moved in bringing an elbow to the back of his head in a fluid motion. The jolt dazed Balaclava and made Carew wince with the pain it caused. The shock shot up his arm to his wounded hand. Balaclava fell onto his hands and did a forward somersault, spinning around as he got up.

His head was framed against a full moon as he crouched and moved in again. A few spots of rain fell diagonally across the two men.

From the rooftop of the opposite tower block, the Biker watched the scene through a pair of Bushnell PowerView 10x50 WA Porro Prism binoculars.

The Biker was thinking that Carew was on good form, considering his hand injury. Looking down, the Biker could see that LeBeau had arrived in the vicinity but didn't know where Balaclava was. LeBeau was looking at Pascal and Farrow laying on the tarmac and pointing frantically in different directions to direct Jackson, McMullen and Meaden. Jackson and McMullen were running into Fallon tower. Meaden was doing a general sweep of the area. Further away and in a car park, behind a large hoarding board, Nigel and Debbie stood observing.

Clouds swiftly covered the moon and the night became darker.

Carew wasn't about to be sucker punched again, like along the track or at the funeral, and kept a safe distance from Balaclava. Balaclava gave a kick to Carew's hip. Carew grabbed the leg and spun Balaclava to the ground. Suddenly, Balaclava pulled a flare gun from his jacket and fired it at Carew. Carew fell flat on his face and the flare exploded between the tower blocks. Bright pink light drew all eyes upward.

"There. On top of the tower," shouted LeBeau.

All he could see was Balaclava. From his line of sight, he wasn't aware that Carew was there. Carew now knew that attention would be on the tower block. He didn't want to be seen. He decided to keep central on the roof and low.

He leaned against the central roof exit door awaiting Balaclava to lunge at him. He was not wrong. Carew used a different move to disarm him because he realised that Balaclava would anticipate his moves based on his style. Carew ducked under the stabbing arm and wrapped his right arm around Balaclava's shoulder. With a flick of the heel behind Balaclava's knee he pivoted him around and onto the floor. At the same time he ripped the balaclava off revealing Martyn beneath.

Martyn screamed insanely and with an extremely contorted expression, "No! No! No! Give me Tom! Give me Tom! Cunt! Cunt! Give me Tom! Give me Tom! Give me Tom! Give me Tom! You cunt!"

Carew ran and crouching down to avoid being seen, threw the screwed up balaclava over the edge of the roof. The gusty wind carried it far out above the street. A crowd of people had gathered to look. From below, all that could be seen was Martyn reaching over the building to grab the flying balaclava.

Carew dropped onto his back and kicked Martyn's ankle. It cracked. Then, Carew kicked again at Martyn's backside, propelling him over the edge of the building. The onlookers, including LeBeau, only saw Martyn make a grab for his balaclava and apparently trip, then topple over the edge of the tower block. The crowd gasped. There were screams. A girl vomited. Carew ran to the central exit.

Martyn fell with arms outstretched as if mimicking an aeroplane and without uttering a sound. His torso hit the top of a lamp post ripping open his stomach. The metal lamp post juddered under the impact. His flare gun went off burning his genitals off.

"Boomshot," came a voice from the crowd. There were screams.

Martyn's body hit the ground splintering bone and splattering body juices. It began to rain heavily. The blood and rain made a pink rivulet in an 'L' shape into the gutter and down the drain. The corpse twitched.

LeBeau and his men removed spectators from the scene and recalled Meaden, Jackson and McMullen to assist. Nigel and Debbie 'high fived' each other. The Biker, from the opposite roof was gone, having seen everything.

Carew slowly dragged himself down the stairs. He was exhausted. Carew constantly rubbed his hand. There was a patch of blood where the knife of Balaclava had caught him. The cut was very sore now but not deep.

He exited via the back door not paying much attention to anything. Suddenly, he heard a 'thunk, thunk!' behind him. Startled, he looked around to see two jet black, mini throwing knives were embedded in the door. They had landed either side of his head. He knew these weren't meant to hit him but were a signal. 'You have been noticed.' it indicated.

He looked out across the grass to the car park below. Farrow and Pascal still lay there. An ambulance was arriving with lights flashing. Abruptly, the lights on a BMW motorbike went on and the engine revved. Carew saw the Biker give him a thumbs up, waved goodbye and shot off. It all happened too fast for Carew to ask who, what and why. He stood there with his mouth open not knowing if the Biker was male or female under those leathers and helmet. He knew he would hear more from this mystery biker.

His phone vibrated. It was Debbie.

In the rain, his hair was getting bedraggled. Cold rainwater ran over his face and down his neck. He ignored the discomfort.

They both asked each other at the same time, "Where are you?"

Carew made his way over to the car park whilst avoiding the police. He met Debbie and Nigel.

"Thank fucking god you didn't use that gun," Carew said to Debbie as they hugged. She laughed.
"Colonel. You've been stabbed," Debbie said looking horrified as she pulled away from Carew.
"It's just a scratch, Debs," Carew smiled.

***

Debbie drove Pete's car to A&E to get Carew's hand looked at again. Nigel drove home.

LeBeau and Meaden had a wearisome night.

Dangerfield sat and smiled when the news arrived of Martyn's demise. "Carew," he said nodding his head.

"Better get the Citroen back, if it hasn't been half inched," Carew said. Debbie agreed. For now it wasn't important so she said, "Perhaps Nigel will give us a lift over there, to get it, but your hand gets first priority."

Carew knew that all this would take some explaining away, but it was mission accomplished. He hadn't been implicated in Martyn's death but had caused it. It wasn't murder. This was justice of the kind the police could not enforce.

There were unanswered questions but that was typical of life. People's actions are not always logical and so often, nothing will fit the mould.

LeBeau would have questions for Carew, Debbie and Nigel but there was nothing to tell. There is no law about driving through a city to retrieve your car that's been stolen. The only violation may well be driving a vehicle uninsured. Then there was the chase through the garages and the resulting damage but LeBeau wasn't about to pursue that line of enquiry.

The headless corpse found in Martyn's cellar remained a mystery. The sale of Krok ceased in the area.

Nigel went home to comfort Moira. Moira got on her knees and prayed, "Father, I abandon myself into your hands; do with me what you will. Whatever you may do. I thank you; I am ready for all, I accept all. Let only your will be done in me, and in all your creatures. I wish no more than this, my Lord. Into your hands I commend my soul; I offer it to you, with all the love of my heart, for I love you, Lord, and so need to give myself, to surrender myself into your hands, without reserve, and with boundless confidence, for you are my Father. Amen!"

***

"Carew is a fucking nobody!"

The words never more echoed from the past.

Carew dismissed the insult thinking, "No, I fucking am not. I am a man and I have become somebody!"

In his pocket Carew felt the wood carving. He took it out and looked at it.

Debbie looked at Carew and gave a knowing smile.

Nigel opened his car door and they climbed in.

"So, we'll get the car. It's just you me and the sky" Debbie said to Carew as Nigel drove them to the power station near the viaduct.
"Yeah," Carew smiled. "What could possibly go wrong now!"

The Biker was sitting astride the BMW, and waiting for Carew when he went with Debbie to collect the Citroen.

Nigel dropped them off near the gates to the viaduct area, after Carew and Debbie agreed a walk would be good.

As they rounded the corner. Carew was surprised.

"How did you get here?" Carew asked. There was no reply from the Biker that sat astride the BMW Enduro.

Sunlight glanced from the Biker's helmet. The rain spots looked like rainbow gems shimmering in the light. Carew accepted a folded note from the Biker. He opened it, read it and looked up as the Biker sped away, spraying mud from it's tyres.

"Fuck me!" Carew laughed ironically, "It never fucking ends!"

A bird flew over and squawked as if mocking Carew.

Carew looked up, laughing he flicked a 'v' sign at the bird. He looked back at Debbie. She winked at him and said, "Let's live happily ever after, Colonel!"

"That would *really* be the boomshot," replied Carew. He began to sing to Debbie,

"Lick shot. Boomshot. Boom boom shot.
Police brutality, in dis ya society.
Boomshot. boomshot. Nuh man.
A wah me seh. Ban diddly, ban diddly.
Mash Babylon to rasclaat. A so me seh!"

10934381R00110

Printed in Great Britain
by Amazon.co.uk, Ltd.,
Marston Gate.